Dear Reader

I was happy with my career as an officer in the United States Marines, stationed at Quantico, Virginia. I *was* happy, that is, until Mollie Devlin arrived on the scene—because from that moment on, my life was never the same.

Mollie is an intriguing combination of playful prankster, serious student and warm-blooded woman. And she's the only recruit I'd ever had the urge to see out of uniform.

For her, I had almost been willing to break every rule of the Marine Corps code of conduct. And then I learned that the delightful Ms. Devlin's latest practical joke was the deception she was practicing—on me.

David Talmadge
Captain, USMC

CATHY GILLEN THACKER

Cathy Gillen Thacker married her high school sweetheart and hasn't had a dull moment since. Why, you ask? Well, there were three kids, various pets, any number of automobiles (some of which worked and some of which didn't), several moves across the country, his and her careers, and sundry other experiences (some of which were exciting and some of which weren't). But mostly, there was love and friendship and laughter, and lots of experiences she wouldn't trade for the world. You can find out more about Cathy and her books at www.cathygillenthacker.com.

MEN MADE in AMERICA

Cathy Gillen Thacker

The Devlin Dare

HARLEQUIN®

TORONTO • NEW YORK • LONDON
AMSTERDAM • PARIS • SYDNEY • HAMBURG
STOCKHOLM • ATHENS • TOKYO • MILAN • MADRID
PRAGUE • WARSAW • BUDAPEST • AUCKLAND

ISBN-13: 978-0-373-36049-9
ISBN-10: 0-373-36049-5

THE DEVLIN DARE

Published Harlequin Enterprises, Ltd. 1986, 1993

This edition published by arrangement with Harlequin Books S.A.

www.eHarlequin.com

Printed in U.S.A.

Prologue

"Are you crazy?" Constance Vanderbilt paced frantically back and forth across the carpeted expanse of her editorial office at *Super Women* magazine. "This is the U.S. Marines we're talking about having you join, Mollie, not some silly summer camp for kids! We're talking about sending you to boot camp! And not just ordinary boot camp at that, but boot camp plus, for officers!"

"It's called officer candidate school, or OCS," Mollie Devlin corrected quietly, enjoying the fact that she was able to maintain her composure while her editor was completely blowing her stack.

"OCS. XOE. TFW." Constance's arms flailed wildly at her sides as she paced back and forth. "I don't care what it's called. It spells torture, Mollie. Physical and mental torture."

"You think I'll never make it, don't you?" Uncrossing her legs, Mollie put both feet flat on the floor and leaned forward, cupping her clasped hands around one knee.

Constance said nothing to disagree with Mollie's assessment.

Mollie let out a heartfelt sigh. Resentfully, she countered, "Look, just because I'm twenty-eight doesn't mean

I'm over the hill. Like my ex-husband said, Constance, I've got a lot of miles left in me.''

Constance couldn't keep from smiling back at Mollie's comical expression. ''Your ex was a jerk.''

''Agreed. So why are we fighting?''

''Because you're my friend. And you're about to make a giant mistake, one I don't want to see you make or sanction by giving it editorial approval.'' The red-haired magazine editor continued more gently, ''Let's be realistic here. You're an attractive woman...a capable woman...a wonderful beginning writer—'' Constance looked Mollie up and down, her gaze critically surveying Mollie's slender five-foot-six height, her shoulder-length, chestnut-brown hair and wide green eyes.

''If hitherto unacknowledged.''

''Only because thus far you haven't been able to come up with a story idea that is timely and sensational enough.''

''But you do agree, joining the marines as an officer—and writing about it as I live it, à la George Plimpton—is worth reading about!''

''Heavens, yes. Otherwise I wouldn't be standing here talking to you about it. I think an article like that could be just what this magazine needs to boost its flagging circulation. But Mollie, couldn't you just hire someone to take the military training for you and maybe keep a journal or something? You could still coauthor the story—''

''Without the pain.''

''Right.''

''No pain, no gain.''

''Mollie!''

''Come on, Constance, you know that would never work. No nonwriter would ever observe and record all that I wanted and needed to do the article. Besides, I want to do this on a no-holds-barred basis. Plimpton would have never hired someone to take football training camp for *him*."

"Did you ever see the television footage of what happened to him when he tried to run the quarterback sneak twice in a row?"

"He got pulverized."

"Exactly. And not once, Mollie, but twice." Constance's voice rose with the intensity of her emotions.

"That won't happen to me, Constance." Mollie sat farther back in the sling-style canvas chair, putting one booted, wool-trousered leg across the opposite knee. The narrow black pants were stylish, comfortable and warm in the New York City winter. Above them she wore a soft maroon lamb's wool sweater that reached just below her hips.

"Oh, no? OCS lasts ten weeks. And after that comes what?"

"TBS. The basic school." Mollie's voice was nonchalant.

"And what do they do there?"

"Teach us about marksmanship and map reading. Combat intelligence. Helicopter-borne and amphibious operations. Patrolling, logistics, military law..." The list went on and on. Mollie had pored over it and all the information her recruiter—an officer-selection officer—had given her for hours.

Constance had seemed to grow paler at the lengthy recitation, but she was also increasingly subdued and reflective. Seriously, she said, "You've really studied up on this?"

"I wouldn't be here asking for your approval if I hadn't."

"Okay, you've sold me on the idea. It would make a

marvelous story for our magazine. Heavens knows we haven't done anything remotely like it in the past. But are you sure you can handle it, Mollie? Are you sure you want to commit yourself to something this…difficult?''

To Mollie, the challenge presented by joining the marines was most of the allure. But there was also truth in what Constance was saying. Mollie bit down on a silent curse. Secretly, to her the lengthy stay sounded like a death sentence, too. Before all was said and done, she was talking about at least eight or nine months of her life, more if she elected to stay and get special training. But she wouldn't admit it or give in to her fears. She'd done enough of that in the past, compromising and backing down—with disastrous results.

''Look, Mollie, I care about you,'' Constance began softly.

Much as an older sister would have counseled her, Mollie thought.

''I know that.'' Mollie echoed her mentor's soothing tone and was rewarded with an exasperatedly wry look.

Nonetheless, Constance continued. ''I know your divorce was hard on you.''

''You're damn right about that much.'' The corners of her mouth turned down unhappily as she recalled how she had drifted in the two years since. Truthfully, she wasn't sure yet what she wanted to do with her life, except maybe write for a living. The idea of having an identity crisis at twenty-eight seemed ludicrous, but that was exactly where she was.

''But to do this—what happens when you get all the information you need? Are you just going to quit? Will they let you do that?''

About that much, Mollie wasn't sure. ''My recruiter said if I want out, all I have to do is resign before I finish

OCS, that the Marine Corps has no interest in keeping unhappy, unproductive people on the payroll.'' He had also assured Mollie she would not be unhappy. ''Back me on this, Constance. Please? I need to prove myself, to know I can do this.'' And after that, Mollie thought hopefully, maybe she would have all the answers. Or at least a better idea of what she wanted to do. And in the meantime, she would get paid, have a place to stay, free meals and medical care....

''And if you can't hack it?'' Constance asked gently.

''At least I will have given it my all. I'll have tried. And that's more than I've done in a long time. Besides, it's the quickest way to get me to literary stardom.''

''Or death,'' Constance said dryly, adjusting the pearls looped around her neck.

Mollie paused to take in her editor's navy wool suit. Classically tailored, it was done in a power color that suited the forty-eight-year-old woman perfectly. Constance's assurance, gained from years of working at something she was good at and loved, was a quality Mollie wanted for herself in greater abundance.

''Surely you exaggerate, Constance. I've checked into it. All I have to be able to do to graduate is to run a mile and a half in ten minutes, do a flexed arm hang for up to seventy seconds and fifty sit-ups in less than a minute. I can do two of the above three items now, as we speak.'' She had been practicing from the day she had decided to join the marines. She had always been slim and since her divorce had no trouble keeping weight off. She exercised daily and in addition ran two miles three times a week. Lately, she'd added weight lifting to her regimen. ''I admit I still need to increase my upper body strength and work on the flexed arm hang, but I promise you I'll have that much down pat, too, before I leave for OCS.''

Constance stopped arguing. "Which is when?"

"March fifteenth."

Constance covered her face with her hands. "Three weeks." Silence fell briefly in the room. Then she let her gaze meet Mollie's. "What about your teaching job?"

"I've already told the district I won't be back. They have to find another high school English teacher."

"You're that serious about this?" Constance walked back to her desk and stood gazing out at the smoggy, skyscraper-filled skyline.

"I've given up my apartment."

Constance arched both brows curiously. "Why not just sublet?"

"Because the military might check into my background. They'd wonder why I would elect to keep an apartment if I was serious about staying in the corps." And then, too, secretly it had been an act of faith on her part. She hoped to be able to afford a much better place when she returned to New York after writing the article.

"All right. You'll keep in touch?"

"I'll call or write you from Quantico, Virginia, first chance I get."

Constance walked her to the door, then faced her apprehensively. "Good luck."

"Thanks." Mollie smiled broadly. "I'm going to come back a winner; you'll see."

Chapter One

"Tell me again why I let you talk me into working out on our Saturday afternoon off when I could be in town, enjoying liberty, or back in my bunk, sound asleep," Greta Dunn pleaded with characteristic high drama.

"Because you want to be commissioned a second lieutenant as badly as I do," Mollie replied. Dramatically, she thumped her open palm against her chest. "And don't blame this lung buster on me. I only suggested we work out on the confidence course."

"Don't remind me," Greta moaned. "If it had been up to you, we'd have been climbing those ladders, negotiating heights, swinging on ropes and dropping down poles all afternoon."

Instead, Mollie thought, they were out in the hills and fields of the military base, bypassing the regular paths and running trails for a more challenging workout. A workout that might kill her yet.

Greta continued defending her choice of activities. "Doesn't this make a good change of pace from our normal daily routine?"

"I admit I enjoy running when we're not in formation, for once," Mollie said between evenly spaced breaths. "As for the other, what wouldn't be a nice change of pace from our Monday-through-Friday routine? We're up at three forty-five in the morning to put the barracks in order and dress. Breakfast. Then into running gear and two hours of physical-fitness training. Showers. More class. Lunch. Another two hours of class, two hours of drill. Dinner. Another hour of class or more drill. Even the two hours of free time before lights out at ten o'clock are filled with more activity—rifle cleaning, boot polishing, studying. On Saturdays we're expected to put in half a day before going on liberty for the rest of the weekend.'' Mollie paused reflectively. Comically, she made an expression of supreme distaste. Maybe her editor at *Super Women* magazine had been right. Maybe Mollie was crazy. ''What was the point of this run again?'' Mollie puffed as they encountered yet another hill. Despite her excellent physical condition, her face was flushed and hot with exertion. Her feet felt like lead in the heavy combat boots.

Greta grinned and shook her head in mock exasperation. ''I wanted to get us ready for the stamina course. You remember. The triple event we've got to be able to master to graduate. The two-mile run on hills with obstacles. Only then we'll be carrying our field gear, packs, rifles.''

Formerly married to—and now divorced from—a marine, the twenty-three-year-old Greta Dunn was more familiar with Marine Corps routine and successful at maintaining the proper image at all times. Her shoes were always shined to a high-gloss black, her clothes always clean and pressed. You could bounce a quarter on her bed. Everything was perfect. Add to that, she had graduated from Texas A & M with an engineering degree and had a way of talking anyone into anything. There was no doubt Greta was a born leader and would go a long way, if her well-known penchant for high jinks didn't get her into trouble. And even then, Mollie felt, Greta would probably talk her way out of it.

Envisioning the heavy gear they would have to carry, Mollie groaned. "Oh, God, I'll never make it." Wearily, Mollie ground to a halt as they reached the top of the hill. Despite the breezy, cool April afternoon, perspiration was dotting her face. Once stopped, Mollie couldn't seem to get started again. "I'm dying. I know it." She bent over from the waist, clutching her side.

"No, you're not, Mollie. Come on, be tough," Greta encouraged as she pulled Mollie upright and dragged her along until they were running again, side by side. Together, the two women trampled down a ravine, jumped a small stream that wound down toward the Potomac and agilely stormed up the opposite bank. "Remember what your recruiter said, now. When you're finished here, you're going to be one of the few...the proud...the marines."

Greta made Mollie laugh and lose her concentration. She broke stride slightly, and Greta raced on ahead of her. Pumping her legs hard to keep up, Mollie chased after Greta, not catching her until the next vibrant green hillside. Dotted with pine and spruce, it was thick with lush undergrowth, inundated with the fresh scent of spring. Mollie had to be careful not to trip over the labyrinth of vines and wildflowers. But she didn't mind the adversity, not really, not when it was such a beautiful day and she had such an intense case of spring fever.

Because bantering and camaraderie made a late afternoon's voluntary trek go faster and easier, Mollie continued griping and questioning her friend's advice with a theatrical flair she knew Greta would get a charge out of. "What do you mean, be tough? I was tough. The day I signed up for the marines. Since then it's been all downhill."

"Don't I know it, since I've been right by your side every step of the way—Grandma."

Mollie grinned at the name given her by the other members of the platoon—a nickname Greta rarely resisted a chance to use. The truth was that Mollie didn't know what she would have done without Greta. The two candidates regularly buoyed each other's spirits, helped each other, shared both their worries and hopes.

Several other younger candidates, also working out in hopes of gaining a competitive edge over their peers, passed both Greta and Mollie, and scowling with competitive frustration, Greta picked up her pace to a killer rate, forcing Mollie to speed up her steps, too, if she wanted to hear what her friend was saying.

"I'll bet you graduate at the top of our OCS class despite all this griping and moaning."

Mollie smiled, her speed unconsciously picking up even more. "I am doing well on the written exams, aren't I?"

"Too well. You're making the rest of them—myself excluded, of course—look like morons."

"Well, I gotta excel in something."

They pumped along for the next one hundred yards in silence. Sunshine fell from a brilliant blue sky, bathing their heads and shoulders with warmth. But despite the dazzling quality of the day, Mollie's side finally began to ache interminably.

With a sidelong glance, Greta assessed Mollie's struggle and grinned through her concern. "Hey, Devlin, want to bet a week's worth of polished boots that I do better than you do on the obstacle course next week?"

Betting on anything, everything, was Greta's way of easing the stress of OCS. "No way, pal!" Mollie had enough trouble polishing her own boots, though she'd be damned if she was going to cheat and use floor wax, like someone swore the regular recruits did.

"Come on, Mollie—" Greta edged closer as they started down another incline.

The ground dipped suddenly, turning marshy, then hard by turn, as a result of the recent rains. "Greta, you'd bet on anything. I, on the other hand... Ow!" Mollie lost her footing unexpectedly and tumbled headfirst down an incline. As she landed in a heap at the bottom of the hill, half on top of an old rotted-out log, her swearing began in earnest. That was the one thing she could do marine tough already, Mollie noted with satisfaction, slowly sitting up. Where she had fallen down the incline, her camouflage pants were torn and muddied, and both her knees were badly scraped and bloodied, and dotted with splinters. Trying hard to ignore the brutal stinging sensations radiating up and down her legs, Mollie noted with relief that nothing seemed to be broken or sprained.

Greta walked slowly back to Mollie's side and offered a hand up. She shook her head with mock graveness. "What some people won't do to get out of a little exercise."

Despite Mollie's half-hearted insistence she was fine, Greta insisted she go over to the Navy Medical Center on base and have her knees cleaned up there.

"You know I'm amazed," Greta began conversationally as they neared the infirmary, almost half an hour later. "When you first showed up here, I thought you'd be in and out of the clinic so many times you'd set a record—before you attrited, that was. But this is the first time you've been injured, Grandma. Old Doc Talmadge is going to be surprised to see you're the patient this time. No doubt she thought you were just practicing being the self-appointed platoon medic,'' Greta teased.

''I have been over there a lot, haven't I?'' Mollie murmured, deciding her mud-caked knees looked worse than they actually were.

''You volunteer to accompany the injured person nearly every time someone gets hurt. Of course maybe that's because you were married to a doctor. Kind of got used to hanging around a hospital, hmm?''

For four years that was all Mollie had done—aside from work she merely tolerated at a teaching job in the public schools. But all that ended the day her husband had asked her for a divorce.

Mollie mulled over Greta's theory. That was another of her pal's positive traits—the ability to cut through the gauze and find a person's weaknesses and strengths. ''I do feel comfortable there, in a medical setting, I'll admit. And because I was both a doctor's wife and a teacher, I know first aid.''

''Sure you're not looking for a new husband, one with a military bent?'' Greta asked with a grin that indicated she knew darn well she couldn't be farther off target.

''Hardly,'' Mollie said dryly. She glanced back down at her leg, then over at Greta. Giving back as good as she got, Mollie drew her brows together perplexedly. ''Have I told you recently why you're my friend?''

''No, I don't imagine you can recall right now why that is, either.'' Greta grinned back. Without warning, she slid to a halt, not reacting in the least as Mollie nearly missed stumbling into her. ''Hey, Grandma, wait a minute. Check out that action, would you?''

Mollie swore again, but curiosity had her looking in the direction of Greta's ardent gaze. To their left was a tall man in his early to mid-thirties, if Mollie gauged his age correctly. Long limbed and broad shouldered, he was headed into the infirmary. They only saw him from the back, but his physique was superb, his gait rolling and easy and confident. Very confident. The door shut behind him.

"Wouldn't you like to have a date with that!" Greta breathed.

"You haven't even seen his face!" Mollie accused, still staring in the direction of the clinic.

"Who cares! I'll settle for just his body."

Mollie's pulse was racing, too. The guy had been gorgeous. "No big deal." She shrugged off her reaction to him as they started up the steps.

"No big deal!" Greta echoed in amusement. "How often do we see a guy like that who's not off limits because he's an officer or another candidate? Did it register in your brain that that man wasn't in uniform but an expensive civilian suit? Maybe he's one of those network television men always coming around to scout out a story. Why, I'll bet—"

"Whoa!" Mollie held up a silencing palm. "Don't you think you're letting this civilian-watching get out of hand?"

Since getting her divorce a year ago, Greta had been on the prowl voraciously. Admittedly, she saw men as commodities, to be enjoyed and nothing more. Since becoming divorced herself, Mollie had tried to avoid becoming similarly jaded emotionally. Mollie knew not all men were like her ex. Much as Mollie liked Greta, she wasn't about to let herself get dragged into anything outrageous, even if it was her Saturday off.

"I'd like to see you get a date with a hunk like that." A faint note of "I dare you to try" laced Greta's low, amused murmur.

"I could do that," Mollie said in a bored tone, trying to convey to her cohort it was no big deal. Or anything to be worried over or sought after. Sometimes, at twenty-eight, Mollie did really feel like the platoon grandma.

Greta grinned, picking up on Mollie's slightly lecturing tone. "Then let's see you do it."

Mollie had the sinking feeling she'd just fallen into a trap. "Greta, get serious!"

"I mean it. I'll bet you anything you can't get him to talk to you personally before leaving the clinic."

"This is ridiculous!"

"You're afraid!" Greta crowed triumphantly.

To her chagrin, a fiery blush was heating Mollie's cheeks. First to fall down and scrape her knees and now this. "Hell, no. I could have him eating out of my hand if I wanted to. But—"

"Then do it. Before either he or you leaves the clinic. But you'll have to do it where I can see." Greta jabbed her index finger into Mollie's chest.

"Where are you going to be?" If Greta was so interested in the hunk, Mollie felt she ought to be going in with her.

"I'll be out here, in front of the infirmary. I'll stand a good distance away so as not to interfere with your, um, losing the bet."

A simple gamble Mollie could have bypassed easily. But Greta's assumption that Mollie would lose the wager inflamed Mollie into impetuously accepting the risk. "It's not over yet." An out-and-out dare, Mollie never had been able to refuse.

Greta backed off, still laughing and taunting her friend as she headed into the clinic. What Mollie found inside was more disturbing still. She noticed with mixed feelings that the man they'd just bet on was talking to Dr. Blythe Talmadge, the same navy physician Mollie needed to see.

"Hey, Devlin, how's it going?" Dr. Talmadge looked up to see Mollie approach the desk.

"I got tangled up in the underbrush on a run." Mollie indicated her injured knees with a downward sweep of her palm.

Blythe shook her head, then said to the man beside her, "This is one gal who's every bit as old as I was when I went through navy OCS. Candidate Devlin, I'd like you to meet my brother—" she hesitated momentarily before continuing "—Dave Talmadge."

Mollie said a soft hello.

To her astonishment, Dave Talmadge was even better looking up close. He had slightly curly midnight-black hair; cut in two-inch strands, it tapered neatly above his collar, against the strong corded lines of his neck. His face was rectangular, his jaw stubborn and angled slightly in to his chin. His cheekbones were high, almost hidden in the smooth, deeply tanned skin. She focused on his eyes. They were finely lashed, dark blue, under thick straight brows. His lips were full and sensual, his mouth wide, his nose unremarkable except for a slight crookedness to it that made his looks all the more rugged and masculinely attractive. His was a face she felt she could trust. Yet he seemed both wary and strangely receptive to her as they nodded formally to each other in mute acknowledgment.

Their eyes held for another minute; then he glanced away as if with effort before turning back to return her politely issued greeting.

Aware Dave Talmadge was scrutinizing her as thoroughly and swiftly as she had him, Mollie unconsciously reached toward her hair. Cut in a classic dutch-boy style that was easy to maintain and made use of her natural wave, her hair still felt unusually short and somehow not part of her. Though she knew she looked attractive, she wished for a moment she could go back to the security of having long hair again. And then, just as swiftly she realized nothing would have made her feel any more at ease with Dave Talmadge. Nor less assessed on every level.

"Mollie went to Ohio State, too." Blythe paused to make a notation on the chart before handing it back to the nurse, who promptly disappeared.

"Really?" Dave turned back to her.

Hard to tell what he was thinking, thought Mollie, except he didn't really want to get involved. Didn't want to be standing here listening to his sister make introductions. Curiously, Mollie wondered where Dave was from, what he did for a living, but nothing more was forthcoming from either of them.

"Yes, she did," Blythe confirmed.

Dave looked at his sister with a curious mixture of censoriousness and hidden meaning. Blythe returned his look almost defiantly, but nothing was explained to Mollie, who suddenly found herself looking at the floor. Glancing back at Blythe, Dave said, "Well, look, about dinner—I'll just hang around until you're off and then we can go on into Quantico."

"Okay. Mollie's the last person I have to see."

Blythe ushered Mollie into an examining room. The nurse popped in to see if Blythe needed assistance, but the doctor shook her head. "No, I don't. Isn't your son's birthday party today?"

The navy nurse nodded.

"Well, go on, then. Get cracking and put up those streamers. I'll finish up here."

"Sure, Lieutenant?"

"Positive. Mollie and I have a lot in common, we've discovered. We'll have a great time talking about how homesick we both are for the Midwest." They had in the past, which was, Mollie supposed, a minor violation of the no-fraternization rule. But she didn't worry about it too much, for they were in different branches of the military service and neither had anything to gain, careerwise, by knowing the other.

"So, how's it going, Mollie? Are you keeping up?" Blythe asked as Mollie slipped off her trousers and sat up on the examining table.

"Yeah, I am." Mollie winced as Blythe cut away part of the fabric sticking to her skin and washed the whole area with antiseptic. As Blythe worked, they chatted about specific physical-training tests that had given them both problems.

"Well, don't worry about passing the physical part, Mollie. You're in excellent shape. You'll make it. All us Ohio State grads do. It just may take you a little longer than the younger recruits to master some of the more difficult or taxing maneuvers. Unfortunately, age does count against us in some matters. On the flip side, though, I think we gain a certain cachet from being older. A little extra mental wisdom can sometimes go a long way."

"Amen to that, Doc." Mollie winced as Blythe used a variety of stainless-steel instruments to remove a wealth of splinters.

Blythe peered closer to the dual wounds and shook her head in exasperation. "What'd you do here, Mollie? Try and stuff a whole tree in your leg?"

"Just about." Mollie grimaced again. What Blythe was doing hurt like hell, but she wasn't going to cry or let it get to her. She was a marine now. She could take it.

When both her knees were patched up and thoroughly

bandaged, she put on her torn camouflage pants and went back into the reception area. Dave Talmadge was still waiting for his sister. He looked restless, slightly edgy. Blythe noticed it and smiled but did nothing to offer him any respite from Mollie's company whatsoever.

"I'll be right with you," Blythe called over her shoulder, heading back toward the other end of the empty infirmary. "I just have to return a few calls and let the base service know where I can be reached in case of an emergency."

Dave tossed her a meaningful glance, then shrugged and grinned with no faint amount of exasperation. "Okay, take your time." He seemed to wish she would do anything but that.

Dave turned to Mollie, seemingly at odds about what to do or say. Mollie wondered at his odd behavior, because in all other respects Dave seemed like an extremely confident man.

Another awkward moment passed. Mollie pivoted toward the exit, about to leave, when Greta's wager came to mind. She groaned inwardly, recalling what she had impetuously boasted. "I'll have him eating out of my hand." Despairingly, she wondered what had ever possessed her to make such a claim. But the fact remained that she had made it, and now she was forced to carry it through before she got even more of a reputation as the platoon grandma. Glancing past Dave out the window, she saw not just Greta but four more female candidates from her platoon. Mollie bit down on another oath, frowning deeply. Greta hadn't wasted any time using her leadership and organizational skills. Mollie only hoped, desperately, that Greta had managed it without any of the brass knowing about it. She didn't want this on her record. Then again, what could happen to her by finishing the joke?

She was on liberty. And Blythe's brother was a civilian. If he had half the sense of humor of his younger sister, he wouldn't tell. Would he? That was if he even knew what was going on. Mollie resolutely decided he wouldn't.

Dave, misinterpreting her pained look, automatically closed the distance between them with two long strides, and reaching for her elbow, gallantly asked in a low murmur, "Hey, are you all right?"

"Uh, yeah." Mollie swallowed hard, trying to ignore the burning sensation where his hand gripped her skin.

His hold on her dropped. "For a minute there, I thought you might faint or something."

I only wish, Mollie thought. "I assure you, I'm fine."

He nodded vigorously as if pleased, then glanced down at her knees. "Looks like you got fixed up."

"Yeah, there were a lot of splinters." Mollie found herself nodding, too, and was barely able to stifle a groan.

His suit jacket hung open. He let his hands rest loosely on his waist. The edges of his jacket were pushed back, revealing a taut, trim waist.

"You must have really taken a tumble."

Enough to rip open her heavy cotton camouflage pants, Mollie thought. Feeling a similar need to grab hold of something, Mollie nervously shoved her hands into her trousers pockets; with her right hand she unexpectedly encountered a plastic container of mints she'd smuggled in to lunch with her and never opened. For good reason. As a candidate, to be caught chewing gum or sucking on a mint would heave meant instant ridicule from a platoon sergeant or drill instructor. They saw it ostensibly as a sign of lack of discipline in a candidate. Mollie, however, had become hooked on the small confection years ago and refused to give them up. Cut her hair, yes, she would do that, but give up her cherished mints? One of her few pleasures in life? Never.

"I've been fortunate not to get hurt otherwise. Several candidates in our group have suffered injuries. Especially the two lady lawyers. They're really having trouble. And we had one candidate from Massachusetts who had to drop out because of a severed tendon in her ankle."

"You're a candidate at OCS?" he looked intrigued.

"Isn't it obvious?"

He laughed, glancing down at her camouflage pants and gray sweatshirt, the sleeves of which were now pushed past her elbows. "Afraid so, now that I pay attention to what you're wearing. Well, good luck. I hope you make it."

"Thanks."

Although their exchange had been short and polite, Mollie's pulse was pounding. She was acutely aware of every nuance about him and sensed he felt the same surprising sensitivity to her.

Without warning, he seemed ready to turn away. Mollie, ever mindful of the bet and desperate to keep his attention a while longer, said, in all truthfulness, slowly edging her way toward the door, "Your sister, Dr. Talmadge, is really great. She's…well, just everything a navy doctor should be."

Dave turned back toward Mollie curiously. "Thanks. I'm proud of her."

"I'll bet."

Mollie edged toward the door.

"How much longer do you have before you graduate?" Dave asked impulsively.

"Six weeks."

His expression remained implacable. He seemed to be

fighting some sort of silent inner battle with himself; about what, she couldn't decipher.

"And after that, then what?"

Mollie couldn't tell whether he was asking for himself, out of real curiosity, or inanely, to pass the time while he waited for his sister. She wet her suddenly dry lips and found her voice. "Two weeks' leave, which I plan to take in South Carolina. And then back here for TBS."

"Well, good luck."

His voice was sincere and filled with encouragement, but he made no effort to continue the conversation; indeed, he was backing away from her in a polite way that made Mollie wonder if she had imagined his interest in her, after all. Now slightly aggravated at his eagerness to be rid of her, Mollie determined she would win Greta's wager, after all.

She moved to the door. Frustratingly, he made no effort to go with her. She began limping. The only way she'd win the bet was if he was seen with her. And thus far her fellow candidates outside hadn't seen anything.

As her limp increased, he remained motionless and made no effort to assist her. Finally, she turned to him directly, giving him her most theatrically helpless look, and fluttered her lashes. A frown puckered his forehead. Finally, he sprang chivalrously into action, striding across the empty reception area to head her off at the door. Even so, his attention seemed reluctant, as if he would've preferred not to have anything to do with her.

"Here, let me get that for you." His eyes radiated amusement. His wide grin said he knew full well her limping had been a ploy for male attention. Her walk had been normal when she'd come out into the reception area.

"Thanks." Mollie lingered in the open door, positioning herself in the portal so he couldn't begin to try to close the door but had to remain there, his back holding the door open. Spring air circled all around between them. She reached into her pocket, withdrew the unopened wintergreen mints and opened the top of the package. "Care for a mint?"

For a long moment she thought he wouldn't take one. His eyes read hers: he knew something was up. Mollie felt bad about using him, yet her determination to win was stronger. She wanted to be known as a woman and an officer candidate who got things done, who thought on her feet, who was capable of quick action and faster thinking, no matter what the circumstances.

Dave still look mystified. It was too bad he was a civilian, Mollie thought, surveying the impeccable lines of his muted brown tweed suit, striped shirt and tie. He certainly had the build for it. More so even than some of the pumped-up, weight-lifting male recruits in the four other platoons in her company with whom she took military-history classes. "Why not?" he finally said softly.

Reaching for her palm, he shook out a single mint. Wordlessly, Mollie took the container from him, shook out several more, then placed them in the palm of his hand. Her heart was racing. She'd never been more forward or somehow blatantly suggestive. Out of the corner of her eyes, she could see the candidates dying of laughter in the distance. Greta was the worst, having to hold on to the base of a tree to remain upright. Other candidates were silently holding their sides and covering their mouths. It was an effort for Mollie herself to keep a straight face. To her dismay, she felt the corners of her mouth turning up in a totally inappropriate smile, and she knew her eyes were dancing.

Whatever warmth he had been feeling toward her fled.

Regret that she had used him swept over her once again.

"Thank you," he said softly, popping a mint into his mouth. "I think."

Mollie swallowed hard. "You're welcome." She knew she'd made a mistake, but it was too late to rectify it. She turned away, moving slowly until he was back inside and it was safe to pick up her pace.

Mollie hadn't gone ten yards before she was surrounded by the officer candidates.

"God, I don't believe it," Greta squealed with delight, giving Mollie a joyous hug. "You actually did it."

Enjoying the sudden adoration being offered the "grandma" in their group, Mollie began to strut like the proudest of U.S. servicewomen. "No big deal, candidates!" Mollie spread her hands wide in a gesture that said what she'd accomplished had been absolutely no trouble at all. "I said I'd have him eating out of my hand, and I did." And she looked at Greta, enjoying her turn to gloat. "Sorry you lost your bet."

"What do you mean lost? I bet *on* you, not against you, idiot. They bet against you!" There was another round of screams and more laughter. The jokes continued, each more ribald than the last. After another minute of laughter, they began disbanding, some candidates ambling slowly toward the mess hall for dinner. Greta and Mollie started in the direction of the barracks to change.

"Well, no problem with your reputation as a winner now, is there?" Greta asked, slapping Mollie on the back.

"I can't believe I did it," Mollie groaned, once out of earshot of the others and safely back at the barracks. "Sexistly exploited another human being—"

"Ah, hell, he probably loved it."

Talmadge had looked interested, at least initially, Mollie thought, as she disrobed quickly and stuffed her dirty clothes in the laundry bag at the end of her bunk. But just as swiftly he'd turned unaccountably cool, as if he didn't want to have anything to do with her. Why? She hated to admit it, but the feeling of being pushed away or ignored by him stung.

"So what do you say I polish your boots for a week?" Greta proposed a solution to the bet as the two headed for the showers.

"Thanks, but I think I'll keep doing it. I need the practice," Mollie shouted over the spray of the water.

"Want to go into Quantico with me tonight? Some of us are going in to party," Greta said, slipping into clean clothes.

Mollie considered the offer briefly as she began shampooing her hair. Dave Talmadge was having dinner in the little military village adjacent to and within walking distance of the base. No, Mollie didn't want to go into Quantico and chance running into him. After what she'd done, she wasn't sure she could face him, even if he didn't know how he'd been used. She knew. And she felt guilty as hell.

"No, thanks. I think I'll just study, catch up on some sleep."

"You sure?"

"Positive. Thanks for the invitation."

"Okay, Grandma. But if you change your mind, you know where to find us." Greta disappeared.

Finishing her shower, Mollie relaxed slightly. Greta's joke had eased the tension of a long week of classes and rigorous physical and mental training. But now it was back to business for Mollie. They were all serious about becoming Marine Corps officers. And of those left in the platoon, Mollie was willing to wager that every one of them would make it to graduation. Only Mollie wanted to be at the top of her class.

"SO, HOW'D IT GO with Mollie Devlin?" Blythe teased slyly as she joined her brother seconds later in the infirmary reception area. "You notice this once I didn't introduce you by rank and government service."

He'd noticed that little slip, all right. "Just because you didn't tell her and she doesn't know I'm an officer doesn't make it all right for us to fraternize." As a result, Dave'd been very cool toward her, so much so that he knew he'd probably hurt her feelings, at the very least wounded her feminine pride. But it had been a move on his part that couldn't be helped. He turned back to his sister. "That was a damn awkward situation you put me in."

"I'm sorry." Blythe shrugged unrepentantly. "But you are off duty."

"That doesn't make any difference, Blythe, and you know it. As a candidate, she's off limits to me, and vice versa."

Blythe didn't even try to hide her disappointment in his attitude. "So you told her you were a captain?"

Dave scowled. "No." For the life of him, he didn't know why he hadn't. All he'd had to do was inject his rank and branch of government service into the conversation and the impromptu tête-à-tête would have come to a dead halt. Instead, he'd let it go on, watching her all the while. The truth was, Devlin was good-looking, apparently intelligent, too. But not smart enough to know who not to tangle with, he thought, his ire toward Mollie increasing again without warning.

To Blythe, he explained his omission vaguely. "I didn't want to get into all that with her." He clamped his teeth together and impulsively added, "Though considering the way the meeting turned out, it's just as well you didn't tell her I was a marine, too.''

Blythe tilted her head in a speculative manner. ''Why? What happened?'' She watched Dave's face closely for any hint at what he was feeling.

''I'll tell you what happened.'' Dave's teeth were still clenched. His spine was stiff as a board, and the rest of him was just as untouchable. ''I think—I'm not sure—I was the object of a little bet. The moment I walked back into the clinic, she was surrounded by other female candidates. They were laughing and talking and looking this way and money was changing hands.'' He'd wanted to strangle her for making a fool out of him.

''You don't think—'' Blythe began to laugh. ''Mollie Devlin! No, she wouldn't.''

''She sure as hell did.'' Curious as to the excitement he'd heard going on outside, Dave had moved to the window, where, after a moment, he'd been able to hear enough through the glass to confirm his immediate suspicions. ''I couldn't catch all of it, but apparently it was something about getting me to eat out of her hand. She gave me several mints.''

''And you took them?'' Blythe was clearly disbelieving as she slipped off her white lab coat and grabbed her purse and keys.

''Like the proverbial Adam accepting an apple from Eve.'' He was furious he'd been used that way, and amused. And most of all, he found he wanted to get even.

Dave was still standing at the window, his fists planted firmly on his hips. Casually, he inquired, ''What do you know about her, anyway, on a personal level?''

Several seconds passed. ''Only that she seems like an awfully nice person. That she's divorced, like you—and, like you, never had children during the marriage. Why do you want to know?"

Dave was too wrapped up in his own musings to answer. So, she was divorced, he thought. That explained her manipulative approach toward the opposite sex. He himself had been though a romantically distrustful phase, which he had largely gotten past—until Mollie Devlin had appeared on the scene. Damn her, anyway, for bringing all his negative feelings right back to the fore.

Blythe moved closer, zeroing in on the intensity of his expression. But he wouldn't meet her gaze directly. Rather, Dave concentrated on the future. Several contemplative seconds passed as all sorts of possibilities for evening the score between himself and Mollie Devlin passed through his mind.

Blythe pulled on her trench coat. "Oh, come on, Dave. Stop looking so upset." She tried to coax him out of his vengeful mood. "You know Devlin didn't mean anything by that prank. You know how much pressure those candidates are under, especially at the beginning of OCS. They were probably just letting off steam after a tough week."

"Well, too bad for Devlin she chose me."

Blythe paled and turned wary. She knew enough about that hard-edged tone of his to realize he meant business. "Dave, no! What are you going to do?"

"I don't know yet." Speculation laced his tone and his gaze.

"Dave, don't do anything hasty, anything you'll regret." Blythe might have been two years younger than him, but at the moment she was acting more mature.

"I don't intend to," Dave said silkily, raising both his palms in a surrendering gesture. Certainly his career was too important for him to jeopardize with any infractions of the non-fraternization rule, especially for a little know-it-all like Mollie Devlin. On the other hand, though, there was little chance she'd complain against a man she *thought* was a civilian, especially when she herself was clearly guilty of "conduct unbecoming an officer." No, not when she was still trying to get through OCS. Ten to one, no matter what he did, she wouldn't say a word. And that gave him plenty of license. Damn, but he was going to enjoy this retaliatory gambit, after all.

He turned to his sister in all seriousness and again declined to let her in on the plans forming in his brain—until the time was right, anyway. "But you can count on this much," he finished, watching as Blythe's face grew even paler. "I am going to give Mollie Devlin what she's got coming to her for what she did—in the form of a lesson she'll never, ever, forget."

Chapter Two

"Mollie? This is Dr. Talmadge, over at the Navy Medical Center. Look, I know it's late, but, uh, we've had a..." Blythe paused to clear her throat rather harshly before continuing, and when she spoke again, it was as if she had a frog in her throat and was having extreme trouble getting the words out. "...problem with your blood tests, the ones you took upon your arrival several weeks ago. Due to a mix-up in our records, I, uh, didn't see the results until just this evening. Anyway, I'd like to get this straightened out as soon as possible. I know you're on liberty this evening and that you were just here this afternoon, but could you come over to the dispensary? You know where my office is. I'm here now. It, uh, won't take long. And you don't have to tell anybody about it until I'm sure there truly is a problem. The way the lab's been operating lately—well, you understand. I don't want to get anyone in trouble when it may turn out to be nothing."

"Sure, I understand." Mollie's heart was pounding and her throat was dry, but because she was on a public phone, there was little more she could say. She would have to save her questions for the meeting. Fortunately, most of the other candidates had elected to spend their Saturday night off in one of the bars or restaurants in Quantico.

Only Mollie and another officer candidate, who was asleep at the far end of the dormitory, were in the barracks.

"Good, I'll expect you in fifteen minutes, then." Dr. Talmadge hung up the phone.

Mollie raced the distance to the infirmary, arriving breathless fifteen minutes later. Blythe met her at the door, then locked it behind them. Most of the lights in the medical center were out. "No one here at night, hmmm?" Mollie said. For some reason she couldn't determine, she felt chills running up and down the length of her spine. Nerves, she told herself firmly; this spooky feeling she had was all nerves.

"No, we've got a doctor on call, of course, but we don't get many calls Saturday nights." Blythe stopped just short of the nurses' station on the other side of the reception room. Beyond was a long, darkened corridor with examining rooms on either side. An X-ray area was visible in the distance, as was an opened-door lab where routine blood and urine tests were done.

"Were you called in tonight?" Mollie asked. Blythe seemed unusually distracted. She looked pale and harried. There were splotches of something red on the surgical clothes she wore beneath her lab coat.

"Earlier this afternoon." Blythe was riffling through a stack of manila folders, finally locating the one with Mollie's name. "Listen, the reason I called you in is that mononucleosis showed up on your lab tests. Have you been sick recently?"

"Well, n-no!" Mollie stammered. "Mono!"

"I know. I had much the same stunned reaction." Blythe patted Mollie's arm but didn't look at her directly. "But you have been tired, haven't you? Maybe a little clumsier than normal because of the fatigue?"

"Well, yes, I've been tired. But everyone's been tired. My God, we're up at three forty-five every morning. Lights out are at ten, but I rarely get to sleep before eleven-thirty."

"I know. OCS is tough. Frankly, I'm amazed you were able to carry on, if you were sick."

"So am I." Mollie's mouth formed a perplexed moue.

"Have you had any other symptoms? Headache? Sore throat?"

"No, nothing."

"Hmmm. Well, stranger things have happened." Blythe folded her arms across her chest.

Mollie noticed she was holding a circular white tag. On it was written in black magic marker "Franklin, Bud H.—DOA."

Blythe continued to frown as if in deep thought. "The funny thing is, you've been here...what...four weeks now? And, uh, mono usually runs its course in four to six weeks. However, in any case, I thought I would do another blood culture and give you a shot of antibiotic to ward off any secondary infection just in case... Oh, blast." Blythe looked down at the tag she held in her hand. "I must be more tired than I thought. And still so much to do!"

"Anything I can do to help out?" Mollie was more grateful than Blythe knew for calling her in unofficially. Otherwise, she would have probably been kicked out of OCS. And she'd come too far to drop out now. Only if she were actually commissioned an officer and made it through basic school, would her article be saleable.

"Yeah, as a matter of fact." Blythe shoved the white tag in Mollie's hand. "You can take care of this for me while I go get the necessary supplies." Taking Mollie's elbow, Blythe began walking her down the hall to the very last examining room.

It was dark as Blythe pushed open the door, but enough light filtered in from the hall for Mollie to be able to make out a long draped form on the examining table. Mollie gulped. It looked like a dead body. "Is it...?" The chills Mollie had been feeling earlier came back full force.

"Yes, unfortunately, Bud H. is no longer with us," Blythe said, shoving her hands down into the pockets of her lab coat. She looked at the still form glumly. "He was brought in dead on arrival a couple of hours ago. That's why I'm here so late. I've been waiting for the morgue to come and pick him up. I called them again half an hour ago. They assured me the ambulance would be here in thirty minutes. And that tag has got to be on before they move him. So if you don't mind, why don't you do the honors and place that around his ankle. Just lift the sheet. And don't worry. You won't hurt him. Right now he can't feel a thing." She laughed.

Mollie felt as if she'd walked out of a time warp and onto a strange planet. Blythe was acting awfully weird. However, in retrospect, Mollie could hardly blame her. Perhaps that was what handling DOAs did to one.

"You can handle that, can't you?" Blythe asked, patting Mollie's arm, hardly giving her an opportunity to refuse.

Mollie nodded reluctantly, feeling a little sicker with every passing moment. Like Alice's odyssey through the looking glass, this evening was getting stranger and stranger.

Blythe turned toward the door, not really giving Mollie a chance to refuse. There was a sink and several cupboards that ran perpendicular to the gurney. Blythe reached for a switch beside the sink and turned it on. The room was lit with a very dim glow. At that point, Mollie wasn't sure whether she wanted less light or more. "I have to run across the building, to the offices at the end, to get the keys. All our drugs and supplies are locked up after hours. I'll be right back. Stay here, would you, just in case the guys from the ambulance arrive? I'll be back in a minute." Just that quickly, Blythe was gone, the examining room door sliding to a close with a thud behind Mollie.

Mollie turned back to the corpse with the tag in her hand. Blythe's footsteps were long gone. She was alone with a corpse. Reaction set in. Her teeth started chattering. Her hands were shaking so badly that the tag waved back and forth like a flag fluttering in the breeze. "Okay, there's nothing to be afraid of." Mollie took a big gulp of air and continued talking to herself as she approached the body. He was a big man; she'd give him that. His feet fell off the end of the gurney. "He's dead. I can't hurt him. He can't hurt me." Mollie started to reach for the sheet. She'd just grabbed the corner of it when a low, gutteral moan sounded.

She froze.

Just nerves, she told herself firmly.

"This isn't happening. He's dead. He can't talk, can't moan," Mollie said, backing up. She waited another half a minute, ashamed of her own cowardice, yet still shaking badly, sure what she'd heard had been the product of her overactive imagination and nothing more. Yet despite all her assurances, she couldn't bring herself to try to touch Bud H. again. Where was Blythe? What was taking her so long? Mollie didn't want to be alone in there. Yet she knew she was being childish.

She started forward again. The corpse didn't moan this time, but something even more telling happened. Without warning, blood started seeping through the upper portion of the sheet, slowly at first, just a drop, then two. This time Mollie's moan of dismay was audible. She held a clenched fist against her hand to still the anguished sounds of fright coming from her mouth. Corpses that had been dead several hours didn't suddenly start to bleed, did they?

"Tell me this isn't happening," she whispered tormentedly, yet even in the seconds as she spoke, blood continued to gush forward at an ever-escalating rate, the stain spreading across what looked to be the broad surface of a man's chest. At first the jagged-edged pool covered two inches, then four, then six. And a mere five or six seconds had passed. The only sound in the room was the faint rustle of cloth as Mollie's knees knocked together through her fatigues.

She knew what she had to do. Approaching determinedly, Mollie forced herself to overcome her fear and revulsion. Carefully but quickly, she began turning back the corner of the sheet. "Bud Franklin?" she whispered tremblingly as dark black hair and a tanned, perfectly unscarred forehead appeared. She was shaking so hard she could barely manage that much, unsure of what she would find next.

"Guess again, darlin'," came the startingly clear and audibly masculine reply. Without warning, the sheet was wrested downward; Mollie's wrist was grabbed and held in a tight, steely grip. Mollie was so panic-stricken she couldn't think, couldn't move, couldn't seem to do anything but shut her eyes and pray. Just that swiftly, her gasp turned into a scream. A second hand was clamped around the back of her neck and down over her mouth, to muffle the sounds. Despite her struggles, her head was lowered inexorably, until her senses swam with the clean, fragrant scent of her accoster's skin, the temptingly spicy fragance of his after-shave. And something else, something patently artificial. Mollie opened her eyes and found herself staring deeply into the angry, challenging gaze of the alleged victim. Recognition hit her like a hammer blow to the stomach. And still holding her captive, the "corpse" sat up.

IT TOOK HER LESS than two seconds to wrest free of him. "Dave Talmadge!" The force of her shock sent her back against the wall closest to the door. She took in one deep breath, then another, fury flooding her instantaneously, giving her strength. "You eccentric, maniacal, infantile turkey!" Flattened against the wall, her arms spread on either side of her, Mollie was still having trouble breathing, so great was her shock. She felt that her heart was going to leap right out of her chest any minute. Damn him for scaring her so! As it was, her legs were so weak they would barely support her.

"I thought you'd recognize me," Dave drawled indolently. Swinging his legs around to the side of the gurney, he lazily tossed off the sheet and peeled a sticky, wet plastic packet from the front of his water-repellent jacket. With an economy of motion she found admirable, he rose and sauntered to the sink. Seconds later, the offending plastic packet—responsible for the fake blood—was safely ensconced in a bed of paper towels. He had unzipped the light windbreaker that had been protecting the rest of his clothes from the gleaming red liquid and rolled it into a ball. After washing his hands quickly, he stood before her, remarkably spotless and unscathed.

Mollie wanted to punch him in the face. He had planned the whole escapade, right down to the fake blood, the big lug!

Recognizing the intensity of her emotions, he allowed one side of his mouth to curl up. "Care for some cinnamon mints?" He reached into his pocket calmly. Sauntering closer, he held out a fresh pack, waving it under her nose.

"No, thanks." She shoved them away decisively.

He pretended to study the mints in a perplexed manner. "Don't care to eat out of someone else's hand, I guess. It must lose all meaning if it's not part of a public display." He pressed the unopened package of mints into Mollie's hand and curled her resisting fingers around them. Silkily, he warned, "Careful, darlin', they might burn your tongue. They're awfully hot."

As was he, apparently.

But then, so was Mollie. She straightened and pushed back her hair with one hand. She used the other hand as a battering ram against his chest, the flat of her palm pushing him away. She strode past him, feeling trapped and caged in the small examining room. Yet she didn't dare try to run, not yet. For one thing, he was standing right next to the door. For another, he didn't look as if he were inclined to let her go anywhere, not yet, not until he'd had his say.

However, she felt he'd already won retribution enough. "There are words for guys like you!" She shoved the insult through tightly gritted teeth and without warning tossed the package of mints back at him with an underhand throw.

He caught the mints with an effortless flick of his wrist, his eyes never leaving hers. "Yeah." His cynical, appraising glance covered her from head to toe, lingering on her breasts before coming back to rest on her mouth. "And words for women who make bets about men, too." He moved a threatening step closer.

Mollie gulped. How much did he know about that? If he'd overheard even half of her sophomoric boasts to Greta, he had a right to be angry, or at the very least feel resentful, used. "How did you—?" Her words were quiet, uneasy. She had the feeling she'd gotten on the bad side of what could be a very dangerous man.

"I overheard." His voice was as cold as chipped ice. "As did everyone else within shouting distance of the parking lot or dispensary building."

Mollie flushed warmly and said nothing. She knew they'd gone about the wager in a way that had been about as subtle as taking out an ad in the newspaper. And she had no one to blame but herself, that and the pressure they'd all been under.

Blythe entered, looking sheepish.

Mollie was still having trouble regaining her composure. She exhaled tremulously, looking around for something to hang on to. There was nothing within easy reach save the gurney—and a plastic packet of fake vampire blood that had been all used up. "Clever." Mollie picked it up, trying for a voice with some degree of normalcy.

"Lucky I was able to find it. The stores don't carry it much except for Halloween." Dave brought his fists up to rest on his hips.

Mollie decided she was lucky he wasn't in the military himself. He probably could have, and would have, turned her in to her commanding officer. And then she would have been out.

Raising her face to his, she studied him silently. She decided abruptly she'd more than paid for the way she'd used him to win a wager. He hadn't been forced to scare her half out of her wits. "I owe you one, Talmadge." Her threat was cool, as remote and self-possessed as her returning sensibilities.

His eyes narrowed slightly. Half his mouth crooked up in a challenging smile. "You could call it even." The low, soothing masculine tone was inherently deceptive. Everything about him was coiled, ready to jump at her first misstep.

"Even!" She echoed him in a harsh, censuring voice. "I'll do that when hell freezes over and not a minute sooner."

He looked at her in a way that narrowed the world down to just the two of them, to just that moment. He shrugged languidly. "You know what they say: he who laughs last laughs best."

And Dave Talmadge was a man who would never under any circumstances let Mollie have the last word, even if she became a full-fledged marine. Frustration made her blood boil, but she knew when to give up. At least for now, she amended silently.

Mollie looked to Blythe. "Then the…the business about my having mono, the blood tests, was all made up?" Mollie looked from brother to sister inquiringly.

"Every bit," Blythe said apologetically, holding up her hands and spreading them wide. "Mollie, I'm sorry. But I got roped into this…."

"Blythe didn't want to help me, but I told her if she didn't, I'd find someone else who would." Dave was still watching Mollie, amusement playing on his face.

"Someone I'm not sure could have been counted on to keep the joke as in control as it stayed." Blythe shot a censuring look at her brother.

Dave grinned back at Blythe unrepentantly and shoved his hands in the pockets of his jeans. Mollie's attention was drawn to the rock-hard thighs, the muscular calves, the long, lean legs and even slimmer, more tensile-looking torso. No, Dave was not a man she wanted to tangle with physically. Maybe it was best she just forget him. That was, if she could. Somehow she had the feeling he was going to stay in her mind for a long, long time, and not just as a corpse.

"Well, gotta be shoving off," Dave chimed through a smug smile, apparently satisfied that his debt had been paid. "Thanks, Sis." He paused to give his sister a tender kiss on the forehead, then turned back to Mollie, the mints still in his hands. he looked like a devil in a red rugby shirt. He grinned rakishly at Mollie, reading her angry glance. "Maybe it'd be better if the two of us didn't meet again." He picked up his soiled windbreaker with his left hand, gave her a mock two-fingered salute with his right and spun away on his heel.

"And happy trails to you, too," Mollie said, watching his retreating back.

"You're not angry with me?" Blythe asked as soon as he'd left. Swiftly, she righted the examining room, folding the fake packet of blood into the paper towels and depositing it in a plastic garbage sack, and switched off the light.

"Of course not. But you could have warned me," Mollie protested as they walked down the hall.

"Well, frankly, when I started with all that bit about the mono, I thought for sure—"

"No, I didn't suspect a thing." Mollie paused at the nurses' station, inhaling the aroma of freshly brewed coffee. "Well, maybe I wondered a little."

"I knew if the joke didn't work, he'd just try again." Blythe reached into a cupboard and got down paper cups, sugar, packets of cream, plastic stirrers and napkins. "And if he had to do it a second time he'd no doubt think up something even more startling to do."

"Determined, isn't he?" Mollie said, watching as Blythe poured them both some coffee.

"To have the last word? I'm afraid so. Oh, Mollie, he really is a nice guy. If you'd just met under different circumstances..."

Mollie thought the facts of their first meeting had been pretty usual. But she refrained from commenting about how remote Dave had seemed to her, how unwilling to engage in even simple conversation with her while Blythe was otherwise occupied.

"You don't believe me, do you?" Blythe said quietly, pulling up a chair and gesturing for Mollie to do the same.

Mollie grinned ruefully. "Not really, no. I think maybe your brother and I were destined to become instant enemies."

"Enemies or adversaries? It seems to me the two of you are more locked into one-upmanship, marine style, or a battle between the sexes than any genuine ill will toward each other. Look, Dave was divorced a few years ago. It was an unpleasant mess that left him bitter, hurt. He's been hell on women since. Not just you, but all women. Recently he seemed to be over his hurt and disillusionment, but the joke you played on him really set him off. He hates to be used, Mollie."

"I believe you." Mollie exaggerated every word.

"Don't let his prickliness put you off. Underneath it all, he's just as vulnerable and human and caring as you or I. All he needs is someone in his life whom he can care about and who cares about him."

"Your sentiments as a sister are admirable," Mollie hedged. After all Blythe had done for her previously, she hated to hurt her friend's feelings.

"But you think I'm way off the mark?" Blythe asked, seeing through Mollie's evasion immediately.

Mollie decided the best answer in this instance was an honest one. "Yes, I do. I think the last thing your brother needs in his life is a woman, especially the way he's feeling now. And as for the other, well...if I were to hazard a guess, I'd say he had ice water running through his veins."

Blythe tossed back her head and laughed at Mollie's teasing tone. "He struck you as that cold, hmmm?"

Mollie folded her arms across her rib cage and hugged them tightly against her body. She could still recall all too well how unrelenting his grip had been when he'd grabbed her wrist. In those few brief seconds of skirmish, she'd been completely at his mercy, and he had known it. He'd used his maleness, his superior physical strength, as an advantage against her. No, Dave wasn't a man to toy with. Nor did he have a lenient streak or even any vulnerability that she could see. In his own way, he was as driven and grudging and as much a loner as she. "Definitely that cold."

Chapter Three

"So, you really paid that debt in full, huh, buddy?" Percy McCoy wiped the tears of laughter from his eyes and poured two glasses of whiskey. He walked across the living room of his off-base apartment and handed his friend a glass.

"Yeah, I did." Dave stared into his whiskey. He and Percy had been friends since high school. Both had always been fascinated with the military. Dave had chosen the marines as a career; Percy, the navy.

"So why so glum?" Percy stepped around a set of barbells and over a weight-lifting bench to find a well-cushioned lounge chair on the other side of the cramped living room. He picked up a stack of newspapers on the seat of the chair and tossed them haphazardly onto the top of a nearby end table before sitting down. "She had it coming, didn't she?" He cranked the footrest up so he could stretch his legs out indolently.

"Yeah, she did. But I don't know. Maybe I shouldn't have been so hard on her. Blythe was right," Dave said, still torn between amusement and chagrin at his own actions. "That was an underhanded trick to play on her." He took another slow sip of his whiskey and met Percy's knowing look. "But I wanted to make sure she knew who she was dealing with."

"Sounds like you did that, all right. I'm just surprised she didn't start screaming sooner." Percy folded one arm behind his head.

"So was I. Frankly, I thought Blythe would come back before I got a reaction out of her."

"What's she like, anyway, this Mollie Devlin?" Percy asked, taking off his eyeglasses and rubbing the indentation on the bridge of his nose where they had rested.

Dave shrugged, relaxing. He stretched his long legs out in front of him. "Pretty; maybe too damn much so for her own good."

"Come on, you can do better than that," Percy coaxed humorously. "Make me green with envy."

Dave grinned again. That kind of one-upmanship dated back to their college days at Ohio State, when their dorm mates had constantly tried to outdo one another. "All right. Since you asked for it, you'll get the eat-your-heart-out version. She's got brown hair with blond strands woven through it. Big green eyes, long lashes. Fine-boned features…nice chin…good nose. Probably her best feature aside from all that hair and her eyes is her complexion. Her skin looks creamy and soft and has a—I don't know—kind of a peachy glow to it."

"And her body?" Percy asked, his interest warming.

"Better."

Percy made a low growl in the back of his throat. "Too bad for you she's an officer candidate, isn't it?"

Dave nodded. He looked down at his knees, restlessly kneading the fabric of his jeans over his legs. With rueful hindsight, he admitted, "I shouldn't have used the navy clinic as a setting, though, even after hours." Dave knew better; he knew a hell of a lot better. "But it was the only way I could figure to get her in a situation where a joke could be played."

"And what better one for an officer candidate than one involving a corpse?" Percy echoed Dave's sentiments exactly.

Dave nodded. "It all seemed so perfect. And since I'm not stationed at Quantico to begin with..." He knew Blythe wouldn't turn him in. He sensed that, mad or not, Mollie wouldn't either; otherwise, he never would have risked it. No woman was worth the death of his military career.

"Did Blythe enjoy the joke?" Percy reached for his glasses and put them on.

"The beginning, yeah. She wanted to get Mollie over there. But she didn't want me to scare her. I think she's got matchmaking on her mind again."

"That makes two of us," Percy muttered, getting up to add a half-inch of whiskey to his glass. He walked over to hit Dave's glass, too. Putting the bottle aside, he asked genially, "Did Blythe tell you I've asked her out a few times?"

"Yes. She also said she refused to go."

"She says she doesn't have the time to date, which we both know is a—well, it's a mistake that ought to be rectified."

Dave didn't challenge Percy's sentiment. "I think she ought to get out more, too, Percy. But there's very little I can do about it. After all, she is thirty-two and quite capable of making those kinds of decisions for herself. I can't order her to go out three times monthly to keep up her social skills." Never mind pick her beaux for her, Dave thought.

Percy was silent. He went back to the lounge chair and

sat down. He stared at the floor for a long moment. "I guess you know I'm hung up on her."

"You make that clearer every time I see you."

"Yeah? Well, about the only time I see her is when you're around."

Dave took a deep breath. He felt it coming already. "I reckon I know that, too," he said carefully, with humor.

"Do an old buddy a favor?" Percy asked.

"Not another double date fixed up to look like a group outing?" Dread underscored Dave's every word.

"Just one more. Come on. I've done favors for you."

"Yeah, you have at that." Dave paused. "The last 'date' you two had last Christmas ended up with me acting as a referee. I don't fancy myself spending more time in the middle."

"This time it will be different," Percy insisted stubbornly.

Dave's brows lowered like thunderclouds over his eyes. "How so?" He stared at his buddy speculatively. Though Blythe and Percy had known each other since childhood, it hadn't been until recently that something had happened to spark Percy's interest in Blythe. Maybe it was her graduating from med school and finishing her residency. Or maybe just that Blythe was in the navy, too. Or shared a common background. Or all of the above. But whatever it was that was drawing Percy, he was hooked.

"I don't know. It just will, that's all. I think she's mellowing."

Dave guffawed and almost choked on the swallow of whiskey.

"Well, maybe not mellowing," Percy continued reflectively, "But getting used to the idea. A little."

"A little?" Dave echoed, trying and failing to keep a straight face. For reasons unknown to him, the minute

Percy's interest in Blythe perked up, hers had all but gone out the window. Right now she didn't want even to be friends or casual acquaintances.

"You know there's nothing wrong with me." Percy sat straighter, jabbing his thumb into his chest. "It's your sister that's got the problem."

"Don't I know it. All right—" Dave sighed "—I'll see if I can work something out. But then I don't want anything more to do with it. You either manage to see her on your own or forget it. I'm not Blythe's social director."

"Thanks, old buddy."

Dave stayed a while longer, then left to drive back to his own apartment outside Washington. En route, once again his attention turned to Mollie. Why had he acted as impulsively as he had? It wasn't like him to crave revenge, no matter what the circumstances. Yet he'd been unable to get her or her wager from his mind. At first he'd assumed it was because she'd publicly humiliated him, but after he'd seen her again, he'd realized that wasn't it. No, wreaking havoc on her nervous system had more to do with the way she looked and smiled, the way she'd made him yearn for further contact, in just one short meeting. He'd arranged that revenge for one reason and one reason only, so that he might forget her. Instead, all it had done was imprint her image indelibly on his mind. But the fact remained that he would have to forget her. Her rank and his position meant he had no choice.

"COME ON, MOLLIE," Blythe pleaded over the telephone late Sunday morning. "After what happened last night, the least I owe you is lunch. Besides, you don't have any other plans, do you?"

"No." All she planned to do was work on her journal.

"Well, then, what do you say the two of us drive down

to the beach and have lunch. I know a great place about an hour from here. The restaurant is right on the ocean. They serve great seafood. And on Sundays they have an all-you-can-eat buffet. You can't beat the price. It will do you good to get away from the base for a while."

Although Mollie wanted to go, caution tempered her voice. "What about your brother?"

"He took off last night; said something about looking up one of his buddies—no doubt to brag about the joke he played on you. I haven't seen him since." Blythe sounded as relieved as Mollie felt.

"I really should get in a run today." Mollie debated. Exhausted from her dealings with Dave, she'd slept late that morning, thus far only managing to get her laundry done, and little else.

"Then take your jogging clothes with you. You can run on the beach after we eat."

"You seem to be shooting down all my objections," Mollie said wryly. She didn't mind.

"And I intend to keep shooting. Come on, Mollie; what do you say? I'll meet you over at the barracks at noon, and we'll go from there. I've already made reservations."

Mollie agreed, and an hour later they were on their way. As promised, the waterfront restaurant was fantastic. It was situated right off the beach on a cozy inlet. The plush interior was divided into three main dining rooms, all with a view, all surrounded by a deck. No sooner had they entered the restaurant, though, than Blythe froze.

"What is it?" A perplexed Mollie turned in the direction of Blythe's gaze and saw, to her incredulity, Dave and another man seated at the long bar. They still hadn't seen her. Mollie took one step backward and then another, ducking sideways to better shield her face. A litany of swear words ran through her mind. She was swamped with panic. Her hands were perspiring. She knotted them into fists, willing the telltale moisture to evaporate at once. "Did you know they were going to be here?" Mollie asked, her voice wavering tremulously.

But she wasn't the only one attempting to hide. Blythe stepped back beside Mollie. She frowned deeply, looking momentarily as aggravated and nonplussed as Mollie felt.

"I knew about Dave," Blythe said finally. Leaning forward, she peered around a group of people chatting at the bar and hazarded another look at Dave's companion.

Average looking, with dark, thinning hair and black-framed glasses, the tall, stockily built man caught Blythe's shock and smiled back in an encouraging manner.

"I didn't know about Percy." Blythe frowned again and bit down on an oath. Temperamentally, she raked both her hands through her hair.

Mollie was similarly piqued. She was miles from the base on a Sunday afternoon. She had no car. No way to easily make it back. She had no choice but to join Blythe and the others for whatever Blythe had cooked up. Why hadn't she foreseen this? Mollie ranted inwardly. Why had she ever accepted an invitation from Blythe or taken Greta's ridiculous bet? Why had she mercilessly used Dave Talmadge in her joke? More importantly, what was she going to say to Dave now? After what had happened in the clinic the evening before, she had hoped never to run into him again. Darn Blythe, anyway, for maneuvering them into such an awkward situation.

"Who's Percy?" Mollie asked finally, trying without success to slow down the mad thumping of her heart. Calmness, she thought. That was what she needed. An air of tranquility, as if this little get-together weren't going to bother her at all.

The generally unflappable Blythe still looked distracted, upset.

"Lt. Percy McCoy." She answered Mollie's question nervously. "He's with the navy. He and Dave have been friends forever. Percy works at Quantico, too. Damn!" Blythe crossed her arms against her waist and turned away agitatedly.

And it was, unfortunately, at that moment that the group of people temporarily sheltering them from view moved past Mollie and Blythe to the cash register to pay their check. The men glanced up in tandem. Dave's face registered shock. He glanced at Blythe, then back at Mollie. He gave Mollie a slow, unsettling smile—as if he were mentally recounting all that had happened between them since they'd met. And still deciding what he intended to do about it. Mollie's spirits plummeted, and her vision blurred.

Dave was already on his feet. Under the circumstances, she would have expected him to be annoyed. She hadn't expected him to retain his smoldering resentment of her. After all, he'd had the last laugh. But it was in his eyes, in the set lines of his determined white smile, in the taut, poised set of his shoulders. Every inch of him was coiled tight, ready to spring at the slightest provocation.

Before Mollie could do more than draw a breath, he and Percy were standing and sauntering deliberately toward them. Mollie turned and hazarded a glance back at the entrance. She still wanted to run...if it weren't so undignified.

She turned back toward Dave just as he and Percy approached from opposite sides, squeezing the women into the middle of the foursome. The dread Mollie felt was mirrored in Dave's eyes. She took an involuntary step backward. Lazily, Dave put up a hand to stop her from withdrawing any farther. Possessively, he cupped her left elbow with the open palm of his hand. It was an easy, natural gesture, not the least out of line for a man greeting his date in a public place, and yet Mollie was vibrantly aware of his touch. She was aware of him as a man. And she didn't want to be that aware.

"You didn't tell me you were bringing a friend," Dave reprimanded his sister almost indifferently.

Mollie wasn't fooled by Dave's casual tone. He was furious both with Blythe for having tricked him and himself for having fallen into his sister's trap so easily.

She felt a similar anger herself. Why hadn't she guessed what Blythe might be up to, especially after that "Dave's really not so bad" talk Blythe had delivered the previous evening after the retaliatory practical joke. Smoothly, she extricated herself from his grasp. Glancing over and up at him, she favored Dave with her most nonchalant smile. She may not have been prepared for this eventuality, she thought, but she wasn't going to let him get the better of her, either. Not again.

"You didn't tell me you were bringing a friend, either." Blythe turned to her older brother with a dazzling display of cordiality.

Mollie was amused to note that if looks could have killed, Blythe would have slain Dave instantly with her glare.

Dave forced a mock smile, sighed deeply and said, "I guess we're both surprised, then." His steady look told his sister that their mutual actions were going to be discussed later, at length.

Blythe's eyes met her brother's glare for glare; then she let out an angry, exasperated breath. "Surprised isn't the word for it," she murmured haughtily.

Another awkward moment passed before Dave took

charge. Placing both hands firmly on Mollie's shoulders, he turned her wordlessly in the direction of the table he and Percy had reserved. "As long as we're all here, why don't we sit down?" he suggested forcibly. As Mollie walked, she tried to slip free of his guidance. He only tightened his hold on her, in an attempt, no doubt, Mollie thought with a trace of irony, to show her who was boss. Well, she would win this latest skirmish between them yet by ignoring him completely. They seated themselves, Dave and Percy both taking pains to pull out their chairs.

Again, awkwardness fell. Blythe and her brother studiously avoided looking at each other. Mollie glanced at Percy and decided to concentrate on him. She recalled what Blythe had said earlier. "So, lieutenant, you're in the navy, too. What kind of work do you do?"

"I'm with the Navy Investigative Services, the NIS," Percy answered smoothly, as if glad she'd taken the initiative to get the luncheon back into neutral gear. "We handle all security complaints or violations on the base. As you know, the Marine Corps has no organization equivalent to the NIS, so our group does double duty, for the marines and the navy."

"I see," Mollie said.

Who would have thought she could get herself in so much danger so quickly? Yet here she was, with Percy, a man who did investigative work for the marines. Blythe couldn't have picked a worse person for Mollie to lunch with if she'd tried. But of course there was no way Blythe could have known either about her daily diary or that she'd been sending her editor letters detailing some of the more interesting activities at Quantico.

"Something the matter?" Dave had picked up on her loss of color. He was watching her intently.

Mollie shrugged and smiled stiffly. She searched her

mind quickly for some objection that would end the proposed intimacy and came up with the no-fraternization rule. "It's just—I was thinking of regulations. Percy's a lieutenant; so is Blythe.... I'm only an officer candidate."

Dave paused, then turned toward Percy and Blythe. He seemed to be leaving it up to Percy to decide what to do next. Or at the very least, separate Mollie from the rest of them.

"She's right," Percy said slowly, still watching Dave's face intently.

Percy turned back to Blythe reluctantly, as if knowing beforehand what he was going to say was going to raise her ire. "There is a rule against fraternization between enlisted personnel and officers."

"Stop being so 'by the book,'" Blythe countered affably. "The chain of command hasn't been compromised by the fact we're lunching with Mollie. There's no appearance of partiality. Nor has good order, discipline, morale or authority been undermined. Not all contact or association between officers and enlisted personnel or lesser ranking officers is criminal."

Percy agreed reluctantly. "Officers are expected to know their lower-ranking personnel. There's nothing wrong with talking to other marines or navy people when we're on liberty—as long as the association is not on terms of military equality." Percy shot a disquieted look at Blythe. "We both know for us to be sitting here, dining with a candidate—if the brass found out, our actions would be frowned upon. We'd be risking personal and performance counseling, transfer, an administration discharge or revocation of our commissions."

In other words, everything they had all worked so hard for, Mollie thought miserably.

Blythe turned to her brother as if expecting some help

from him. He met her gaze head-on, but whatever he was conveying to his sibling, Mollie was unable to read.

Blythe apparently understood that she would get no help from her brother in extricating them all from the sticky situation. She turned back to her date. "Stop being so dramatic, Percy," Blythe interjected with a frustrated sigh. "You know we're not going to be spotted with Mollie. There's no one else here. We're miles from the base. Even if we did see someone we know, it's very unlikely we would be turned in. Unofficial fraternization like this happens all the time."

"I agree, it's unlikely that we would be reported for one lunch. But if we were reported, we'd all have some explaining to do. We'd all have this on our records. I just think Mollie, as well, should be aware of that risk," Percy finished diplomatically, holding his ground under Blythe's unhappy regard.

Silence fell. Mollie half expected Dave to have lunch with her alone, or at least offer to. That would solve the dilemma. But he made no such offer. Nor did he respond to the curious, half pleading, half reproachful looks he was getting from both his sister and Percy.

For Blythe's sake, Mollie knew what she had to do. She was already reaching for her handbag when Blythe reached over and touched her arm in a staying gesture Mollie felt she had no choice but to obey.

With unexpected gentleness, Blythe implored Percy, "It's not as if we're all on base and in uniform, Percy. We're just taking a little R and R. Mollie has nothing to gain by being here with us. Even if we were turned in for having lunch with her, our superiors would understand that."

Percy vacillated. He wanted to please Blythe.

"Percy, she's my friend. And as for procedure...I don't

give a damn about it. I never have. As far as I'm concerned, the military has far too many rules, most of them unenforceable. I choose my own friends, regardless of rank or service."

Percy's reluctance melted under Blythe's persistent coaxing. "I guess you're right. It's not as if we're instructors at OCS or responsible for her grades there or could smuggle her copies of tests beforehand. Mollie doesn't have anything to gain by being here with us."

Except maybe to get more information from them, Mollie thought guiltily. Information she could use in her magazine article. What would they think of her if they knew about her plans to write a tell-all story about her Marine Corps experiences for *Super Women* magazine? Could she risk staying on and getting closer to these people? Did she really want to lie and misrepresent herself, her motives, any more than was absolutely necessary? Could she manage to even eat anything with Dave Talmadge watching her in that sensual, penetrating way? Abruptly, Mollie knew her first instincts had been right. She had to get out of there as soon as possible. "Look, this is obviously a bad idea. I don't want to cause trouble for anyone. I—" She started to rise.

Dave reached out and captured her wrist. "Sit down, Mollie," he said quietly. The pressure on her wrist remained steady until she did as ordered. His voice dropped an intimate notch. "If this is anyone's fault, it's mine and Blythe's for not leveling with each other about what we intended." He paused, as if irritated with himself for coming to her defense at all, but then, after glancing at Blythe's pleading expression, continued more sociably. "In six weeks, you'll be commissioned an officer, anyway. I think Blythe and Percy… We—" he stumbled over the word that included himself in the tally "—can get through one lunch without compromising anyone's integrity or standing in the military if we keep the conversation to non-work-related matters. Don't you agree, Blythe and Percy?'' He spoke the last sentence as if underlining every word.

Percy gave Dave a curious look, one Blythe mimicked. It was obvious to Mollie that Dave was sending them some sort of message—one both Percy and Blythe seemed to understand. Mollie was left entirely in the dark. In mystified union, Percy and Blythe nodded yes.

''Let's go to the buffet, shall we?'' Blythe said cheerily. ''I'm starved.''

Fortunately, the meal proved easy enough after a rocky start. Dave was remote. He spoke mainly to Percy and simply listened to everyone else with quiet cordiality. Several times he watched Mollie wordlessly. With every glance, a small portion of his anger and resentment of her seemed to melt away.

As much as she could, she tried to avoid looking directly at Dave. But time and time again, she was drawn to him. It was almost as if she couldn't stay away. Mollie didn't like that feeling of chemistry; it wasn't in her plans.

Percy and Blythe were also struggling to remain cordial and relaxed. Still, tension remained between the two. When Percy watched Blythe, hope sparked from his eyes. Blythe responded to that interest coolly at first, then with increasing irritation. And yet several times Mollie noted Blythe looking at Percy intensely, too. But only during the moments when Percy was deep in conversation with Dave and not paying attention to her.

''Weren't you going to run on the beach awhile before we start back?'' Blythe asked as she and Percy lingered desultorily over coffee. She reached for her handbag and opened it.

"Yes, I think I will." Relief flooded through Mollie; at last she had an out.

Unfortunately, no sooner had she spoken than Percy cleared his throat loudly and gave Dave a meaningful look. There was a scraping of several chairs at once as they all moved back away from the table, then a muffled thud. Dave winced, looking as if he'd been kicked under the table. Mollie didn't know by whom. Apparently it didn't matter.

Dave's eyes darkened. He reached forward and rubbed ruefully at his shin. Aware Percy was still watching him steadily, he gave a sigh of resignation. With a decided economy of motion, he placed his napkin next to his place. "Believe it or not, I'd also planned to run. I also brought some jogging clothes. They're in my car. I think I'll go with you, Mollie," he said as he rose to help Mollie with her chair.

"Really, that's not necessary—" Mollie began.

"Oh, yes, it is," Percy intervened with surprising force.

Mollie gave Percy a shocked look, then glanced down and noted Percy had captured Blythe's hand in a staying grip. Blythe had stopped resisting. Dave was still waiting for her. Whether Mollie liked it or not, the matter was settled.

"LISTEN, I WANT YOU TO KNOW I'm sorry about what happened last night at the clinic. I'm not going to say you didn't deserve exactly what you got. You did." Dave's lips compressed together tightly in a self-effacing grimace. "But I am sorry I went through with it."

"Why?" Mollie concentrated on the tall, waving fringe of sea oats anchored in the loose sands of the dune ridge that extended back from the beach by several hundred feet. Beneath them the sand was gray and slightly damp, still bearing the tire tracks of some off-road vehicles. The sky overhead was blustery and gray, filled with fast-moving clouds. It was late afternoon, still early enough in the spring for the beach to be deserted. Around them, the air was brisk and invigorating, laced with the tangy scent of salt spray.

Dave shook his head wordlessly, as if at a loss as to how to answer her question. "I don't know. Maybe because I did scare you. Because it's not in my nature to take advantage of women."

Mollie shot him a sidelong glance, then softened as she saw his confusion. More honestly, she admitted between evenly spaced breaths, "I don't know why I took that bet. I—I don't usually act like that." She lifted her head and let the wind cool her face. "I also had no idea about today."

"I saw the surprised look on your face when you walked into the restaurant." He slowed his pace, keeping his strides small, to match hers better, to make conversation easier.

The wind was blowing his black hair into disarray, making him look more ruggedly handsome than ever. His cheeks were ruddy with the exertion and the cold. His eyes were a dark navy blue against the stormy blue-gray of the sea.

Mollie's side was beginning to ache. He ground to a slow walk, and again he matched her pace, though it was clear to her he could have run on unaffected for several more miles, probably at top speed. "You and Blythe are very close, aren't you?" Breathing deeply, Mollie rested her fists loosely on her waist.

Dave nodded affirmatively, his eyes holding hers several seconds longer than necessary. "Yes, we are." His voice was soft, confidentially low. The reserve he'd exhibited earlier in her presence was fading.

"I envy you that," she said softly, looking out at the crashing white waves pounding down on the shore.

"No brothers and sisters?" Dave asked. When Mollie would have stumbled over a piece of driftwood because she was still looking at the sea, his arm snaked casually around her waist. He guided her wordlessly around the offending object, then just as easily dropped his hold on her.

"No."

"Parents?" Eyes deepening in color, he watched her, mesmerized, as if committing to memory every word she said.

Mollie shrugged. "My mother died when I was ten. My father several years ago. I've been alone ever since."

"So why'd you join the marines? Aside from the slogans you see on posters. What'd you do before this?"

A shiver slid down Mollie's spine. She looked away. "I joined for the sheer challenge of it; I wanted to see if I could do it. Before this I taught high school English for six years." She brushed the bangs from her face ineffectually. They fell in silken splinters over her headband.

"Why'd you quit?" His voice was soft, compelling.

"I discovered it wasn't what I wanted to do in life." His eyes shifted to hers, and held for an intimately long moment.

She moved back slightly, uncomfortable with the idea of getting close to him. Foremost in her mind was that she didn't want to have to lie to him; she didn't want to have to lie to or hurt anyone. Yet she did want to realize her ambition.

"If you hated teaching, why'd you do it so long?"

Mollie sighed. That was even more embarrassing in retrospect. Taking a deep breath, she looked away for a long, enervating moment and then turned back to him and answered honestly, "I was married. My husband was in medical school. I was supporting him. When he finished and began his residency, he no longer needed me. So after four years, we were finished. I was a free woman."

"Did you want the divorce?"

"Not at first I didn't." Mollie gritted her teeth with the memory of that traumatic time in her life. "But when I realized that he'd used me, that he'd never loved me at all, yes, I did." And now she had no regrets; in fact, she felt less burdened, freer, than she had in years.

Dave was looking at her with sudden understanding. She was reminded of what his sister had said about his marital history. "Blythe said you're divorced," she murmured.

If he was surprised by her knowledge, he didn't show it.

After a moment he nodded. "Yes. I've been single for nearly six years, and I intend to stay that way, too. Much to my sister's chagrin, I might note." His mouth turned up ruefully as he spoke, still watching the timeless rush of the waves as they battered against the shore. "She thinks I ought to be married. Probably so I can produce some children to carry on the Talmadge name. God knows our parents would've wanted one of us to marry, and it's not going to be Blythe."

"Why not?"

He shrugged. "She claims men expect too much from a woman when they marry. And she's worked too long and hard to give up her medical degree for housework. I think she's afraid what'll happen to her is what happened to me. She'll pick the wrong person, for all the wrong reasons, and it will end destructively."

"Because you asked too much of your wife?" Mollie knew she shouldn't ask. If he had wanted her to know the reason for his divorce, he would have told her straight-out. But she was consumed by curiosity. She wanted to know what had embittered him so.

At her question, Dave turned toward her sharply. For a moment she thought he wouldn't tell her what had happened to break up his marriage. But after a moment his features softened slightly. He seemed to realize that he had a compassionate, understanding audience.

Softly he related, "I asked my wife to be faithful to me. She...flatly refused...and instead took me for every cent she could get. And no, we didn't have children. I wanted them—eventually. I was just out of college when I married. But it's doubtful my wife ever would have given them to me. She wouldn't have wanted to ruin her figure."

Mollie was silenced by the depth of his hurt. "Why did you marry her?" she asked him quietly at last. What did a man like Dave want in a woman?

He shrugged. "Because I was too young and inexperienced to know the difference between sexual compatibility and love." He turned toward Mollie; his glance darkened and held hers. "Because my parents had died. Because I wanted a renewed sense of family, none of which she could give me, as it turned out. For a while I thought maybe time and effort would solve the problems, but after nearly five years of misery, it still didn't. She wanted out desperately, and I felt miserably trapped, too. So when it ended, it ended. I haven't seen her since. I don't look back."

"But you don't look much to the future, either, do you?" She surprised herself with the impulsive shrewdness of her statement.

"No, I guess I don't. Maybe that's something all divorced people share." He looked at her, the question in his eyes.

He seemed to be wondering how much common ground they truly had, and she knew how he felt. Divorce was devastating, no matter what the circumstances; there was no getting around that. Purposefully, she injected a slight bit of levity into her tone, remarking, "The ones who don't rush right out and remarry."

He grinned and drawled with an insolence she found mesmerizing, "Well, I didn't do that."

Mollie didn't intend to, either. She was finished being trapped in a teaching job she wasn't suited for. Finished fashioning her life to suit a man's. Finished looking to a man for all the answers. She knew now she had to find the solutions, the direction of her life, within herself. That it was up to her to make herself happy. She couldn't keep waiting for a man to come and rescue her. Life didn't work that way. Happiness was something one earned, something one actively sought out. She intended to find her happiness in the fame, fortune and acclaim being a top writer brought.

They began walking again, in the direction he'd parked his car.

Blythe and Percy had waited for them at the restaurant up the beach. "What? No angry glares and insults?" Blythe asked when she saw Mollie and Dave walking companionably toward them.

Mollie noted Blythe looked slightly flushed; Percy was similarly embarrassed. Had they become closer, too, in the interim? Mollie wondered.

Dave sighed and leveled a teasing glance at his sister. "You'll be happy to know I only tripped her twice going up the beach and once on the way back."

Blythe paled slightly, and alarmed, looked at Mollie for comfirmation. Mollie couldn't resist. She shrugged with the same devil-may-care nonchalance Dave had evidenced. "I only slugged him three times. All in all I'd say we got along fairly well. Right, Talmadge?" She popped him playfully in the upper arm.

The grin he sent back to her was dazzling and genuine as he teasingly tweaked her on the nose. "Right, Devlin."

Mollie wasn't sure she could call him her friend at that point, on any level, no matter how casual. Nor were they enemies. She understood him a little better; he understood her. It was a start.

Chapter Four

The next two weeks passed in a haze of hard work and taxing physical endeavors. Mollie didn't hear from Blythe. She did, however, receive an invitation in the mail that came like a bolt out of the blue. It was for Blythe Talmadge's birthday party. Tucked inside the printed invitation was a personal note from Dave. It read simply, "I know Blythe would like you to be there. Hope to see you then. Dave." That was it, two sentences. Yet just glancing at the casually scrawled prose accelerated her pulse.

"So, are you going to go?" Greta asked Mollie when she told her about the invitation Saturday afternoon. Both women were stretched out on their bunks, relaxing after a hard week, still in the uniform they wore all week—green and brown camouflage shirt and trousers, white T-shirts and olive-green socks. Their heavy black combat boots were neatly lined up at the foot of their bunks.

"I'm tempted." Mollie whimsically examined the flat-brimmed green cap in her hand.

"It sounds fabulous!" Greta said, studying the invitation Mollie had showed her on the way back from their voluntary workout on the confidence course. "A moonlight cruise on the Potomac. Did her brother arrange the party?''

''I think so. I know she doesn't have any other family.''

Greta studied her friend's expression. ''You have reservations about attending, don't you?''

''Is it that obvious?''

''I'm afraid so. Is it the no-frat rule? You don't want to be seen at a party for a navy doctor?''

''No.'' Mollie paused and looked behind her to make sure no one else was listening. There was no one else in the squad bay; everyone had gone off on liberty immediately after being dismissed from morning drill. ''Even if I did get caught socializing with Blythe, I don't think much would happen at this point except I'd get a reprimand.'' Which would hurt her military record, Mollie thought, but not her story. An experience like that might even aid her story. She'd get to see firsthand what the military justice system was all about and if the brass was really as serious about the no-frat rule as all the manuals implied. Or if the rule was, as she thought, heavily touted but rarely enforced unless there was absolutely no avoiding doing so because of complaints or an outrageously flagrant violation. ''What I am worried about is her brother.''

''The civilian? I thought you and he had called a truce.''

''Well, we did. I think. It's just...''

''What?''

Mollie's voice dropped to a confiding whisper. ''I haven't been able to stop thinking about him. It's been two weeks since I heard or saw him at all, and yet every time I close my eyes at night, there he is, in brilliant Technicolor.''

Greta laughed. "Sounds to me like you've got a crush on the guy."

Did she? Mollie hated to admit she was intrigued with him. Ever since he'd gone to such lengths to avenge himself, she'd been diverted by him. Learning he was divorced, too—well, that gave them something else in common. "I don't know anything about him, though. I don't even know what he does for a living. Or where he lives."

"Somewhere in the area?"

"I would guess so. But he never said so specifically. Don't you find that strange?"

Greta shrugged uncaringly. "The party's tonight, right?'

"Yeah."

"Then go. If it doesn't work out...well, hey, there are plenty of other fish in the sea. Or men on the Potomac, whatever the case may be."

"I could use a break from the barracks," Mollie replied. "I could use a night in a hotel." Nice starched, nonmilitary sheets, a comfortable mattress on a double bed, room service, her own private shower and bath, time and solitude to write the next day without worrying about anyone looking over her shoulder. It was beginning to sound better and better.

"Well, there are certainly plenty of good hotels in Washington. When does the party start?"

"The invitation said nine o'clock to one."

"Well, get with it, candidate. You've got time to pack a bag and grab a bus into the city, check into somewhere before you have to take a cab to the D.C. boat-company docks. Did Blythe's brother mention anything about picking you up?"

"No, it was just an invitation, pure and simple. For all I know, he's probably got a date." That fact irritated Mollie more than she was willing to admit, even to herself. She didn't even know the man, and she was jealous just thinking he might have a date with someone else.

Greta shrugged nonchalantly. "Well, like I said, kid, there are plenty of other men around."

"Maybe so," Mollie answered. But none of them was quite like Dave.

NINE O'CLOCK found Mollie boarding an old-fashioned white paddle wheeler aptly named the *Potomac Queen.* On board were already some three or four hundred people, most of them either tourists there to take the cruise or members of other private gatherings. The party for Blythe was being held on the enclosed first deck. No sooner had she entered the breezy stateroom said her hello to Blythe and offered her birthday good wishes than Dave was at her side.

"Glad you could make it," he said finally in a casual undertone.

Briefly, his eyes drifted to her softly glossed lips, lower to the deep V and slim skirt of her simple white sheath before returning to her face.

"Thanks for inviting me." Mollie said. Her head tilted back; she told herself it was an involuntary reaction to standing next to a man who was six inches taller than she, not any unsuppressible desire to better see—and again memorize—the lines of his face. From above, the sounds of a live band playing top-forty hits wafted down. Moonlight shimmered in across the dark waters of the Potomac. At the rear of the boat, a bell was clanging, signaling the captain's intention to raise anchor and leave the docks.

"Can I get you something to drink?"

Mollie nodded and named her favorite mixed drink. He

returned moments later with a tequila sunrise for both of them.

"So, did you bring a date?" Mollie asked finally, taking her glass from his hand and trying hard not to touch him. She managed, except for a slight brush of fingers.

"No, did you?"

"No." Mollie's tone of voice was calm, but on the inside she was a bundle of frazzled nerves. Her fingers were hot against the coolness of the glass.

They sipped their drinks in silence. In an effort to regain her equilibrium, Mollie looked awkwardly over at Blythe, who was surrounded by guests. Percy was standing next to her, an arm wrapped around Blythe's waist. Somehow Mollie wasn't surprised. She'd figured Percy's determination would reap benefits. "Did Percy and Blythe come together?"

"Yes. Apparently they've been seeing quite a lot of each other the past couple weeks." Dave frowned.

"Does that bother you?"

He shrugged. "Only in that it might not last." He turned back to Mollie. "I don't want to see either of them hurt."

"I can understand that."

Another silence. Mollie and Dave were joined by a group of men in their early thirties. Most had been drinking. All sported shorter military haircuts, nonmilitary sport coats and ties. "Hey, Dave, some party you're giving here," said a man who introduced himself as Chris Callahan. "Leave it to you to go all out for your sister."

"What I want to know," said the second, "is why you didn't have it at the officers' club at Quantico. Or one of the O-clubs here in Washington. Especially when you're—"

"Not all Blythe's friends are military." Dave cut across

Chris Callahan's voice abruptly. "You know that. Besides, Blythe's always had a fondness for boats." Without warning, Dave seemed uneasy.

"Yeah, well, that's some sister you've got there." Chris looked over at Mollie with interest. He tilted his head sideways and narrowed his eyes. "Tell me you're not Dave's date." He cupped his palms together in prayerful fashion and began to get down on bended knee.

Mollie couldn't help but laugh, his adoration was so comically exaggerated.

"I'm not."

"She is." They both answered in unison, she negatively, he in the affirmative.

Chris raised his brows and lazily straightened to his full height. "Umm-hmm. I see. You want the lady, and the lady doesn't want you." He held up his hands in self-defense before Dave could do much more than take a facetiously threatening step forward. "Okay, okay, we're going." Chris pretended to duck Dave's shadow punch. "We've got to check out the action on the upper decks, anyway."

"You know them well, I take it?" Mollie asked as soon as they left.

Dave nodded, looking uncomfortable again. "They're all marines." He tugged at his tie agitatedly. "Listen, Mollie, we've got to talk."

Before he could continue, a cake was brought out to the delight of a dazzled Blythe.

"But it'll have to wait until later," Dave said as a chorus of "Happy Birthday" began.

As they joined in the singing, Mollie couldn't help but wonder what was making Dave so skittish suddenly. True, she did know very little about him. He had volunteered nothing except a few facts about his divorce and his close relationship with Blythe.

''So, where do you live?'' Mollie asked as they entered an informal line for cake and ice cream.

''I've, ah, got an apartment on the Virginia side of Washington, D.C.''

''You work here, then,'' Mollie ascertained, unable to help but notice he was looking uneasy again.

''Yes. Look, Mollie, I—''

They were interrupted again, by a second group of people Mollie didn't know. Introductions were made on a first-name-only basis all around. Again, Dave was complimented on the spectacular birthday party he was throwing for his younger sister. Chris came down to join the group again. He commented as he stood next to Dave, ''Course to be truly first-class, Dave shoulda thrown it at the O-club, I'm telling you.''

Dave stiffened beside Mollie and turned toward Chris as if to visually cut him off. Missing whatever signals Dave was trying to give him, Chris continued, only slightly slurring his words as he wrapped an arm around Dave's stiff-as-iron shoulders, ''Why, a fine marine officer like Talmadge...''

Mollie choked on her drink. She looked straight at Chris, her mind still laced with shock. ''Did you say...?'' Her voice deserted her, and she looked over at Dave in bewilderment. Unexpectedly, his fingers closed over her wrist.

''Chris was referring to the fact that I'm a captain in the Marine Corps, Mollie.''

A combination of shock and dismay rendered Mollie momentarily speechless. She turned toward him for confirmation, and he met her searching look implacably.

Dave continued pragmatically, more it seemed for the

benefit of others than for her. "Blythe is of course a lieutenant in the navy. If you'll excuse us—" he shot an apologetic glance at the guests clustered around them "—I promised Mollie I'd take her on a tour of the boat."

Mollie waited until they were on the wraparound deck outside the stateroom, away from the noise and laughter of the birthday party, before she spoke. "I don't believe it..." she began angrily, feeling somehow betrayed by the fact he hadn't told her he was also in the service.

Certainly he'd had plenty of opportunities. As had Blythe and Percy. Yet they'd all conspired to keep it from her. Why? How could she have been so unobservant? How could she not have suspected? Sure, he'd been in civilian clothes every time they'd seen each other. His hair was short, she realized, but cut so fashionably she'd paid no attention to its actual length. He was remarkably physically fit for a man his age. Moreover, he had that extremely self-disciplined look common to marines.

His voice was calm, even slightly annoyed as he answered her. "Will you listen to me?"

"No." She yanked free of his grip. "Why didn't you tell me, Dave? Why did I have to find out like that?"

"I was going to tell you."

"When?" Her words were sharp, staccato.

"Tonight. Earlier. Remember when I said we had to talk? Well, that's what it was about."

The fury left her as swiftly as it had come. She realized he was telling the truth and that she was overreacting. She had no right to expect him to have confided anything in her after the way they'd met. She couldn't seem to help it. Somehow, in the time they'd spent together, he had become important to her, an object of her fantasies. To find out he was less than one hundred percent honest had hurt. But perhaps there was a reason for his secrecy.

She leaned against the rail and took several slow, tranquilizing breaths. "Why didn't you tell me when we'd first met? Why didn't Blythe?" All this time she'd thought he was a civilian, never once imagining... And he'd deliberately furthered that image. Suddenly she understood all the meaningful looks, the unspoken thoughts that had gone on between Blythe and Dave and Percy.

He shrugged. "Because initially I didn't want to get involved. I never expected to see you again. Blythe didn't mention it because she knew it would inhibit your feelings toward me—because of the difference in rank and the no-frat rule—and she was matchmaking. After the prank you played, when I decided to get even, I felt it was safer for me if you thought I was a civilian."

"Why weren't you in uniform that first day at Quantico?"

"I had just returned from several days' leave. I stopped by the clinic to pick up Blythe and take her to dinner—hence, the suit and tie. I don't wear my uniform except when I'm on duty. Like most other marines, I prefer to relax in casual civilian clothes. It's easier, because a uniform draws attention."

About that much, Mollie shared his feelings. When she had liberty, off came the traditional camouflage pants, shirts, boots and green cap or the physical-training clothes of gray sweatshirts and pants.

Feeling somewhat calmer and more understanding, she asked, "Where do you work?"

"In Washington, at headquarters. In intelligence."

She realized by the finality of his tone and the classified nature of his job that he wasn't likely to give her much more information about what he did. Accepting, she turned her attention to the second time they'd met. "Why didn't you speak up when we were in the restaurant and the no-frat rule was being discussed?"

"I felt we were all in enough trouble as it was. The less you knew at that point, the more protected you were. At least until we could decide what to do, whether to stay or leave."

Mollie remembered that the conversation between Percy and Blythe had been intense. It would have been difficult, if not almost impossible, to get a word in edgewise. Yet several times Blythe had turned to Dave with a look that pleaded with him to do something. And he had refused steadfastly, keeping his distance from both the argument and Mollie. "And later that day on the beach," she inquired, "why not then?"

"We were still very much adversaries at that point, remember? I didn't trust you not to turn me in for 'conduct unbecoming' regarding my practical joke."

Mollie couldn't help it. Despite her resentment, she started to grin. "Do you trust me now?" she queried with barely checked amusement.

He shrugged. "I'm not one hundred percent certain." He paused and shot her a wary glance beneath lowered brows. "*Are* you going to turn me in?"

"I should."

"And I should turn you in, too."

Her mouth crooked up ruefully. "In that case, we're even."

"Good." He heaved an immense sigh of relief.

For several moments they were silent. It occurred to Mollie that if she were a by-the-book person, she would bid him good-night and never see him socially again. Even in a crowd. But she never had run her life by the book.

Putting all thoughts of self-chastisement and warning

from her mind, she said, "Tell me about yourself. How long have you been in the marines? Do you plan to stay in past your current enlistment?" By unspoken agreement, they circled the first deck and climbed the steps to the second. Dave led her to a shadowed bench that faced the river and the sparkling city lights. A slim quarter-moon rose above the river and glowed luminously against the star-studded, black-velvet backdrop of the night sky.

Dave sat next to her, his thigh nudging hers, his arm curving around her shoulders, resting on the back of the bench. "I've been in the marines since I graduated from college. I've made the corps my career, and I plan to stay in until I retire."

"You're a lifer?" The knowledge shouldn't have mattered to her. She barely knew the man. But it did, if only because it highlighted the difference between them. He was committed to the Marine Corps. She was out to expose it in writing, warts and all.

"You're not happy with my plans?"

"I—I don't know," Mollie lied. "It's just such a shock." Especially when she gave herself a moment to dwell on his specific military occupation. Intelligence! He would have to be in intelligence. Now she would have to be doubly careful. Above all, she didn't want her reasons for joining the marines discovered. For if they were, she suspected she would immediately be given a discharge. And that would mean the end of her article. The end of her hopes for fame and fortune, at least anytime soon. She no longer even had a teaching job to fall back on.

Dave stood and moved restlessly at the rail. Music floated around them. A group of people passed. When they'd gone, he turned back to her and said softly, "My ex-wife felt that way, too. She hated the idea of my being in the service indefinitely, of being on call constantly, of living with the possibility I might suddenly be pressed into service overseas."

"But all servicemen and women deal with that possibility."

"People in intelligence more than others. But you're right. We all run the risk of being drafted into service wherever in the world we're needed on as little as one or two days' notice." His eyes scanned her thoughtfully.

"But you do work here in Washington?"

He nodded. "Headquarters. At the moment I'm something of a troubleshooter. I work with the various embassies in an advisory capacity and occasionally interface with the various NIS people at Quantico. I help tighten security wherever our people are sent, investigate complaints, work with the public affairs people when they need questions answered."

"I see." Mollie said quietly. Someone of Dave's knowledge could be invaluable to her quest. But she didn't want to use him. On the flip side, could she afford to pass up the opportunity to find out whatever information she could from him?

"Does this silence of yours mean I'm forgiven for the secretiveness?"

Mollie nodded. "We all have...facts about us we don't want made public." She only hoped someday he would understand that, in reverse, and be as forgiving of her as she was now of him. Eventually that day would come. She would have to resign from the marines and publish her article in *Super Women.*

Dave smiled and held out his hand. "There's still a party going on downstairs. Do you want to join it—as my date this time, officially, in case anyone asks? I'll see you get home okay."

Mollie smiled back at him, encouraged by the blossoming closeness between them. "I'd like that very much."

"WHAT A PARTY!" Mollie exclaimed, sighing.

True to his word, Dave had escorted her back to her hotel. It was nearly one-thirty in the morning, and the corridors were quiet. By mutual courteous agreement, they kept their voices at a whisper.

"Yeah, it was, wasn't it?" Dave murmured contentedly, watching as Mollie opened her door. "I guess this is it, then. Good night."

Mollie nodded. "I guess so. Thanks for bringing me back to the hotel." She hadn't relished the idea of trying to find a cab from the docks at that time of night.

"You're more than welcome." He squared his shoulders. "So, what are you doing tomorrow?"

"Sleeping in." Transcribing the personally written notes from her journal into the more factual format of professional writing.

"And after that?" he asked, teasingly tracing the line of her jaw with his index finger. "You don't have to be back at the base until evening, do you?"

"Technically, no. But on Sundays I always do my laundry and—" Mollie was dismayed to find her voice was slightly unsteady, her ability to speak coherently similarly diminished.

"You brought your dirty laundry with you?" He laughed softly and shook his head in consternation.

"Yes." She blushed as she admitted to that. "As well as some papers on military history I need to study."

"I could help you study. You could do your laundry at my place. Maybe have lunch with me. If you want, I could even take you back to the base after that."

It was a tempting offer. Mollie did want to know more about him.

Face it, it was more than that. She wanted to spend time with him. A fact that put her in yet another quandary.

"What are you thinking about?" he asked gently, brushing a strand of hair from her face.

Mollie revealed what she was able to. "I was thinking about us, the no-fraternization rule. They've told us at OCS about social contact between officers and enlisted marines or candidates being strictly forbidden. In the past I've disobeyed the rule, mostly on a whim, because I felt a similar situation would never come up again, at least not while I was in OCS. I know Blythe seems to disregard the rule entirely."

"Blythe is only in the service because it pays for her medical training. Once she's served her time, she'll be out." He scornfully outlined his sister's attitude. Seeing her concern, he reassured her gently, "Once you graduate from OCS and are commissioned a second lieutenant, then it will be easier for us to spend time together. We won't have to worry quite so much about being seen together."

"But we do have to worry about that now," she ascertained, watching his face carefully.

Regretfully, he nodded. "If someone were to get wind of our friendship and complain to our superiors, both our motives would be open to scrutiny. It works the same, really, as in any business. If a boss and a secretary see each other socially or romantically outside of business hours, it leads to talk and simultaneously leaves one open to questions or charges of sexual harassment on the part of the higher-level person and charges of sleeping their way to the top on the part of the lower-level officer. Neither of which we need. And yet, I can't help it, Mollie.

I'm drawn to you. Staying away from you does nothing to negate that attraction.''

So he had decided to act on those feelings.

What did Mollie want?

Mollie lapsed into confused silence. What he'd just said made sense and in the civilian environment was all too true. She'd never dated her co-workers in the past for just that reason. Yet here, in the military, she'd already disregarded her previous policy. Not once but several times. Latent rebelliousness on her part? She wondered. Due to being back in the high school-like environment of OCS? Or just plain attraction to the man? She'd been thinking of him constantly the past couple of weeks. That had never happened to her before. She'd never been so obsessed with just a memory. ''Do you feel funny about seeing me?'' she asked quietly.

He met her searching glance with equal intensity. The back of his hand lifted gently, and he brushed her cheek. ''Not enough to stop seeing you,'' he said huskily. He put the tip of his index finger to her lips, cutting off whatever protest she might have been moved to whisper back. ''It's crazy, I know,'' he said softly. ''Even talking to you, never mind being seen with you, goes against every scruple or code of conduct I've adhered to in the past. But I can't seem to help it, Mollie. I think about you all the time. I have since the first day we met.''

She took a ragged breath. ''I think about you, too.''

''Enough to risk seeing me again?''

His honest confession made her decision easy. She nodded. ''Yes.''

''I'll pick you up at noon tomorrow. All right?''

Mollie nodded.

She was in her room, the door shut behind her, Dave long gone, before she recalled the article she was supposed to be writing, the notes she had promised to transcribe from her diary to mail to her editor. Now, in order to make good on her commitment to herself, she would have to get up at dawn. Was she willing to do that just in order to see Dave again? Mollie found she was. On one level, she knew she was acting impetuously, romantically, throwing caution to the wind. But she also knew she was going to enjoy the interlude, that she enjoyed being with Dave. She hadn't felt that way about a man in a very long time. She damn well intended to enjoy every second of pleasure afforded her. Life was too short for her to do otherwise. And she knew Dave felt the same.

DAVE ARRIVED PROMPTLY at noon the next day. Mollie met him in the lobby, her duffel bag stuffed with dirty clothes, her handbag slung over one shoulder and a suitcase filled with writing materials and clean clothes in her hand. In her free arm she carried a collection of texts on military history. "Ready to go?" he asked, automatically reaching for both the duffel bag and suitcase.

She nodded. She'd kept her study materials out, separate from her other notes, so as not to chance having her journal discovered. Her more detailed notes had been packed into a manila envelope and mailed to her editor in New York for safekeeping earlier that morning. By working that way, both had concluded there would be less chance of discovery. A journal was logical to keep. Reams of notes—most of which Mollie wrote on her Sunday afternoons off and promptly mailed before returning to the base—would have been harder to explain.

During her stay at OCS, Mollie had felt guilty from time to time about her subterfuge. But never the guilt she felt now, being with Dave, knowing she was deceiving him every step of the way. For if he had any inkling about what she was really doing at OCS, she knew he wouldn't approve at all.

His apartment was located on the ground floor of a Colonial-style twelve-building complex. It was spacious and new, with a fully equipped galley kitchen and a fenced-in patio off the small combination living/dining room. Not surprisingly, he hadn't put a lot of energy into decorating his abode. There were no pictures on the walls. No plants. But it was clean and neat and sunny. She felt cheerful just walking through his place. Almost shyly, Dave showed her around, ending the tour in front of a double-doored closet that contained a washer and dryer.

Sensing her sudden embarrassment about sorting through her laundry in front of him, he said, "I'll be out in the kitchen while you get things started."

Moments later, when she joined him, he was in the process of making a salad. Wordlessly, he handed her a bunch of carrots and radishes, a vegetable peeler and a small paring knife.

"So tell me about your work," she encouraged. "How is it that you ended up in intelligence?"

"I was always interested in it from the time I was a kid."

"A James Bond fan, hmm?"

"And then some," he admitted readily.

"Did you have any trouble getting into that field?" she asked.

He shook his head negatively. "No, it's not difficult to get in if you're serious about doing that kind of work and have a good record. There's extensive screening done before one is accepted into the training program."

"What attributes do they look for specifically?"

"High IQ, physical strength, the ability to withstand stress."

"And on a personal level, do they investigate candidates there, too?"

His eyes caught hers for a moment as he finished shredding the lettuce. He nodded. "Yes, but that's not really as bad as it sounds. It doesn't matter so much what one has done in the past as long as they're honest about it. In other words, someone with a criminal record is not going to be accepted into the program. But on the other hand, if you had three speeding violations, they wouldn't care as long as you're honest about it. Withholding information or lying about something will immediately disqualify you."

"I see." Guilt flooded her. Defiantly, she pushed the emotion away. She wasn't going to let anything get in the way of her having a nice day with Dave. She could do her soul-searching later, on her own time.

"What do they teach you in intelligence training?"

"How to protect yourself, pick locks, break and enter, ways to withstand torture and psychological stress. The training sessions can get pretty scary and real."

"Do men and women get the same training?"

He nodded affirmatively. "Except for the torture. There are different ways men and women are tortured, so they, uh, handle those classes separately."

"Do you ever get scared?"

"Out on assignment, you mean?" He turned away and rummaged through the refrigerator until he came out with a bottle of vinegar-and-oil dressing. "Most of the stuff I do now is fairly routine."

"But you have worked—I don't know how to say it—undercover?"

He nodded. Seeing the question was important to her, he finally answered, in a quiet, honest tone, "There've been times when I wished I were back in the States and not out on the streets of some foreign country. Blythe wished so, too. And since she's the only family I've got right now, I've tried to comply with her wishes—although technically, because I'm in intelligence, I've got to be prepared to be sent off on assignment, at twenty-four-hour notice, anywhere in the world."

Mollie found she didn't want that to happen. She wanted Dave there, safe, with her. "How do people with families cope with that?"

"Most people in intelligence who do undercover work don't have any living relatives or family. That emotional unconnectedness is important, especially for female operatives, who tend to react most at distressing news of relatives hurt, etcetera, and hence have the potential to become less effective at their jobs and/or open to emotional blackmail. By being a loner—or just able to cut that part of yourself off when necessary—an operative is less open to blackmail. That trait is essential for anyone working in the field."

Did that also mean if something came up, an objection, he would stop seeing her at the snap of a commanding officer's fingers? Mollie wondered. How did she feel about that? Easy—distressed. She didn't want to be left behind either because he was on assignment or had been ordered to stop illegally fraternizing with her.

"I see." Her guard went up again. All things considered, she was letting herself get too involved with this man, too interested in who he was as a person, a marine, a man.

He watched the play of expressions on her face. Finally, he said in a low, soothing voice, "There's probably something I should mention. Because I am in intelligence, my files are reviewed and scrutinized periodically as a matter of security. My relationship with you could conceivably come up."

"And if it does?" Mollie asked.

"I'll be honest about it."

"You don't think anything would happen?"

He shrugged. "I might be told to stop seeing you socially." His troubled glance said he would find that particular order very hard to follow.

As would Mollie.

"I think the washer's stopped," he said finally. "Do you want to put your clothes in the dryer? I'll set the table. We can lunch on the patio."

"Do you plan to work in the field again anytime soon?" Mollie asked minutes later, taking a sip of iced tea. The salad was light, delicious, perfect for the midday meal after a late night.

He shook his head negatively. "No, right now I'm happy with desk work. I like being back in the United States. I've been approached about becoming an instructor. I'm thinking about it. For now I want to be close to Blythe, stay in Washington, D.C."

Mollie was surprised to find she wanted that, too.

Interested in both what he was revealing about himself and his line of work, Mollie kept up the steady stream of questions throughout the meal. Many of her inquiries were too specific. For security reasons, he couldn't answer her. She accepted that readily but still wanted to learn as much as possible from this fascinating man. "So what should I do if I'm ever taken hostage by terrorists?" she asked lazily as, after completing the dishes, they lounged on cushions scattered over the floor and listened to the pulsating beat of rock 'n' roll.

"First, stay calm." He shot her a sideways glance and rolled towards her. A teasing grin spread over his face without warning. His hands grasped both her wrists and drew them slowly to a level even with her head. "Consider yourself captured," he said throatily.

Mollie laughed. She couldn't help it; his demeanor was so obviously unthreatening. And yet, within seconds, the playfulness had become something more potent. Electric sensations shot through her and intensified everywhere their two bodies touched.

Trying hard to maintain her composure, she asked, "And when I'm being scrutinized, what then?" He was looking at her as if memorizing everything about her for all time.

"Nod your head and speak as little as possible. *Avoid* eye contact," he stressed. "Stay neutral."

Neutral? How could she be even remotely indifferent when he was drawn over her, when the muscled wall of his chest was against hers, when she could feel both his arousal and the accelerated thump of his heartbeat blending with hers. "I...don't think I can do that anymore," she whispered, lacing her fingers through the soft, thick hair at the nape of his neck.

"What?" His mouth lowered until it was poised over hers.

"Stay neutral," she murmured.

He kissed her then, his mouth catching hers, lightly at first, then more persuasively, until her lips were parting helplessly and she was returning the embrace, giving fire for fire, touch for subtle, persuasive touch.

When it ended, she was trembling, as was he. He moved away from her reluctantly, got to his feet and offered her a hand up. She took his hand, her fingers shaking slightly as they twined with his. With a hand on the midpoint of the back of her waist, he drew her against him. His lips touched the top of her head. He inhaled the fragrance of her hair and hugged her against him tightly. Not as much desire flowed through her then as need—raw, unadulterated emotional need. The yearning to love and be loved in return.

"Mollie, what are we going to do about this?"

The military said it was wrong. Nothing had ever felt more right to Mollie than her attraction to this strong, sensitive man. "I don't know..." she whispered back. "I just don't know."

"YOU KNOW, we never did get around to studying your military history," Dave remarked as he helped Mollie pack up her belongings and carry them to his car.

"That's okay. I've already got most of the material memorized, anyway. I can study on the bus back to the base and again in my bunk tonight after lights out, if need be."

"Sure?"

"Yes. No problem." She smiled up at him with an inner confidence that was both dazzling and remarkable. Dave could only too well remember how he had been forced to cram for some of the OCS tests on mundane names, dates and places. But maybe, being a former schoolteacher, Mollie was more able to easily prepare for written tests than he. No, his expertise was in the field, in gut reactions to people, when they were lying and when they were telling the truth.

Which brought him to an interesting observation. Mollie Devlin was scrambling all hell out of his character-scrutinizing radar. There were times when he felt she was almost baring her soul to him and other times when she seemed to be hiding almost everything about herself. Maybe that was due to shyness, he thought. Maybe just a reflexive cautiousness in the aftermath of divorce. But whatever it was, it was disabling his innate abilities; he found it perplexing to say the least.

At the moment, her behavior was normal. She seemed open and relaxed. Except for one brief skirmish over her suitcase—she mysteriously, inexplicably, refused to let him carry that but handed him her books and duffel bag filled with clean folded laundry—she was quiet and uncommunicative. A fact that made him wonder belatedly if he had rushed her, kissing her so passionately. He hadn't thought so at the time. Acting on their mutual passion had seemed what they both wanted. Now he wasn't so sure. Now she did seem to have doubts. She didn't, however, explain why or what those reservations were. And sensing she needed time and space to sort out her feelings about their growing involvement, he didn't press her. "I wish I could drive you back to the base," he said, putting his keys into the ignition.

The truth was that wasn't all he wished. He wanted to keep her there with him, for that night, the day after, however long the magic between them kept growing. She was an extremely mesmerizing woman, Mollie Devlin, more complex and courageous than any woman he'd ever met.

"It's better you drop me at the bus station," Mollie said, fastening her seat belt. She'd erased all evidence of their passionate kiss on the floor and looked remote, in control. *Neutral* was the word he would've chosen. He damned his own advice on how to daunt terrorists. Why was he teaching her how to cover her emotions when all he wanted was to uncover them?

"Can I see you again?" he asked.

"Dave—" Again she seemed unsure of herself, almost afraid.

"Next weekend."

She looked over at him, her expression both thoughtful

and disturbed. Eventually she shook her head in confusion. "I...don't know what I'm going to be doing then."

Dave understood how rigorous the demands of OCS were, both physically and mentally. He could understand her not wanting to make a date too far in advance. "Promise me this. You'll call me next Saturday afternoon, at home?" He scribbled his phone number down on a piece of paper and handed it to her. "That way, if you do feel like going out...well, we can make plans. It would be less attention getting than if I called you at your barracks." Seeing her hesitate, he continued in his most persuasive voice. "If you don't want to do anything, I'll understand, but at least we'll have touched base with each other."

"All right," she said finally, smiling again. "I'll call."

"I'll be waiting to hear from you."

Chapter Five

As it turned out, though, Dave didn't have to wait a week to see her. Unfortunately, the circumstances under which they did see one another again weren't the best.

"I'm glad you stopped by today while you were on the base," Percy told Dave quietly early Tuesday morning. "We've got a potential problem. This morning I was given the assignment to look into a problem concerning Mollie Devlin."

"Why, what's she done?" Dave asked. He leaned against the wall, his eyes narrowed in perplexity. He was still harboring good feelings from the weekend they had spent together. He didn't want anything to spoil it. Nor could he imagine Mollie in any major trouble. Pulling a prank, maybe, but doing anything that would warrant an NIS investigation? Never! Which either meant he was more smitten with her than he thought, Dave supposed, or he was slipping—in both his character evaluation and surveillance skills.

"Nothing so far as I can ascertain at this point. One of her classmates has accused her of cheating on tests." Seeing Dave's disbelief, Percy hastened to add, "I've talked to every one of her instructors. None of them substantiates the candidate's claim. So at this point it could be a case of simple jealousy, envy on the part of the candidate who turned Devlin in. The other candidates are constantly cramming. Devlin's gotten almost perfect scores but rarely studies. She does, however, spend time after lights out with what appears to be a diary of some sort. She writes in it and appears to be studying whatever she's written very intensely. Always under cover of darkness, always with a flashlight."

"That's not unusual," Dave broke in defensively. "A lot of candidates are still catching up on various chores after lights out. I studied by flashlight on many occasions myself."

Percy looked as if he wanted to side with Dave and Mollie, but the requirements of his job kept him neutrally determined. Levelly, he continued. "She keeps this diary—which has a lock on it, by the way—at the bottom of her laundry bag at the end of her bunk. And when one of the other candidates—Greta Dunn—teased her about it and wanted to have a look at what she'd written, Mollie got very upset. It was then that the complaining candidate suspected her of cheating. She feels Mollie may have gotten copies of previous tests—or information covered on them—from someone else."

"And is keeping them in a diary?"

"Apparently, from the report, it's a rather large journal—nearly the size of theme paper. And filled with writing. How many candidates do you know of who had time to keep a diary during OCS, Dave? Or even the inclination to write in it regularly?"

"She was a high school English teacher."

"I know that."

Dave recalled Mollie's insistence on carrying her own suitcase and the fact that it had been heavy. Was it possible Mollie was involved in some sort of cheating scam, to smuggle information in or out? Emotionally, he wanted to rail at Percy for even suggesting Mollie might be guilty. Years of experience in the military prompted him to dig for more information, just as Percy was doing. ''What does Candidate Devlin have to say about all this?'' he asked quietly.

Percy tossed down his pen. His lips were set. He shoved his hands in his pockets and looked out his window at the red, white and blue flag whipping in the wind. ''I haven't called her in yet. I was about to.''

Dave's next words were unaccustomedly impulsive. ''Mind if I sit in on the meeting?''

Percy turned to face Dave incredulously. For a moment he said nothing at all. ''It would be highly irregular—'' Percy hesitated. ''At this point, it's a matter for the NIS and her drill instructor or company commander only. Thus far they don't even have enough information or evidence against her to go through office hours.'' Percy casually referred to the lowest level of military justice, imposed by commanding officers on members of their commands. ''As always, prior to the imposition of office hours, or nonjudicial punishment, a preliminary inquiry must be conducted, to gather evidence. I'm still doing that now.''

''Has Devlin been informed her CO is contemplating office hours?''

''She was told a short time ago, yes.''

''And?''

''She waived her right to legal counsel, at least for the moment, insisting she could clear everything up. She's willing to bring her journal in for scrutiny.''

Dave heaved a sigh of relief. ''Then she's innocent.''

''Or more clever than any of us have suspected. But as for your staying to sit in on the meeting—Dave, I don't know. At the very least, as I said, it would be highly irregular.''

Dave was behaving recklessly, even asking to be included. ''You're probably right,'' he agreed readily. He searched for a reason that would hold up under the scrutiny of their superiors. Casually, he continued, ''On the other hand, if someone is amiss on the information she's keeping in her diary—who the hell knows, this might turn out to be another Pentagon Papers-type scandal for the Marine Corps. If I sit in on it, I could personally report back to the proper authorities at headquarters. Besides, she might be more inclined to talk if we're both there. Strength in numbers, all that.''

Percy frowned.

Decorum was against it, Dave knew. If Candidate Devlin were to complain to her commanding officer, there could be hell to pay on his part. Realistically, he doubted she would. After all was said and done, she might even be grateful for his presence. He only knew he couldn't walk away from the situation or Mollie at that point.

''All right, you can stay,'' Percy finally relented. ''But do me a favor and make your presence look official. Don't say much. Just stand there with your arms folded across your chest.''

Twenty minutes later, a pale Mollie walked in the door behind a base MP. She had come directly from the morning's physical training and was dressed in gray sweatshirt and pants. The fringes of her short hair were dampened with perspiration and clinging to her head. She reeled in shock when she saw Dave. Her mouth opened, then shut. She looked from Dave to Percy and back to Dave again. When Dave saw that there was fear in her eyes, he told himself it was natural. In her place, as a candidate, he would have been shook-up if unexpectedly called in.

"Sit down, Candidate Devlin," Percy instructed. He waited while the MP exited the room and closed the office door behind him. Their privacy assured, Percy explained what the charges were, then, looking at her steadily and with unrelenting scrutiny, asked, "Have you been cheating on your tests?"

"Sir. No, sir." Mollie sat up straighter in her chair. She met Percy's scrutiny with a resentful, angry glare. A fury that, if she was innocent, Dave thought, was all too easy to understand.

"What's in the journal you've been keeping?"

Abruptly, Mollie paled. She looked embarrassed. Her hands tightened over the arms of the straight-backed chair. She steadfastly refused to meet Dave's steady glance and did a good job of lifting her gaze only as far as Percy's chin.

"Personal thoughts. My—" she swallowed hard "—impressions of what it has been like to go through OCS."

"But you have been writing in it after lights out?"

"Yes, I have." Her tone remained neutrally respectful.

Percy contemplated her silently for long moments before continuing. "Can you explain your high test grades?"

"I was a high school English teacher before I enlisted in the marines. I know how to study. I have a near photographic memory. Book learning has always come easily to me."

Percy was silent.

Dave noticed, though Mollie was well aware of his presence, that she hadn't looked at him again once; rather, she had kept her eyes trained on Percy's face. Was she hiding something? Was she afraid to face him? He hated the mistrustful direction of his thoughts but was powerless to help her. He had been trained to trust no one, to evaluate people, to determine who was lying and who was not. And right now Mollie had the body language of a person who wasn't being entirely honest. She vacillated between shifting nervously and sitting still. She was avoiding direct eye contact with him entirely and Percy whenever possible. As the questioning went on, there were pauses where he would have expected quick, heated answers. In retrospect, he noted, it was almost as if she weren't all that surprised to have been called in about her diary. Now that was odd. Damned odd.

Dave broke his word to Percy by injecting quietly, "You knew this was going to happen, didn't you?" he said.

At that, Mollie's head snapped up. Her mouth hung open slightly, incredulously. She paused—a fraction of a second too long again.

In a subdued, surprisingly pleasant tone, she admitted, "There's been some resentment that the academic part of the curriculum does come so easily to me. The truth is I don't have to study as much as some of the other candidates. I do have to work almost twice as hard on the confidence course, though."

Percy was unmoved by either her confession or her cooperativeness. "Would you mind handing over this diary for us to look at?" His tone was cool and commanding.

Mollie didn't look happy about Percy's request, but she quietly did as ordered. She swallowed once, twice, as Percy thumbed through the pages.

"What was your purpose in keeping this journal?" Percy asked. Still looking at Mollie, he handed the journal over to Dave.

As Dave thumbed through it, the entries looked harmless enough and indeed reported mainly on trivialities.

What they'd done at PT, what food they had to eat. Occasionally, something about the backgrounds or personal histories of other candidates.

"I wanted to keep track of my progress here. I...I knew I might get discouraged. I thought if I recorded all I had done, day by day, that when and if I did get discouraged, I could simply look back and see how far I'd come from my first day here. Then, too, this has been one of the most memorable experiences in my life. I wanted to keep a record of it."

Dave handed the diary back to Percy. The interview was concluded, and Mollie left to return to her platoon.

An hour later, Dave and Percy both had skimmed through the entire journal. Dave was relieved to see there was no mention of her meetings with him.

"Well—" Percy flipped the diary closed on his desk "—doesn't seem to be any sort of code or confidential information in here." He looked up at Dave. "Do you think she's telling the truth?"

Dave hesitated. "She seemed very nervous," he said finally. Was he being overly suspicious, or was Percy thinking the same thing?

Percy shrugged, abruptly believing in Mollie. "Wouldn't you be? She knew that if there was any truth to the allegations, she risked being thrown out of OCS on an honors violation." Percy pointed to the personnel file on his desk. "She was an honors student in college. Maybe she is one of the lucky people who don't have to study much."

"If her memory is so good, why is it necessary to record it all on paper?" Dave wasn't sure why. He had a lingering feeling of suspicion that despite her surface candor, Mollie Devlin had been holding back a hell of a lot.

Percy shrugged. "Maybe she's sentimental. I hate to bring this up, buddy, but you know her better than I."

"Not that much better." Dave scowled. He realized belatedly, that she'd told him very little about herself, very little that counted.

Percy shuffled through the papers in her file, shrugged and noted seriously, "On paper her profile looks good. There's nothing on the forms she filled out upon enlisting that would cause us to red flag her. She passed her National Agency check and the local police records check. Nothing to implicate her there. I'll go ahead and have the FBI run a routine security clearance on her. They'd do it, anyway, after she was commissioned a second lieutenant. But as far as I'm concerned, the case is already closed." Percy shut the journal and shuffled papers about Mollie's history back into her file. "I'll tell her CO she's clean; there's nothing to warrant the holding of office hours. But just to be on the safe side, we're going to go ahead and run her security clearance a few weeks ahead of time."

Dave rose to leave. He was glad the FBI would be handling the check on Devlin. He was too involved with her as it was.

Percy stopped him with a question before he could open the office door. "You gonna see her again?"

Dave scowled. "I probably shouldn't. Common sense tells me I'm already far too involved with her. But, on the other hand, it does look as if she's innocent. And we did have an agreement to spend time together over the weekend."

"So you're going to risk it?" Percy asked.

Dave hesitated only fractionally. The rational part of him knew he was being a fool to continue breaking the no-frat rule to see Mollie Devlin, that he was putting his own career and reputation on the line. But he was past the point of being able to walk away from her. Like it or not, he cared about her. Maybe more than he wanted to admit, even to himself. "I'll see her as long as I possibly can, yeah. As long as she's here in Virginia, I'll see her whenever, however, I get the chance."

"SO, YOU WANT TO TELL ME what all that business was about this morning, why you got pulled out directly after PT?" Greta asked softly. She and Mollie were sitting on the floor of their barracks, embarking on the nightly ritual of polishing their boots, cans of black polish and combat boots spread out around them.

"Someone turned me in for keeping a diary," Mollie whispered back. Finished rubbing in a good coat of black polish on each combat boot, she quickly began to buff her shoes.

"You're kidding." Greta glanced up in surprise.

Mollie shook her head negatively, her serious expression mirroring the depth of her worry and unease. God, she'd about died when the drill instructor had called her out and informed her only that office hours might be conducted against her, then accompanied her to the barracks so she could get her diary. From there it had quickly gone from bad to worse. An MP had arrived to escort her to the NIS offices; she discovered that it was to be Percy investigating. A triple shock had occurred when she'd seen Dave Talmadge standing by Percy's desk, his arms folded across his chest. She'd wanted to give up, or give in, right then and there. But characteristic grit had kept her hanging in there. Only by keeping her eyes trained on Percy—as well they should have been, since he was the officer interrogating her—was she able to get through the interview.

"What did they say about the diary?" Greta asked, her eyes round with continued amazement.

Mollie shrugged, and dipping cotton balls in water, began "spit shining" her freshly glossed boots. "Not much. They just wanted to make sure I wasn't cheating on tests, that I didn't have copies of previous exams hidden in my diary. When they found out I didn't, they let me go."

"Did they give you your diary back?"

"Not right away." Mollie recalled a day spent with a pounding heart and perspiring palms. Talk about stressful—every second she'd felt as if she were on the verge of a major anxiety attack. It hadn't been that hard on her when she'd found out her husband was suing her for divorce. She took a deep, enervating breath and let it out in a long, heartfelt sigh. "Still, it was a relief to get my diary back tonight." At the moment, her journal was safely ensconced in the bottom of her laundry bag.

"Are you still going to write in it?"

"After being turned in for it? You bet. Besides, the drill instructor said I wasn't doing anything wrong—except writing in it after lights out. For that infraction, I've got two hours' extra drill Saturday afternoon."

"Too bad. I'm glad it was nothing more serious than that," Greta confided.

"Yeah, me, too. I'd hate to be kicked out of here now."

Finished, Mollie looked down at her boots. They were shined to such a high gloss that her image was reflected back perfectly.

An hour later, lying in the darkness of the barracks, her hands folded behind her head, Mollie's mind was still on the events of the morning. Had Dave Talmadge known she was lying through her teeth about the reasons for keeping the diary? What would he have thought had he known? And why had he been there during the interview?

Was headquarters involved in this? How would she manage to continue on with her information-gathering with so many people looking over her shoulder? She now felt she was being watched constantly.

But maybe that was her imagination. Certainly there'd been no major punishment inflicted on her. Mollie would simply have to write in the diary in broad daylight. She'd also have to watch out for whatever candidate was watching her. She couldn't take any chances of ending up in the NIS offices again. She wanted to graduate from OCS at the top of her class, or as close to it as possible.

"WE THINK WE KNOW who turned you in for keeping the diary," Greta and a group of other candidates confided early the next evening.

"We've eliminated everyone else. It had to be Nosy Nellie," Candidate Morrison continued.

They were probably right, Mollie thought. "I'll steer clear of her from now on," Mollie said.

"Don't you want to get even?" Greta asked.

Mollie thought briefly of revenge, then shook her head. "Not really I—I've been in enough trouble as it is." She didn't want to be watched any closer than she already was.

"Well, I want to get her," Candidate Morrison said, moving in closer. "The tattletale turned me in for using floor wax on my boots."

"And she turned me in for taking bets on who would get the highest test score on our last military history exam," Greta grumbled.

"So..." Morrison stepped forward and pulled a small brown plastic medicine container from her pocket. Inside was a triangular-shaped foil packet that looked suspiciously like cheese! "Greta and I have devised the perfect revenge for someone who can't help but stick her nose in everybody else's business. Limburger cheese. We're going to put some in her shampoo. That way, when she goes to take a shower tonight, she won't be able to smell anything but herself."

There was a round of laughter. Mollie was amused by the inventiveness of the prank. She didn't want them to go through with it.

"Don't you think that's kind of mean?"

"Now, Devlin," Candidate Morrison said, "don't get all softhearted on us. Besides, you won't have to do a thing. We've got it all arranged."

Moments later, their plan was in action. Mollie, still uneasy about what they were doing, and worse, almost positive the prank was going to get them all in trouble, stayed on her bunk for the duration.

It didn't take long for trouble to start. Five minutes after Nosy Nellie hit the showers, her screams of rage could be heard echoing through the squad bay. Still dripping wet, with a robe clutched around her and the now open and undoubtedly foul-smelling-shampoo bottle clenched in her fist, she marched back into the squad bay, cussing at everyone in sight.

Everyone involved in the prank looked remarkably innocent except Greta, who was wearing a complacent grin, and Candidate Morrison, who was doubled over on her bunk, wiping tears of laughter from her eyes.

Nosy Nellie headed straight for Morrison and dumped the rest of the shampoo on Morrison and her bunk. Morrison screamed and flew toward Nellie in a rage.

Mollie, seeing the beginning of a brawl, got to her feet immediately and tried to put a stop to it. But it was too late; everyone in the platoon was already taking sides. Push led to shove, then hair pulling and punches. Only the sudden intrusion of their drill instructor put a halt to the ruckus.

They snapped to attention. Their drill instructor inspected the premises with a look of disgust. When she turned to Mollie and the others, Mollie felt a deep sense of shame. She could have stopped the prank, and the fight, before it had started. But she hadn't. And look what had happened. They'd made fools of themselves, wrecked their barracks, and the infighting had literally destroyed whatever group morale their platoon had previously had going for them.

"Get your boots on, candidates," the drill instructor said with a total calm that was all the more fear inspiring. They all knew that the madder their DI got, the less was said to them. "We're going for a ten-mile run with full field gear."

Someone in the foreground had the bad judgment to utter a very small groan.

The DI turned in the direction of the sound. She smiled even more sweetly. "Correction. An *eleven*-mile run. Anyone else?"

Dead silence filled the squad bay. And what followed was no less than the punishment they all deserved for their lack of esprit de corps and lack of judgment.

"So we made a mistake in the timing of the prank," Greta said wearily the next morning at breakfast in the mess hall. "I still say Nosy Nellie deserved exactly what she got."

Mollie'd had plenty of time to think about that during their eleven-mile run. No more was she holding her tongue. "The only person we hurt with that prank was ourselves, Greta."

The group looked up in amazement.

Mollie put down her fork and faced them all equably.

Thinking about what had happened made her furious with herself and with the others. "Look at us. We've all got bruises or sore scalps from the fight. None of us needed an eleven-mile run in the dead of night. The prank all but destroyed morale. And worst and most damaging of all, that slip in group behavior has now earned our platoon the worst reputation in the company."

Morrison nodded glumly. "The men's platoons were buzzing with word of the cat fight. You ought to hear the jokes that have started about us already. The whole fiasco is very humiliating!"

And humbling, Mollie thought. Because it had made her stop and think about everything she'd done, what the Marine Corps stood for, and most importantly, all that their instructors had been trying to teach fellow men and women. "Our DI was right. The prestige of the Marine Corps depends on the appearance of its officers. Last night we wouldn't have made a bunch of hooligans proud of us. Let's face it; we botched it up bad."

For long moments, everyone in the group was silent. Across the mess hall, Nosy Nellie was sitting with her group. The continuing separation of their platoon couldn't have been more obvious.

"So what are you saying?" Greta asked glumly. "That we apologize to Nellie after what she did to you and me and Morrison and the others? I'm not saying what we did was right. On the contrary, it was stupid and mean. But if it teaches her not to mess with us, then I say, job well done."

Others murmured their assent.

Mollie was silent. She toyed with her scrambled eggs, her appetite all but gone. "I only know how I feel, and that's very ashamed of myself—and the platoon. Regardless of what Nellie did to us or didn't do, we had no right to treat her that way. What we did was wrong."

"It's all black and white to you, isn't it?" Greta said sarcastically.

Mollie shrugged. She knew she was sounding like a schoolteacher or a Girl Scout—or a leader. She didn't care. It was past time she stood up for what was right and saw that others did, too. Calmly, she countered, "Maybe it goes back to the golden rule. You know...do unto others as you'd have them do unto you. I only know I wouldn't have wanted anyone to put Limburger cheese in my shampoo. We're supposed to be officers here. If we don't set a good example, who will? How can we expect to have respect from the men and women we're assigned to lead if we don't act in a manner that earns esteem? I think we should apologize," Mollie said firmly, deciding that was the answer.

"Are you crazy?" Morrison asserted. "Are you forgetting what she's done to us in the past? If we apologize now, she'll think she can go on tattling with no retribution coming her way."

"Maybe, and maybe not. Maybe if we're kinder to her, she'll feel more included in the group and won't feel the need to tattle on everyone to score points with the instructors."

The silence around Mollie was stubborn and grudging.

"I only know peace has to start somewhere. And that if we don't do this—well, we can hardly expect the friendships within the platoon to repair themselves magically." Mollie stood. Whether anyone went with her or not, she was going to apologize.

Reluctantly, everyone else got to their feet. Finally, even Greta and Morrison.

"You know, Devlin, you're crazy to be doing this," Greta said.

Mollie disagreed, and for the first time in her life she wasn't afraid to speak up and say so regardless of the peer pressure to conform. "You know I'm right." She made eye contact with everyone in her group. "This backbiting has got to stop now."

There was some grumbling, but finally everyone agreed with Mollie. In tandem they went over to Nellie's table and delivered apologies all around. Nellie was stunned, resentful, but less angry somehow when everyone left.

Mollie felt better, too. She knew she'd made a mistake the previous evening. But the animosity within the platoon didn't have to continue. And with any luck it wouldn't, now that the first step toward peace had been taken.

Fortunately, the rest of the week was both demanding and absorbing. By Friday night, the fracas had all but been forgotten, so delighted was everyone to have passed their rigorous day/night compass test. And though the working relationships were not exactly flawless, everyone was trying harder to work together as a team, to not be so petty or self-involved. Mollie saw that as a very positive sign for all of them, especially their platoon as a whole. It was important that by graduation from OCS they really be able to work together as a group.

"I think we should all go out and whoop it up this weekend. You, too, Devlin," Greta said as they all prepared for lights out. "I know you always think of a reason why you can't go. But this time, I think you should go with us."

Mollie had been supposed to call Dave, to decide whether or not they wanted to do anything together, but after the way he had looked at her in Percy McCoy's office... No, she doubted he wanted to hear from her again.

Greta was watching Mollie curiously. "You've got plans this weekend?" she asked.

"Not anymore." Once the decision was made to break it off with Dave, Mollie felt relief. Unable to resist the opportunity to tease Greta, Mollie pretended to waiver briefly. Eyes sparkling, she said, "I don't know, Greta. Are you sure the others will want Grandma to come along?"

Greta grinned back. "Grandma can leave her rocking chair at home. Come Saturday night, our whole platoon is going to party."

Chapter Six

Party wasn't the word for it, Mollie thought several days later. More like celebrate, as in riotously. Greta had been placing bets right and left all night from everything to who would get the highest score on their upcoming reaction course the next week to who could drink the most watered-down beer. Through it all, Mollie had remained the quietest participant, sipping her beer slowly, coaxing life histories out of some of the other candidates. She considered her evening to be one of true R and R—recreation and research.

"So why did you enlist?" she asked Candidate Cindy Mueller. With her peripheral vision, she watched Greta down another glass of beer.

"My father was a lifer in the marines. My brother refused to enlist, so I'm here to carry on the family tradition."

"Any other reason?" Mollie asked, beginning to enjoy the totally female company she was keeping.

"The travel." Cindy grinned. "The men..."

There was a raucous and lecherous whoop from their group. At several other nearby tables, a group of male candidates—some of whom they knew from their coed academic classes—turned around to look. Before Mollie quite knew what was happening, half her group had defected to join the men. Cindy got up to go to the ladies' room. Not wanting to be approached, Mollie got up and went over to study the selections on the jukebox. She was halfway down the list when the drift of masculine cologne sent her senses spinning.

"Find anything of interest?" a low voice asked.

Mollie glanced up into Dave Talmadge's eyes. He was angry with her—that much was clear—and disappointed. She felt a wave of guilt wash over her for not having contacted him earlier in the day, as she'd initially promised.

"Got change for this?" he asked casually, for the benefit of whoever might be watching as he thrust a crumpled green paper into her hand.

Mollie nodded, then reached into her pockets and produced four quarters.

He didn't take them from her. Rather, he curled them back tightly into her hands.

"Well, now that we know you have the money and the access to a phone—" he looked behind him at the pay phone on the wall "—suppose you start with an explanation."

Remembering how suspicious he had been during the investigation into her diary, she realized she couldn't risk being with him again. She had never been comfortable lying. She was uneasy about deceiving anyone, and to further it— No, it just wasn't possible. The more deeply involved she became with military people, the more she would have to lie. And unnecessary fabrications could escalate. She could trip up and eventually jeopardize her whole writing project. She'd come too far to let that happen, no matter how attracted she was to Dave.

"I changed my mind about seeing you, that's all."

His disappointment in her evident, he reached past her and deposited fifty cents in the machine. With decisive movements, he punched in his selection. Rock music clicked on, loud and energizing, further drowning out the voices.

She started to step past him. He moved, subtly enough not to attract anyone else's attention but enough to block her way. "Something happened between now and the last time we were together to make us sworn enemies?" He leaned back to look at her intently.

She dropped her gaze to the bar's scuffed and scarred wooden floor. "You ought to know," she muttered beneath her breath.

"This place is crawling with military people." He stepped past her, turning sideways. His back to everyone else, he said, "My car's out in the lot. I'll be waiting for you. We can talk there."

"I can't—"

"Just do it," he issued tersely, then turned and walked away.

Mollie stared impotently at his retreating back, then pivoted in frustration toward the jukebox. She ought to leave him out there alone, forever. But if she did, he'd doubtless come back in to get her. And she could do without a public scene.

Angry with herself that she was giving in to his demands so easily but seeing no other course of action possible, Mollie waited about a minute, then slipped out after him. The parking lot was cold and dark. She shivered in the night air as she spotted Dave's car. As she neared, she saw he was seated behind the wheel.

"We have to stop meeting like this." Mollie was only half joking when she climbed in beside him.

"I'll welcome the day when we can." He was serious.

Mollie paused, refusing to let herself get drawn into any romantic conversation. She looked down at her hands and knitted her fingers together nervously. "What were you doing in Percy's office?"

"I was there on other business, so I dropped in to say hello. He alerted me to what was going on."

"Then your presence wasn't official?"

"It was and it wasn't." He flashed a roguish smile.

"Then why stay?"

He looked at her as if surprised she had to ask.

"You could have been in a helluva lot of trouble."

Depression swamped Mollie as she remembered. "Tell me about it," she said glumly. "I wasn't cheating."

"Then why were you so uncomfortable?"

"Have you ever been accused of something you didn't do?"

He shook his head negatively, started to speak, then stopped. "I was going to say no…but yeah, I have been. When I was about ten, I was accused of stealing apples from a neighbor's tree."

"And did you?"

"No."

"How did it make you feel?"

"Humiliated, embarrassed."

"Exactly. Look, I know I acted peculiarly. I always do in situations like that," Mollie explained in a low, passionate undertone. Catching herself, she tried to remain calm and react in a more self-possessed manner. "It's involuntary paranoia, I guess. I felt the same way when I took the exam to get my driver's test. I knew how to drive and could parallel park but was still convinced I was going to fail. Add to that the cloak-and-dagger stuff of my trying to see you when I know I'm violating the no-frat rule." She paused and ran a hand through her hair. Her next thought was harder to admit but maybe just as necessary to voice in order for him to understand why she'd been against seeing him as planned. "I saw your reactions, your suspicions. I'll be honest with you. Your lack of faith in me stung." All the more because of the partial truth. She'd been swamped with guilt and fear all week, two emotions she could not afford to have. And she'd been angry, too, because as far as Dave knew—on the surface, anyway—there had been no basis at all for either his or Percy's suspicions. She hadn't been cheating on her tests; she would never have even considered it.

"I'm sorry about that. I'm guilty there as charged."

"Why? Why were you so quick to believe the worst of me?" She turned toward him. "How could you believe even for an instant I'd cheat?"

"I didn't, not at first. But then, when I saw you, I began to wonder if something wasn't amiss." He held up a silencing palm to stop her instinctive retaliation. "Maybe that's because of the way I've been trained to be super-alert to every nuance of a person's behavior, and you were acting nervous and guilty as hell, Mollie." His tone lowered an introspective notch. "And maybe, too, because I had a wife who was an expert at lying, deceiving. I didn't want to think I'd made the same mistake twice, of being attracted to the same kind of woman."

Mollie felt as if she had been sucker punched in the gut. Was she the same as his ex-wife? Was cheating cheating, no matter what or why the reason? True, she hadn't cheated on her exams, but she had lied about why she wanted to join the marines. Not to serve or defend her country but to further her own journalistic aspirations.

"Add to that," he said tongue in cheek, borrowing her introductory phrase, "always before you struck me as quite together… You were very nervous, Mollie. Trying not to show it, but still very nervous."

What could she say to that? It was the truth. Gathering her wits about her, Mollie continued evenly, "I may be 'together' under normal circumstances—in the clinic, even around bodies that I presume to be dead—but not when I'm singled out of my platoon, picked up by the MPs and told to report to NIS. I sweated all the way over there! I couldn't think what I'd done. And then to see you and Perry—I thought I was going to be kicked out of OCS!"

Dave was silent. "I'm sorry to have put you in an awkward situation."

"And yet you're pursuing me again!"

"I felt we had to talk!"

At least they'd cleared up any misunderstandings between them, she thought. She knew how he felt, what he'd thought—or suspected. It was a relief to be able to tell him she was no academic cheater at least. Yet she was still in danger every time she was with him. She wanted to tell him the truth about everything, but she couldn't. Knowing he was bound to disapprove of all her actions only made her more miserable.

"I've got to go—" She started to open the door.

He stopped her with a hand to her arm. "They'll be running a security check on you," he warned at last.

Mollie's hands began to tremble. She dropped the idea of leaving immediately and decided to stay and find out what she could about what was going to happen next. She shoved her hands in the pockets of her jacket and adopted a casual air. "What's involved in that?"

Dave shrugged, apparently unconcerned about her failing. "They'll check out everything you said on the forms, make sure you've never been involved in any terrorist or radically political activities."

"And if I haven't been?"

"They'll let it go at that."

"And if I have?" She said this in a challenging voice.

His gaze narrowed. "Then, depending on what you'd done, or were suspected of doing, you'd answer to the NIS, your CO, maybe even the FBI or the CIA."

Oh, God, Mollie thought. *What have I done?*

"Something is still bothering you, isn't it?" he observed.

Mollie couldn't deny she was upset at his latest revelation, but she concentrated on what they could discuss. "How could I not be upset," she volleyed back softly, "when I'm out here whispering with you in the parking lot? I feel as if I've suddenly stepped into a scene from *Indiscreet.* I can't tell anyone I'm seeing you. And when I do—well, every time I'm with you, it's a risk for me."

She watched as he opened and closed his fingers, circling the steering wheel.

"The sordidness of our relationship bothers you?"

"Doesn't it you?"

He nodded and looked away. "I've never put so much on the line for any one person. My whole record is at stake, too."

"Then why are you pursuing me?" she asked.

For a long moment he didn't respond. "I enjoy being with you. I think about you when I'm not."

"And that's all?"

He turned toward her and his eyes, searching hers, seemed to gentle, as did his voice. "I want to get to know you. I don't feel like I do yet." There was a conciliatory pause, and he continued. "Physically, I'm very attracted to you."

His hand tightened above her elbow. Her arm was guided from her pocket until he was able to link fingers with her. The touch of his fingers, his warmth, was very reassuring.

"But I think you know that."

How could she have forgotten, after the way he had kissed her and the way she had responded?

Mollie took a deep breath and shut her eyes. It was getting harder with every minute that passed to resist him. She struggled to hang on to the pragmatic "this is all our relationship will ever be" attitude that had carried her through the weekend and kept her from calling him earlier. "I'm not in the market for a lover or a relationship or even a male friend. I'm not at a point where I can tolerate demands; there are enough made on me at OCS." Stubbornly, she faced straight ahead. The windows had fogged up around them. She felt as if they were ensconced in a soft, foggy cloud. Nonetheless, knowing no one could see them, she began to relax.

"I understand that. I can help. I just want to see you, maybe spend Sundays together in D.C."

Part of Mollie wanted that, too. More badly than she wanted to admit. The truth was that Mollie didn't know what to do. She had lied, and he had believed her. How much longer could she keep it up?

She didn't want to experience his disapproval, his distrust. She would be better off without him. Without warning, she had a lump in her throat, and tears were blurring her eyes. *I'm not cut out for espionage,* she thought. *I'm not, I'm not, I'm not.* She disengaged her hand from his. "Look, I've got to go. My friends will be wondering what happened to me."

"Damn it, Mollie, don't do this to us. You know breaking it off isn't what you want." He moved toward her, caught her by the shoulders and dragged her into his arms. His warm breath brushed her temples. She felt his lips in her hair. "I want to see you again." His arms tightened around her possessively, emphasizing the depth of his determination.

Her pulse raced and everywhere they touched, she melted into him. The attraction she felt for him was as simple as chemistry and a thousand times more complex. She only knew that she'd met many men in her life and that none of them had made her feel as vulnerable and simultaneously cared for as Dave. "Dave—"

"Don't say no. Just think about it. Think about spending time with me in a neutral setting. We could go sightseeing tomorrow in D.C. I could meet you wherever you say, for however long you want. I want to see you." His free hand cupped her chin and lifted her eyes to his. His other arm tightened over her spine possessively.

Warmth rushed through her. "All right," Mollie said finally. "The Lincoln Memorial at noon." Part of her knew she was being foolish. The other half didn't care. She'd waited a lifetime for a man like Dave, and she wasn't going to disregard him without at least becoming better friends. And as for the no-frat rule, well, she wouldn't be in the service forever. Until she was a civilian again, she would simply have to be careful.

"You're sure?" he said quietly, searching her face.

Mollie nodded. She knew that seeing him was a risk, but one she very much wanted to take. "I want to be with you, too," she said softly. "I won't deny that any longer."

SUNDAY DAWNED SUNNY and beautiful, a perfect spring day. Dave was waiting for her as she approached the white marble monument on foot. "Want to go inside?" he asked, taking her hand.

"Yes."

They walked up the steps together. Other tourists and their families were roaming the rectangular Doric temple, taking photos of the seated Lincoln. Together Mollie and Dave read Lincoln's Second Inaugural Address and his Gettysburg Address, both of which were engraved on bronze plaques on the walls. He was in no hurry to leave the impressive monument, and she liked that.

"There's such a sense of history here," Mollie remarked.

As they started down the steps, Dave offered his arm. "Being here in Washington gives me a real feeling of what this country is all about. There's a sense of pride here, a commitment to protecting the population of our nation as a whole, as well as to freedom."

"And the marines are here to help." Mollie was surprised to find that although her comment had been meant to be facetious, she was half serious.

He slanted her an amused glance. "You'll get used to admitting publicly to feelings of deep patriotism. Duty, honor, country. That's what life is all about."

"For marines."

"For everyone. They just don't all know it."

They moved down the walk leading from the monument and out into the sunshine. It was a possessive feeling, holding on to a man's arm the way she was holding on to Dave's. She liked it. She liked being the one doing the holding.

In the foreground was the reflecting pool. Some distance away was the Washington Monument, and on the other side of the Tidal Basin, the Jefferson Memorial. "Anything in particular you'd like to see?" Dave asked.

His eyes scanned hers. He seemed to be beseeching her...to what? Her breathing quickened, and her throat felt taut. She couldn't have answered him then if a passing pedestrian had offered her a million dollars to do so.

"How about Constitution Gardens on the other side of the Mall?"

Mollie nodded her assent.

As they strolled the park, they passed many joggers. "If I'd have thought, we could have brought our running clothes and run here," Dave said.

"Maybe next time." Mollie spoke before she had time to think.

Dave nodded, seemingly not repelled by the idea. "Maybe next time," he agreed softly.

The forty-two-acre park was indeed worth seeing. Gravel walkways meandered through the proliferation of colorful flora. There was even a six-acre man-made lake.

"It's lovely here," Mollie said, stopping to admire the many multicolored blossoms that glistened just like jewels in the sunlight. "The azaleas are especially beautiful." Several minutes later, she stopped again to admire a particularly dazzling display of roses.

"You like flowers?"

Mollie nodded. "When I was a kid living in Ohio, my mother had a spectacular flower garden out back. And there were flowers planted up the walkways, beneath the trees, around the front porch, as well as African violets inside. When I see flowers—or smell them—I always think of home."

"You grow them, too, then?"

"No, I...never have."

"Why not if they bring you so much pleasure?" He watched her curiously.

She was dimly aware he was coaxing facts from her

she had previously revealed to no one. "Not enough time, I guess. When I was in college, flowers were the last thing in the world I wanted to mess with. Later, there was no time. And when I was married and wanted—needed—to make our apartment more of a home, there was no money. My husband's tuition alone was over ten thousand dollars a year. That left barely enough for us to scrape by on, even with me working full-time teaching and summers as a waitress.

"Your husband never bought you flowers?" He sounded as if this disturbed him.

"When we were courting, sure, but after we were married? It's my understanding not many husbands do that."

"True. I guess not." He lapsed into silence. They wandered along the paths, across the small footbridge to the island in the middle of the kidney-shaped lake. The views there were spectacular, too. He wrapped his arm around her waist, and Mollie leaned against him, content momentarily to draw her strength from the reserve of his. She realized abruptly she hadn't felt so at peace in years, so comfortable with any man.

"What was the financial arrangement in your marriage?" Mollie asked. What did a man like Dave really want in a woman? she wondered. Could she be there for him someday, or were they already hopelessly mismatched?

"We lived on my income only. My wife didn't work."

"Did you want a stay-at-home wife?" Mollie asked. She found the whole idea of being a housewife repugnant.

His reply was clipped, cautious. "I wanted her to be happy. I wanted children. So I'll admit the arrangement was fine with me. In a sense, her not working made it easier when I was transferred. For example, she enjoyed living in Europe, because we were able to do some limited travel on my time off. But the moving around, the conditions under which I worked, were hard on her, hard on the marriage. I know there were times when she was very lonely."

"When you were away?"

"That, or exhausted from overwork, stress." His face tightened as if the memory of the time upset him.

Mollie found herself wanting to comfort him as they moved back across the footbridge, to the outer fringes of the park once again. "Did she understand?"

"As much maybe as a spouse can be expected to understand. If she had worked—well, maybe it would have been easier for her, maybe not. At any rate, her loneliness led to her infidelity."

"How'd you find out about it?" Mollie asked.

"There was some talk around the base...jokes. I...ignored them. She was very beautiful. I thought it was only natural guys would make remarks, out of jealousy if nothing else. One day I came home and—well, it all became very clear. She wasn't there, but several miles away, at a motel; my car was parked in the lot."

"You saw it?" Mollie tried without success to suppress her horror.

"A friend did. He also saw my wife come out of a room with some guy. He didn't want to see me cuckolded any longer, so he told me about it. I confronted my wife. There was a helluva scene. It was the only time in my life I've ever been tempted to beat up a woman. But somehow I kept a lid on my anger and got out of there. I was drunk for several days after that. Finally, I went home. I couldn't believe it." He laughed harshly. "She was still there."

"Then what happened?"

Dave shrugged, as if it were of no consequence. "She

was frightened, said she was sorry. I didn't know whether to believe her or not.''

''Did you try to work it out?''

''Yes.''

About that much he seemed to have no regret, Mollie noticed. She understood his ambivalence. Having a marriage fall apart hurt. Yet similarly strong was the involuntary denial that almost always followed, at least for a while. No one wanted to admit a mistake had been made in entering into the union.

''We went to a marriage counselor. In the course of the joint therapy I discovered my wife had never wanted children and had gone along with it verbally to please me. But she felt pressured, unable to raise a child alone. The counselors suggested she become self-sufficient, get a job. I was willing to do whatever I could—give up hopes of having children indefinitely, request assignments only in the States. I felt responsible for what happened, as responsible as she. Like I should have realized sooner how unhappy she was. I really wanted it to work. But she was unwilling or unable to change. And without trust, there was nothing left to salvage. So we ended it.''

''And you've been bitter ever since.''

''Yes. Less so, though, since I met you.''

His gaze darkened, turned penetrating, promising somehow.

Mollie's legs turned to mush. She put a hand up to steady herself and came in contact with hard male flesh, evident beneath the soft cotton shirt. She swayed again, and his palm came up to rest against her waist. His response simultaneously steadied and aroused her. And still his eyes held hers, coaxing from her, silently, revelations about her emotions and her attraction to him that she never could have been prompted to admit. Suddenly, the world seemed filled with possibilities, romantic and otherwise.

Other pedestrians and tourists passed. They became aware it was time to move on.

Dave asked, "If you had it to do over again, your marriage, what would you do differently?" He dropped his hand on her waist, and they began walking again, aimlessly this time, neither making any pretense about wanting to see any sight in particular.

Mollie wrinkled her nose comically. "Besides choose a different mate, you mean?"

He laughed. "Besides that."

Mollie shrugged, thought about it a moment, then finally responded soberly. "I guess I would've cared more for myself, fought for my rights as an individual, forced my ex-husband to work more at our being a couple. I would have pursued my own happiness actively, not left so much to chance or counted so much on my happiness stemming from his success as a physician. Does that make sense?"

"Yes."

From the way he was looking at her, Mollie knew he truly did understand. "What about you?" she asked. "What would you do differently?"

"I'd choose a woman who possessed the courage to be honest with me and herself. Who knew what she wanted and went after it. Who could be happy with me, or without me, but who wanted to be with me, who wanted to have children. But again, honesty is the quality I need most. I want to know that whoever I'm with, I can trust her implicitly."

Mollie thought of her diary, how she had lied to Dave and to Percy. By entering the marines, and OCS, with the intention not so much to serve her country as to serve herself, hadn't she violated every ethical and moral standard? Hadn't she done a disservice to them all? Resolutely, she pushed the feelings of guilt away. She wouldn't allow anything to spoil this day.

"Has all this talk about our past marriages upset you?" he asked.

"No." *It's my dishonesty,* she thought. Wanting to change the subject, she glanced at her watch and was amazed to see the afternoon was already half over. "Have you had lunch?"

Half an hour later, they ended up at an international fast-food emporium in Georgetown. For very little money they were able to sample food from a variety of stalls. As they finished up the last of the Peking duck, Dave commented, "You know, you're the only woman I've ever known who can eat more than me...and still stay in such great shape."

"Is that a compliment?"

"I think so."

Teasingly, he let his gaze drift over her, slowing his perusal at every pressure point until her senses quickened and her heart pounded warmly to life.

"No, I know so," he corrected himself.

Mollie took a shaky breath and finished the last of her soft drink. If he could stimulate her with just a look, ten to one, the man would be a superb lover. Dare she ever let their relationship progress to that point? And would she forever regret it if she didn't?

Finished, they disposed of the remains of their meal in the trash. Dave drove her to the bus station and parked at the rear of the building. Overhead, the sun was still bright, but his car was surrounded by shadows. Rather than get out or move around, he stretched languorously, or as languidly as his small car would allow. One arm landed behind her, on the back edge of her seat. She turned toward him and read immediately the desire in his eyes.

She'd been expecting him to make his move all afternoon. He'd nearly kissed her the evening before. And if she were honest with herself, she knew she had wanted him to kiss her thoroughly. That if it had been years ago, before her marriage and divorce and subsequent loss of confidence, she might even have taken the initiative herself. Part of her craved the intimacy he seemed to be offering her, the luxury of knowing another human's touch, something she'd denied herself for so long. But there was danger in opening herself up to physical affection, because then she might want more. She might begin to want commitment and permanence and marriage again.

She had cut off those feelings; in fact, she had been successfully, happily, celibate since her divorce. Did she want to alter that?

Panic got the better of her. "Dave, no—" She put both hands against his chest.

"No, what?" His voice was a soft, melodious drawl.

She faced him, and his left hand reached across her to cover her left wrist. His right arm, still stretched along the back of the seat, moved down to cup her shoulders. He held her loosely enough not to hurt her, tightly enough not to let her get away—not without one hell of a struggle and probably not even then. Mollie took in a deep draft of air. She'd known he was a determined man, bent on getting what he wanted, the way he wanted, when he wanted, once he'd made up his mind.

A tension radiated through her, from the two points of contact to her toes, her fingertips, to her face. She felt hot and cold all at once, decidedly on edge.

"Don't run from me," he said softly. "Don't run from this. We've both waited too long to find it."

Slowly, he folded his arms around her and drew her to him.

She meant to protest but his lips on hers were the sweetest invasion; touching and caressing but never taking her farther than she wanted to go. He kissed her so carefully, more gently than she would have ever thought possible, offering her comfort, tenderness, warmth, ingredients that had been missing from her life for far too long. Her need for him intensified. Her arms closed around his shoulders, and she got as close to him as the configuration of the seats would allow. He reacted with a low murmur or approval, and the sweet bliss went on and on, until they were both breathless, vaguely disoriented, thoroughly mesmerized with each other.

As slowly as they'd come together, they drifted apart. His eyes scanned her face; hers scanned his. They both began to smile, shyly at first, embarrassingly, then more broadly.

"Well—" he cleared his throat "—I guess that answers my question."

"What question?" She felt the heat of a blush warm her cheeks.

"I wanted to know what it felt like to hold you in my arms again. To kiss you."

"And?"

"It was heaven. Sheer heaven."

Chapter Seven

Mollie faced away from the reaction course, her rifle at sling arms. She was dressed in fatigues and was wearing her equipment belt, two canteens, her first-aid pouch and a magazine pouch with two magazines. Her helmet was on and buckled. She was ready for the reaction course, a test that was designed to simulate the pressures and conditions that could be found on the battlefield and therefore determine the candidate's ability to use troop-leading steps to solve problems. Appointed the team leader of this specific task, she listened intently as the course evaluator read the problem to her, out of earshot of the rest of the team.

He pointed to a designated red area as he spoke. "These pilings represent the remains of a bridge that has been blown up by enemy nuclear artillery. Portions of the pilings and the stream have been contaminated and cannot be touched. You are a part of a squad operating in enemy territory. One of your party has been critically wounded in the back. You know that in an abandoned ambulance on the other side of the stream there is a stretcher that you will need to transport your wounded across the stream. Your task is to cross the stream, return with the stretcher and transport your wounded across the stream. An enemy patrol was sighted operating in the area.''

The evaluator pointed to a stack of timber and continued, ''You have brought these six planks from the basement of a nearby house. Use what you need and be careful not to touch either the contaminated pilings or the stream with any piece of equipment or any part of your body. Now, any questions?''

Mollie had one. ''Are we allowed to use the first-aid equipment we're carrying to treat the injured man?''

''No. Individual 782 gear cannot be used in solving the problem, but it must be with the team when the problem is finished. Equipment, especially rifles, will not be thrown, nor will you be allowed to jump to or from any obstacle with your rifle.''

Mollie had two minutes to make her reconnaissance. On one side of the stream, Mollie saw an ammo box and six eight-foot planks. The stretcher was on the opposite bank. The dummy was next to her. The distance to be crossed was approximately fourteen feet. White posts—the remains of the bridge—were sticking up out of the water. At the end of the time allotted, she returned to her evaluator, and briefed him of her preliminary plan. He nodded his approval and gave her ten minutes to accomplish the task.

Mollie spent two minutes briefing the other five members of her team on what was to be done. One person was to stand watch for the enemy, another apply first aid—pressure to stop the bleeding—to the dummy. She and Greta placed the planks across the white posts until a makeshift bridge was formed. The fifth and sixth candidates swiftly crossed the makeshift bridge and passed the stretcher back. Mollie directed the placement of the dummy on the stretcher, admonishing, "Be careful! The woman's been shot in the back."

As Mollie directed, and in deference to the location of the alleged wound, the dummy was placed face-down on the stretcher and strapped in securely. The fifth and sixth people moved the dummy across the stream and carefully placed it on the opposite shore. Team members three and four crossed, taking the ammo box with them. Greta crossed next. Mollie went last, taking the planks with her as she crossed, passing them forward to the opposite bank where her team members waited. According to her directions, during the activity one team member was still on guard for enemy activity in the area; a second was watching over the injured marine. Mollie made it to the opposite bank and pulled in the last plank just as the ten-minute time-up was called.

While remaining members of her team returned all equipment to the starting point and prepared to move on to the next starting point in the reaction course, where another candidate on her team would be appointed team leader, Mollie was debriefed by her evaluator.

"Candidate Devlin, your plan was simple and understood. You assigned all team members appropriate tasks, positioned yourself at a vantage point, made sound and timely decisions and avoided excessive physical involvement. You maintained tactical integrity of the team by having someone on watch continuously, showed ingenuity in removing the makeshift bridge and preventing the enemy from reusing the equipment you had just used. Additionally, your wounded received the best of care. There were no fouls. No one touched either the contaminated areas or the water or dropped the wounded dummy. You forgot to ask for suggestions from your team when you initially briefed them, but you didn't appear to need them, either. All in all, it was a task well done, Candidate."

At the evaluator's praise, Mollie glowed with pride, both for the excellent leadership she had displayed and the true teamwork her group had managed.

"SOUNDS LIKE YOU REALLY ACED the reaction course," Dave commented the next weekend, when Mollie told him about her efforts. They'd spent the early part of the day out sightseeing and now were lounging on a blanket, enjoying a warm and sunny May day in the park.

"Yeah, I'm really beginning to enjoy it here at Quantico." Mollie rolled over and lazily folded her arms beneath her head. She stared up at blue skies and white clouds. The faint smell of freshly mown grass and recent rain hung in the air.

"You say that as if it surprises you." He shot her a curious look. From the picnic basket between them, he removed a thermos of lemonade and poured them both a cup.

Mollie sat up to take the beverage he offered her. In the month that had passed, she'd become increasingly more relaxed around him. "You know how hard OCS is. I felt initially I might have all I could do just keeping up, never mind enjoying what I was doing."

"But you are having fun?"

She nodded. Much to her surprise, she was beginning to enjoy the military. She would hate to see it all end.

Dave glanced at the tree overhead. "It's hard to believe you graduate from OCS next weekend."

"Yep, I'll have my butter bars." Mollie used military slang to denote the gold bar that indicated the rank of second lieutenant.

"What are you going to do on your break?"

Judging from his interested gaze, Mollie thought, he had all kinds of plans for them. Was she ready to get that serious with him? She didn't know. She did realize she couldn't hold him at bay indefinitely, with her pleas for friendship. No, Dave was an adult man with adult yearnings. He was patient, true, but no cardboard saint. Eventually, she would have to decide whether or not they were ever going to become lovers. And if she did so in the negative, something she knew instinctively wasn't very likely considering her passionate response to his kisses, she had to be ready to lose him. At least in the increasingly intimate way she knew him now, on a personal level. Sooner or later they would either have to go forward or go back.

"I have plans to go to New York and see a friend, then spend some time down in South Carolina at a friend's beach house there."

"Is this friend male or female?" he asked jealously.

"Constance? She's my—" Editor, Mollie almost blurted out. Giving her head a slight shake, as if that would clear it, she said, "Well, just a friend I made while I was living in New York."

"You taught at the same school together?"

"No, she's in publishing. We were both English majors in college."

"What does she think of you joining the marines?"

Mollie grinned and sipped her lemonade. It was very tangy, exactly the way Dave liked it. "That it was some sort of post divorce lunacy, a delayed reaction to stress on my part."

"And was it?"

"No, I knew exactly what I was doing." *Then, anyway,* she ammended silently. Since Dave had come into her life, it seemed she was constantly bewildered. Confused because she was truly beginning to care for and about him. And resentful that he was taking up time that she had reserved specifically for her writing.

"I'd like to meet this Constance," he said finally, breaking her introspective mood.

"I'll...try and arrange it." Mollie promised finally.

He shot her a quizzical glance. "You don't think we'd get along?"

Obviously he'd picked up on her reluctance. Mollie shrugged, then answered honestly. "I'm not sure you would have a whole lot in common. Constance is very...well, not exactly cynical but pragmatic in her attitude toward men. She thinks men are to be enjoyed but not catered to unduly." Constance wouldn't change the course of her life for a man, Mollie thought.

"Meaning what? That she would disapprove of me?"

Dave looked unhappy about the possibility of any conflict.

"She already thinks I'm crazy for having joined the marines. I don't think she feels the service is any place for a woman. To go so far as to get involved with another marine...sheer lunacy! Of course, if she knew I was breaking a rule to see you, she'd probably like that much of it—forbidden passions and all that." Constance would probably think it would be great for the story, Mollie mused. But Mollie had no intention of taking advantage of her relationship with Dave. She drew the line there.

"Then why go to see her?"

Mollie's jaw jutted out stubbornly when it seemed as if he were about to launch an equally narrow and one-sided view of Constance. "Because we're friends." *Because I have to discuss business with her.* "And it's her beach house in South Carolina I'm going to be using. I'll need to pick up a key."

"Oh, okay. It makes sense now."

She sighed her relief that he'd given up the third degree.

"Speaking of that beach house, I'd like us to spend some time together. Alone." Dave rummaged through the picnic basket for something else to eat and finally decided on a second chicken sandwich.

"Just you and me?" Mollie swallowed around the knot of emotion in her throat. She was both leery of and tantalized by the prospect.

"You've got it." His eyes met hers directly and held until she had to look away.

There was no mistaking his message. He was being very adult about it, very patient, but he was talking AFFAIR in capital letters. And why shouldn't he? Mollie thought a trifle desperately. They'd spent enough time together the last few weeks, every Sunday. They were both adults. There was no denying that their relationship had a sexual hue to it. Every time she was with him, she felt the inevitable physical pull to be with him, to be closer, to do more than simply hold hands or kiss goodbye. Yet what she'd told him earlier was true. She wasn't looking to have an affair or even get involved with a man.

"Dave, I—"

"I've got time off coming to me, too. I'm not asking you to cancel your plans, just alter them to include me. If you don't want me to stay at the beach house with you, I can bunk at a motel."

"Dave, it sounds lovely, but I can't." *Be firm,* Mollie encouraged herself pragmatically. *Use your head, not your heart, your…desires.* An all-and-out affair with Dave still spelled danger—for herself, her feelings and her project.

"Why not?" As he spoke, his jaw jutted out resolutely.

Because I have to work, she thought. *I've got to make sense of all those notes I've been taking and at least make a rough draft of all that's happened to me at OCS.* And she had to do it while it was still fresh in her mind. She couldn't concentrate with Dave around.

Mollie stalled him. "I need time to think about us." Restlessly, she got up to move around.

"What about us?" He followed, skirting the perimeter of the blanket they'd spread out over the grass.

"I'm not sure.... Dave, I don't want to be hurt again, and as far as I can tell, there's no future for us. Your duty is to the marines. I'll only be here in Quantico for a few more months. And then I'll be off to who knows where." *That's it,* she thought. *Keep to the facts. Tell him what you can.* Except the most vital statistic of all—that once she got all the information she needed, she would resign from the corps.

Putting both hands on her shoulders, he turned her toward him. His voice was low, coaxing and so very gentle. "I disagree. I think there is a future for us. And I think your time off is the perfect time for us to find out exactly what that future is." As he continued, his voice dropped another compelling notch. "Mollie, I care about you. I don't have all the answers. I just know that I'll never be able to figure it out unless we do have time together, time away from the base."

He continued persuading her softly, devotedly, for several more minutes, and in the end she couldn't refuse him. Not entirely. Nor was she willing to give up all work on her article. "I do want to see you, but I was serious when I said I needed time alone." To emphasize the point she was making, she separated herself physically from him. He made no move to recapture his grasp.

"Time to recuperate from the rigors of OCS, to rest.

But also to think about what direction I want my career to take next. I'll have to decide that in TBS, and right now I haven't got the faintest notion. So—'' she took a deep breath, trying to ignore the disappointment he apparently felt ''—maybe the last weekend, before I come back?''

''Three days?''

He seemed crushed that was all she was offering.

''It's the most I can do. Dave, I have to be sure.''

''I understand. All right. Three days it is. I'll arrive the Friday before you return.''

Relieved that was settled, Mollie gave him the address of the Vanderbilt beach house.

''YOU REALLY ARE GETTING OFF on all this military stuff, aren't you?'' Constance asked a week later in her New York office.

''I've enjoyed it more than I thought I would,'' Mollie admitted honestly after telling Constance in detail about the rigorous parts of OCS, the pride she had felt upon graduating the previous day. To emphasize the changes in her since she'd left, she'd gone to the meeting dressed in her service-green uniform—a dark green skirt, matching jacket and khaki shirt. Constance was impressed that Mollie had actually earned her commission as second lieutenant and was now proudly wearing her butter bars to prove it.

But now, minutes later, Constance was all business as she asked, ''Then what's the problem? You're troubled about something, Mollie. Don't deny it. I can see it in your eyes.''

Only because of their friendship could Mollie confess, ''It's a man I met.'' She went on to tell Constance how committed Dave was to being a marine and how guilty

Mollie felt about having to deceive him, if only by omission.

As predicted, Constance wasn't the least bit sympathetic to Mollie's plight. "Oh, Mollie, spare me! Don't tell me you're making the same mistake with him that you did with your first husband."

Mollie stiffened defensively; she felt a lecture coming on, one she didn't want to hear. In the past, she would've been overjoyed to have Constance talk some sense into her, to dispel her natural romanticism and help Mollie get down to business, to concentrate on what was really important, the building of her writing career. Mollie still felt she needed that—at least on a rational level. Emotionally, she didn't want to hear anyone speak one word against Dave. He was too special to her. "I care about him."

"Fine. Just don't let your feelings for him affect your work!"

"My writing has never been better!" Dave had helped her get more in touch with her emotions.

"I agree. The notes you've sent me are marvelous. But it remains to be seen whether you can string it all together in a coherent, publishable article. Mollie, you're aware there's still a risk involved in this endeavor of yours. That until you've actually presented me with publishable pages of your experience and not just an interesting string of notes disguised as personal letters, I can't offer you a contract from the magazine."

"I know that."

"Then you're taking me up on my offer and going to my beach house in South Carolina to work?"

"I'm leaving on the morning plane. I'll work straight through until I'm finished with the section on OCS."

"Good."

They spent the next few minutes going over Mollie's

plans, clarifying details, discussing article emphasis, word count.

Finished, Mollie placed her papers back into the manila file. "I'm sorry that my outline wasn't typed, but under the circumstances, I had to work with as few real tools as possible."

"It's fine," Constance murmured distractedly. Her eyes scanned the pages. "There's a typewriter and plenty of pens and paper, a dictionary and thesaurus at my place." She looked up. "I want this to work as badly as you do, Mollie. You've worked too hard for it not to pan out. We're all hoping what you turn in will be sensational enough to really boost sales of *Super Women,* at least for one banner month." Constance's expression was both determined and enthusiastic.

Her enthusiasm was contagious. Mollie was filled with the desire to write—as never before. Now all she had to do was grit her teeth and do it, turn in an article with prose so dazzling it would practically sell itself.

Chapter Eight

"I knew before you left you needed looking after. Now I'm sure of it," Dave said from the porch of the beach house.

Mollie was seated in the combination living room, dining room and kitchen. Exhausted from days of writing, she was dressed simply in shorts and a T-shirt. Her legs and feet were bare in deference to the June heat. Although her hair was shiny clean and sparkling, she wore no makeup.

She put the morning newspaper aside and walked over to let him in, still not sure it was really Dave she was seeing, in all his civilian splendor, and not a mirage. "I—I thought you weren't coming until tomorrow evening."

"I decided to surprise you. Do you mind?"

No. Yes. A thousand responses went through her mind simultaneously. She was glad to see him but felt guilty for the subterfuge, the fact that he had no real knowledge about what she had been doing there. Somehow she regained her composure. "No, of course not. It's just… I'm surprised.… I thought—" Mollie stammered as he approached her languidly, his eyes dark with passionate intent. She had no more chance to speak. She was drawn against him and held there for a lengthy kiss, one she participated in fully.

"I'm glad you don't mind," he murmured when he released her moments later. "Because I've missed you so—"

"I've only been gone ten days."

"Ten days too long!" There was another silence. This one spoke volumes about loving and being loved in return. "So, what have you been up to? Not getting much sun, I see." He looked at her pale skin.

Mollie ran a hand self-consciously through the tousled ends of her hair. "I don't particularly like the heat."

"Hmm." His eyes scanned her face. "You look tired, Mollie." His tone was soft, solicitous. He turned and took in the simple decor and vaguely nodded his approval of all he saw.

Mollie used his momentary inattention to gather her wits. The truth was, she was exhausted. She had been writing, revising and rewriting her entire vacation. To say she wasn't was pointless. She would, however, have to cover up the reason why. "I am exhausted." Before she could come up with a reason, he'd pivoted back toward her. His brows were knitted together in a perplexed fashion.

"How come? I would've thought you would be rested up by now."

Mollie would've been if that had been all she had done—rest. Having no answer for him, she just shrugged, turned away and strode into the kitchen. "Must be a delayed reaction to OCS," she said finally. "The stress I've been under. It took a while for it to catch up with me, but now that it has—I'm sure a few days rest and I'll be as good as new." Thank goodness all her writing materials were upstairs, she thought. Thank goodness she'd managed to finish the first section of her article—the section Constance needed to put her under contract—that very morning. "Listen, would you like some iced tea?"

"Iced tea would be great." He followed her into the kitchen and leaned up against the counter, watching as she worked. "Got plans for dinner? I'd like to take you out."

"That would be fine."

"I checked into a motel about five minutes from here." He gave her a level glance, and said softly, "I don't want you to feel pressured."

"Thanks."

He nodded, stirred sugar into the glass she handed him and sipped at his tea. Apparently he was very thirsty. Half the liquid in the tall glass disappeared. She reached for the pitcher and poured him some more.

"So, what have you been doing?" he asked again. As he talked, he turned a chair around and sat facing backwards, his arms folded over the top rung.

Again, Mollie flailed. She had no ready answers prepared for him. But he seemed to take no notice of her unease, he was so busy absorbing the sight of her.

"I've been reading; I took in a few movies," Mollie fibbed finally.

"Oh, what?" he asked with genuine interest.

She swore inwardly. She was no good at lying, and since she hadn't even glanced at the movie section in weeks, had no idea at all what was playing at local theatres. If she lied to Dave, he would know it. And having him try to figure out why would only mean more trouble for her. She decided to tell him the truth—or as much of it as she could. Proceeding very carefully, she said, "Actually, my trip here isn't all pleasure. I've been doing a little free-lance work for Constance on the side. I've, umm wanted to become a published writer for some time and haven't been able to sell anything. I'm assured I have the talent. It's just coming up with something timely enough, and saleable.'' By the time Mollie finished her impromptu speech, she was fire-engine red with embarrassment.

For a moment he was too stunned to speak. ''So what are you writing about?'' he asked finally.

''My experiences as a divorced woman.''

Abruptly, he whitened. Several tense seconds passed. ''You didn't put me in there, did you?''

''No!'' Mollie said. ''I didn't put anything about my romantic— There's really been nothing to write. No, this is more of a...well, a mood piece. Constance thought it might be interesting—might work—so that's what I've been doing.'' Ruefully, she acknowledged, ''I've found out writing is very hard work.''

''Can I read it?''

''No!'' Her refusal was swift.

''Why not?''

''Well, it's... I'm embarrassed. It might not be any good. Constance hasn't even read it yet.''

''When will she read it?''

''Hopefully in a week or two. I express-mailed what I'd come up with this morning. So, maybe I'll know something soon. I would appreciate it if you didn't say anything to anyone, not even Percy or Blythe. If this doesn't come through for me—well, let's just say rejection is hard enough to take without having everyone in town know about it to boot.''

''I promise. I won't tell a soul. I am curious, though. Why didn't you tell me about any of this sooner?''

''I wanted to. But...''

''You were embarrassed.''

''Yes.''

He stood and hugged her to him briefly.

Mollie relaxed against his warmth, realizing she had missed him, and that she was very glad he'd come down to see her early, after all.

"SO HOW ARE THINGS back in Washington?" Mollie asked two hours later over a dinner of scallops and white wine.

"Percy and Blythe have some interesting news. They're getting married."

"You're kidding."

"Nope. And they want us to stand up for them."

Mollie was terribly excited. "When is the wedding going to be?"

"November. Blythe wanted to elope, but Percy insisted his parents would want to come out for the ceremony. He also had a little church in the country, where he sometimes attends services, picked out as the place where he'd like it to be held."

"And Blythe agreed to all that?"

"Only on the condition that the wedding be small and very private. Just a few close friends, his family. She didn't want a 'three ring circus'—I think she called it."

"How did Percy take that?"

"Very well. Which isn't surprising. He's getting everything he wants."

Especially Blythe, Mollie thought. Without warning, she felt envious of Percy and Blythe. She wished her own situation could have been worked out so easily. She wished she'd never been forced—by her own ambition and the project she'd undertaken—to deceive Dave.

"A penny for your thoughts?" he murmured as he took her hand and led her to the dance floor.

"I was just thinking about Blythe and Percy. I can

hardly believe they're engaged—and so soon! She always seemed too scared of marriage to take the plunge."

"I guess Percy convinced her otherwise. God knows the man has been in love with her for years."

"And she never paid any attention to him?"

"Let's just say she spent a good deal of time and effort ignoring him."

They spoke very little during the rest of the evening. They didn't need to. It seemed enough just to hold each other, to dance to the strains of the soft, lulling music.

They drove back to the beach house in introspective silence. There was tension between them, Mollie noted, not exactly sexual tension—although the sensual element was certainly there. How could it not be with them both dressed up, she perfumed and powdered, he well shaved and scented with cologne? Both of them needed to touch and be touched. Endlessly. Yes, the sensual element was there between them, but something else was there, too. The purely intellectual/emotional need to understand and be understood. That, in Mollie's estimation, was love. The reaching out between two people, the yearning, the never-ending need to keep building on what they had, to make their relationship better, stronger, deeper. She wanted to build on what they had, but she, like Blythe, was afraid. Afraid to love...more afraid not to.

What would Dave give her if she were to listen to the dictates of her heart and enter into a love affair with him? She sensed his gifts would be generous. He'd already bestowed her with the discipline to go slow, to wait until the time was right. The freedom to be herself, to react as vivaciously or shyly as she chose. And the security of knowing he cared about her. She felt safe with him and at the same time pleasurably on edge.

He was unpredictable, possessive, persistent. And, as

his retaliatory practical joke had proved, also imaginative and wild. One moment he was leading her into a slow, dreamy state; the next, tempting her effortlessly toward passion. With every kiss and caress he made her realize they needed, and wanted, the same. Security, trust, elation.

So what was she waiting for?

Only the right moment.

Only that.

As for the other—her continued dishonesty with him—well, that would have to be dealt with eventually. She could only hope he would understand, when the time came. For the moment, she'd told him as much as she dared. In the meantime, she needed what he had to give. And she needed to give to him.

His steps were lazy, reluctant, as he walked her to the front door of the beach house. He was happy and relaxed, content to be with her again, yet wanting something more. Every time he looked at her, his eyes radiated messages only she could decipher.

I knew you needed looking after.

I think there is a future for us, and your time off is the perfect time for us to find out exactly what that future is.

It seemed natural for her to ask him in. They got no farther than just inside the closed door before he was reaching for her, inexorably guiding her against him. The tight rein of control they'd both been holding on to, the long weeks since they'd met, finally snapped. She felt caught up between hope and despair and forces that had long since been out of her control.

He studied her, his eyes impassive. Then, ever so slowly, he smiled. His head bent, his arms closed around her, holding her close. His kiss was tender, deliberate, seeking permission even as he took it. "You're sure?" he said finally, when they could breathe again. "I could go...."

If he stayed, they would make love. It was a given. It was what she had been waiting for. This was the man she loved, and he loved her. No, she wouldn't turn him away, send him out into the dark and lonely night, not ever again.

"I want you to stay." *With all my heart.* Mollie leaned her forehead briefly on his shoulder and shut her eyes, savoring every second.

His arms tightened around her. "You know what I wish?" His voice was soft and husky, his breath warm against her hair.

"Tell me." She drew him closer still.

"That everything could have been simpler for us from the time we first met. No complications, no outside pressures."

He was describing an ideal, one that would never come true, no matter how much they yearned for it. "What would that have changed?" Mollie drew back to look at him.

"Everything. Nothing. I'd still find myself wanting to spend every waking moment with you."

"I'm not much for wishes," Mollie confessed. Her hands curled around the lapels of his sport coat, drew him nearer still until they were touching in one long, tensile line. "I've never held much faith in hope alone. But I wish just for once in my life time could stand still, that we could shut out the outside world, everything; past, present, future."

"And just feel what's in our hearts?" He knew what she was trying to say.

Mollie nodded.

He thought about that, and his mouth curled up at the

corners. His eyes glinted with humor as he said, "I'm not able to mess with the time, unless you want me to stop your watch and all the clocks in the house."

"No, no..."

He grinned again. "But I can do something about shutting out the world. Making time and space just for you and for me. I want to love you, Mollie."

"And I want to love you."

The touch of his hands on her skin was fire, burning away the last of her shy reserve. She had time to draw one quick, halting breath, to stare up at him in mesmerized fascination. And then he was bending his head, touching his lips to hers.

She'd never felt anything like that first heady contact. It was electric, jolting and so ultimately satisfying on an emotional level that she felt tears of joy sting her eyes. How she had yearned for this passionate, wonderful love. And love her he did. She could feel his tender caring flowing through her. It was in the warm, lazy pressure of his mouth, the gentle, expert penetration of his tongue, in the way he held her, as if sheltering her from all harm.

She arched against his body, allowing herself to melt into his strength, letting herself go with the ebb and flow and give-and-take in a lover's paradise. The silence was broken only by the rough whisper of their breath as they kissed more and more hungrily. And suddenly it wasn't enough. They were undressing themselves, each other, laughing as they fumbled over buttons and left a trail of clothing to the master bed.

In the dim light of the bedroom they saw each other for the first time. He was as beautiful unclothed as she'd known he would be. And he made her feel beautiful, very beautiful indeed. He drew her to him reverently, his hands kneading her body, filling her with liquid waves of pleasure. She swayed against him, touched him, savored every masculine plane, every muscled slope, and still it wasn't enough, not nearly enough.

"Tell me what pleases you," he urged softly, pressing damp, heated kisses over the nape of her neck, behind her ear, above her breast.

"You please me." She felt her head drop back. Her hands rested on his shoulders. She gave herself up fully to his sensual ministrations.

"This?" he said, touching her tenderly.

"Yes," she whispered. Her breath lodged in her throat as she felt herself open up to him, as a flower opens its petals to the sun.

"And this?"

She arched against him ardently, feeling his lips move across her abdomen. No one had ever treated her that gently before or with such barely controlled desire. Sensation swept through her, leaving her weak-kneed and trembling. "I want you," she whispered as he kissed her thoroughly again and again.

"And I want to make love to you over and over until we no longer know what it's like to be apart." His legs moved against hers. His arms caught her against him until they were touching with maximum pleasure. He buried his face in her hair and breathed deeply of her perfume. "I want you, Mollie. I love you."

Joy filled her at his revelation. She drew away from him slowly, looking up at him with luminous eyes. "And I love you." She was just beginning to realize how much. In the short weeks they had known each other, he'd already become an intrinsic part of her life. The physical loving would bring them closer yet. It was an intimacy she yearned for and could no longer do without.

They tangled together on the bed. He held her while

his free hand caressed her, his fingers sliding into her warmth, moving until she moaned, arched, writhed. Anticipation shivered along his skin as she touched where she pleased. Gentle kisses, his and hers, unleashed the primitive in them both. They came together in a fiery cloud of passion, of ragged sounds, shudders, of heat and wild sensation. With a soft, exultant moan, Mollie gave herself to the experience, to him, and accepted wholeheartedly the tempest that engulfed and drove them both.

They had created their own world, a secret garden of passion and fulfillment, and she wanted never, never, to leave.

THE FIRST RAYS of sunlight filtered in through lacy white curtains and spilled across the bed. The coolness of night was fading. The warmth of a new June morning was blowing in through the open balcony doors. In the distance, the ebb and flow of the tide could be heard as the Atlantic rolled in timelessly to crash against the sandy shore.

Mollie was aware of a supreme sense of well-being, and a warm form next to her that was rock solid, shifting restively into wakefulness.

Not wanting him to leave her or the bed just yet, Mollie shifted toward her lover. Her thigh touched a hair-roughened one. Softly sighing her contentment, she snuggled against Dave and was rewarded with a hand that coasted across her and cupped her breast. He stroked, teased and adored it until it throbbed with a taut ache that spread to the center of her body.

"Dave?"

"Hmmm?"

"What are you doing?" She tried but couldn't entirely keep the rich amusement from her voice.

"Waking you the best way I know how." His tone was just as deliberate and lazy as his hand moved over her lightly, evoking an immediate response. His lips touched her shoulder. She felt the curve of his smile against her skin.

Teasingly, she pretended reluctance. "Mmm...I wanted to sleep late." Mollie rolled over and burrowed into the covers, lying half on her side, half on her stomach. She hid her face—and her own laughter—in the pillows.

A tickling sensation moved across the nape of her neck, to her shoulders, down her spine. Mollie began to tingle erotically everywhere he touched. As much as she was trying to retain her difficult pose, he was fast luring her into a dalliance. She sleepily turned on her side, allowing him access to her other breast, not willing to end the game just yet.

He seemed content to continue on indefinitely. "Well, heaven knows I never want to deny you anything, Lieutenant. Do you want to go back to sleep?" He leaned over her and searched her face with an exaggerated solicitousness that was all too reminiscent of his roguery the night he'd played his practical joke.

Mollie arched her brows in silent admonition. "If I said yes?"

"I'd let you—eventually."

"Aha!" She spoke as vehemently as if she'd just discovered a major character flaw.

"Tell me you don't want me to stop." His warm breath coasted across her shoulder and was followed by a string of kisses, each one more passionate than the last.

His intimate knowledge of her and what pleased her made her flush. "I, uh, do...ah...Don't...Dave—"

Pretending not to hear her pleas for mercy, he rolled her over and trapped her beneath him with his weight.

Her face was tenderly cupped in his hands. He pressed light butterfly kisses across her brows, down her cheekbones, above her mouth. She knew if he continued much longer she'd be lost. And Mollie was a person who hated to lose. So she tried, for show, to fight both what he was doing to her and her own inclination toward indulgence.

He, in turn, enjoyed the sensual tussle immensely. And to her frustration, expended not one quarter the effort.

Her half-hearted efforts to break free of him physically were totally unsuccessful. Her arms and legs were trapped beneath his stronger, hair-roughened limbs. He was easily able to hold both her wrists in one hand, which left his other hand free. He used it to the best of his ability, and before long, despite the tussling that was still going on, the lower half of her was suffused with moisture and heat. It was a passionate wrestling match filled with fun and ardor and unlike anything she'd ever experienced before. When she was active, he was still. And when she was still, he was active—devilishly so. Eventually, as she had known they would, the rules blurred. She no longer knew or cared who had started what or when; she only knew she wanted it to continue indefinitely.

Her arms were free, her hands stroking his back, lingering below his waist. She throatily whimpered her pleasure as his hands moved over her in turn, touching wherever possible, languorously relearning her curves. His palms slid beneath her, cupped her, lifted her until they were touching as intimately as interlocking pieces of a puzzle. Mollie was about to forget the game altogether when, without warning, he resumed.

"Oh, well—" he pretended to sigh his disappointment comically "—if you want me to stop..."

"No..." Mollie's answer was quick, frank and unrepentant.

"No?"

"Definitely no." Mollie let her hands sculpt his shoulders, his lower back, his thighs.

"I'm glad."

"Mmm." Mollie concentrated on doing to him what he did to her.

A half-hour later, he said, the growl of satisfaction thickening his voice, "Think we could do this every morning?"

Mollie smiled. "For the weekend?"

"At the very least." He kissed her with incredible tenderness.

Her eyes were misty with love when the embrace came to an end. But she couldn't resist one more teasing remark. "I don't know." She made a funny face and pretended to deliberate unnecessarily. "I have a very hard time waking up in the mornings…."

"I'll help you." He was quick to volunteer. He gave her a tight hug and another gentle kiss.

"As you did this morning?"

"Exactly as I did this morning. Well, maybe not exactly…." Thus inspired, he began to be creative again.

Between exultant gasps Mollie said, "Uh, you can be my personal alarm clock. I promise…."

"You promise?" Again there was laughter in his voice. That and soft, generous affection.

Having no qualms at all, Mollie said, returning his loving embrace, "I promise…."

Chapter Nine

Dave knew Mollie was up to something the moment he saw her the last Saturday in June. But she waited until they were leisurely downing an early lunch of hamburgers and fries before she told him what was on her mind. "Now that I'm into the second part of my officer training, I'm allowed to have a car on base. I thought I'd look around, see what I can find. I don't have a whole lot of money to spend, but I want to pay cash. Do you think I can buy a good car for under three thousand?"

"Depends on what you're looking for, but yeah, you could definitely get something."

"Would you help me look?"

For the first time, she seemed hesitant, as if unsure of the exact boundaries of their relationship. He knew how she felt. Once burned, twice shy—the phrase applied to both of them. Their divorces had left them both leery of marriage. And though they were lovers, Dave knew intellectually it was still too soon for anything but the most tenuous of commitments. Dave had to admit, if he were honest with himself, that the more cautious part of him was content to take life and their love on a day-by-day basis.

But there was also a part of him that wanted more from

Mollie. The temptation to somehow further the bond between them was there every time they were together. The inclination to lean on each other as more than friends or lovers, as...what? Soul mates? Husband and wife? He only knew the bond between them was powerful and unique. He never wanted to be without her again.

"Sure, I'll help you." For the rest of the day, they visited every reputable auto dealership in the Arlington area. By nightfall, Mollie had found three cars she liked. But to Dave's consternation, she refused to test-drive even one of them personally.

"When was the last time you owned a car?" Dave asked, unable to suppress his amused grin as he noted the increasingly dismayed expression on her face.

"About...five years ago."

"When was the last time you drove?"

"On a regular basis? Five years ago, I guess."

"No wonder you don't want to drive." He opened the door and waited for her to slide in, across the seat.

"I can do it." Mollie settled herself in the passenger seat beside him. "I just don't want to test-drive the cars. I'd rather observe while you drive. As for my driving skills, it's like riding a bicycle. I'm sure I still know how. I just don't want to wrestle with a strange dashboard."

Mollie Devlin. Afraid of something. The idea was hilarious and oddly endearing. Dave suppressed an ironic smile. "Okay. Enough said."

Despite his accepting attitude, Mollie bristled during the rest of the test-driving. He thought—hoped—she would finally sit behind the wheel herself. She didn't. Rather, she picked out a fire-engine-red coupe that was mid-sized and moderately economical to run and arranged to close the deal and pick it up the following weekend.

The following Saturday, when it came time to pull the

car out of the dealership, at Dave's insistence, Mollie was seated behind the wheel. To his surprise and delight, she turned out to be an adept driver, if a little rusty. She was less enthusiastic, however, about giving her new car the tender loving care it deserved.

"What I don't understand is why we're doing all this for my car when it's clear yours hasn't been similarly attended to in ages," Mollie drawled an hour after picking up her car. As Dave watched, she dipped a sponge into a bucketful of sudsy water. It came up dripping, and she sloshed water up over the hood. Excess bubbles dripped down her bare legs and on her sneakers. Dave stepped around the mess she was making and began working on the right front wheel, rubbing at the hubcap until it gleamed.

"We're doing this because the car is 'new' and it's yours. You deserve a car that sparkles."

"Why not just take it to a car wash?"

"Because they wouldn't treat it with the care we are. And because none of them look as good as you do in shorts, fair lady."

She tossed the sponge at him. He ducked. Retrieving it from the ground behind him, he straightened lazily, and hands behind his back, stalked slowly toward her.

Laughter bubbled up immediately in her throat. "Now, Dave—" Mollie held both hands out in front of her.

Dave kept stalking, his steps measured, deliberately predatory.

She waited until he got almost in touching distance of her and then whirled and began to run. He caught her easily. Looping one arm around her waist, he pulled her back until they were touching from head to toe, her back to his front. Her head rested against his shoulder. She braved a look at his face. "I give up!" she shouted breathlessly, trying in vain to extricate herself from his arm around her waist.

"But Mollie, I don't want you to give up. Not yet, anyway." He walked her forward, until they were at the bucket. She was squirming madly as he reached forward and with his free hand dipped the fat yellow sponge into the cold, soapy water.

He wriggled the soppy sponge in front of her.

"I give up, I give up, I give up...."

"It's not nice to throw things."

"Oh, I know. And I'm sorry." She could barely get the words out she was laughing so hard.

He scowled mockingly down at her. "How can I believe you, Mollie?"

"Uh...?"

"What possible way is there for you to convince me?" He wriggled the sponge again with exaggerated deliberation, splashing them both.

"Let me finish washing the car by myself?"

"No. No, I don't think that would do."

"Let you continue to wash to wash the car by yourself?"

He said nothing, merely assumed his most somber, distressed look.

She laughed again. "Umm, why don't we wash the car together?"

"Can I trust you?" He dropped the sponge and turned her to face him.

For the briefest of seconds she seemed to pale. Fearing he was hurting her by playing too rough—he hadn't meant to—Dave loosened his hold. But his actions had no calming affect on her.

"Of course you can trust me." Mollie dropped her eyes and crossed her heart with her fingers. She took a deep breath and looked up at him. "The question is, can I trust you—not to get me wet?" Whatever fear she'd had seemed to have fled.

"You're wet already," Dave pointed out.

"Drenched, then."

Dave handed her back her sponge. "Okay. But you're on your honor, Devlin. No more horseplay. Promise!"

"I promise."

Mollie was surprisingly subdued as the car-washing resumed. Whether it was because she was out of breath or wary of rowdying him further, Dave didn't know.

"How thick should I put this wax on?" she asked minutes later.

"A thin coat is best. I'll rub it in if you apply it."

She seemed to like the idea of Dave doing most of the elbow work and made several teasing remarks, all of which he volleyed right back into her court. He liked roughhousing with her. There were times when she made him feel like a kid again, and before they'd met, he hadn't ever supposed that to be possible. Yet here he was, in many ways recapturing the fun—and optimism—of his youth.

He also liked watching her. Mollie made quite a picture in cutoffs and T-shirt. She was radiantly healthy and looked it, from the shimmering strands of her hair to the silky, touchable quality of her peaches-and-cream complexion. Her legs were long and supple, with slender thighs and muscled calves; even her knees were great.

But his was more than just a physical attraction to her. He liked her spontaneous wit, her sense of humor. She was quick to smile, stubborn about not crying. She was vulnerable. She was smart. And she was a free spirit. Sometimes almost too free.

They had become lovers; and with that, certain aspects

of the intimacy between them had naturally deepened. Yet, Dave mused, as one wall came tumbling down, another was erected. No matter how freely she gave of her body, a part of her was still holding him at bay. With any other woman he would've wanted to maintain some distance, some separateness. But not with Mollie.

He wanted her heart and soul. He wanted to know he could always go to her, always be welcomed, comforted, loved, appreciated. He wanted to be able to anticipate her moods, to be aware of her thoughts and feelings almost before they happened; he wanted to know her that well. Now there were still times when she shut him off, when he felt they were still strangers.

He wanted that barrier destroyed.

He was glad when she had asked for his help. Yet he felt frustrated that for the most part she was oddly content, maybe even relieved to leave their relationship undefined, casual. He knew that in some ways she was still very innocent, that she didn't make love casually. So it puzzled him that she wouldn't want some tangible commitment from him; if not marriage, then an engagement, or even continual declarations of love.

She asked for none of that.

She wanted to be with him on the weekends. She didn't speak of the future, of anything past her graduation from TBS.

Dave continued to ponder her elusiveness for the duration of the day. After dinner, as they sat sipping coffee in the twilight, he asked her, "Do you ever see yourself getting married again?"

Her head lifted and her eyes widened in surprise. The coffee cup had been almost to her lips, but she lowered it to her lap without taking a sip. "No, I don't."

"Are you ruling it out because your first marriage ended badly?"

"Not necessarily, though I'll admit my experience doesn't make me too eager." She paused. Her teeth raked across her lower lips. "I guess it's more a result of the way I look at life now than anything else. When I was married, I held out a lot of hope for the future. I had a lot of faith in what would happen. I had a lot of plans for the future and hope that the realization of those dreams would make me happy. None of them came true. Now I just take it day by day, moment by moment. I realize, in retrospect, that I asked for too much, and not just from my husband but from the idea of marriage. I was too needy. I depended on him—and his successes—to make me happy, figuring that if he was content with his work and life, I would be content with mine. In short, I was your average modern-day Cinderella. I lost sight of myself, what I wanted, needed. And when he dumped me, I just fell apart.

"I picked up the pieces, of course, but it was a slow, painful process. I never want to go through anything that devastating again. But I learned from my mistake. I know now I have to go it alone, that it was a mistake to rely on others, on my marriage, to sustain and fulfill me. It hasn't been easy. I've had a lot of soul-searching. I've had to figure out what I wanted to do with my life and go after it. I've done that. I know now I can handle life as a woman alone."

"Then you've ruled out any serious involvement?" He was surprised at the depth of his hurt.

"No, I can see having a lover, a friend. I can see having you in my life. But I want to keep our love affair in perspective. I think the secret to success would be to not give too much of myself."

Dave's heartbeat had quickened. He had a sour taste in his mouth, a worse feeling in his stomach. "I disagree. I don't think you ask enough of our love affair or of me." She seemed taken aback by his revelation, and he continued. "I've done a lot of soul-searching, too, since my marriage ended. I don't think I ever gave of myself as I should have. I was too involved in my own career, my own desires, to work at building a solid relationship. I wasn't there enough for my wife."

"And as a result she strayed?" Mollie ascertained skeptically.

"Yes."

"Do you still love her?"

"No. In retrospect, I don't think I ever did. At least not enough to sustain a commitment like marriage. I don't think your husband loved you enough, either."

Mollie didn't disagree with his assessment.

"The past few weeks have been so nice," she said after a pause, as if she were loathe to spoil it by discussing it too much. "What more could we want?"

"Permanence, for one." Candidly, Dave continued. "Mollie, before you came along, I was perfectly content to live alone, to be alone. But not anymore. Since we've been together, and I know it hasn't been all that long, I've realized just how empty my life was. I've realized what a difference you make. When you're not with me, I'm thinking about you." *Dreaming of you.*

"What do you want from me?"

She looked frightened.

"Exclusive rights to your heart, for starters."

"That you've got. What else?"

Good question. He knew without a doubt it was too soon to even broach the idea of marriage, not when she'd turned skittish at just the thought of the future and publicly admitted commitment. "Maybe just more of a good thing," he said softly. "More time with you. More contact. More give-and-take. I'd be willing to meet whatever demands you might make on me. But I'm also going to want the license to make a few demands of my own."

"And those are?"

"I want you to start being more honest with me, to stop censoring everything you say." He held up a hand traffic-cop style, cutting off whatever she was about to interject. "I see you thinking sometimes, Mollie. Your brain's going ten times faster than your mouth. I want to know what you're not telling me." She looked so miserable he was prompted to go on. "Mollie, whatever I'm guessing is bound to be ten times worse than whatever it is you're actually worried or apprehensive about."

She got up to restlessly prowl the patio. "How can you say that? You don't even know me!"

"That's just the point. How can I know what you're thinking if you won't tell me what's on your mind?" He knew by her emotional reaction he'd guessed at the problem correctly.

"Sometimes...I'm...well, I'm trying to get over the habit of speaking before I think. I want to say what I mean and simultaneously filter out—"

"Filter out what?"

"Whatever shouldn't be said." Mollie turned a faint shade of red as she struggled for an example. "Uh, smart remarks. Ungenerous thoughts. Since my divorce I've been very bitter...impulsive at times. I'm trying to get hold of that impetuousness, and I've started with my... speech. I'm an officer. I'm an adult. I can't just blurt out whatever's on my mind anymore."

He had the strange sensation she was holding much

back from him again. That annoyed him. "I'd like it if you'd blurt out whatever's on your mind."

Mollie shook her head. She didn't pursue the argument. Wearily, she ran her hands through her hair and turned away. When she faced him again, she was composed. Her tone was thoughtful. "Okay, I understand what you're saying. But you need to realize that as much as you need certain things from me, I need space. Time to be alone, to think…whatever…without revealing the nature of my thoughts to anyone. So much is going on in my life right now. I'm so busy during the week. Sometimes during the weekend I just want to drift, to sit and daydream or—or…"

"Fantasize?" Dave interjected hopefully.

"That, too." She gave him a sexy once-over before turning serious again. "The point is, for better or worse, I'm simply not able to see or think much past the here and now. What you're describing to me sounds—well, suspiciously like marriage."

Dave had never meant their discussion to turn that serious. But what the hell! He'd gotten that far with her; he might as well continue. "I'm beginning to see marriage as a possibility for us." More than a possibility, if he were honest with himself. The more she held herself aloof, the more he wanted solid ties forged between them. He wanted fidelity, commitment, love, trust. He wanted a sense of mutual caring. He wanted to announce their love for each other to the world.

Contrary to his expectations, his avowal did not delight her. Rather, it seemed to distress her.

She turned away from him and paced the small patio restlessly. "I know what you're saying is not that extraordinary. Maybe I should have expected it, once we became lovers, knowing what kind of man you are—honest and forthright.''

''Except when playing practical jokes.''

She laughed, agreeing. ''Except then. And I know our continuing to break the no-frat rule dismays you.''

''Doesn't it you?''

''Well, yes, it's a nuisance for you not to be able to come and pick me up at the base or call me on the phone every night. I don't like worrying about one of us being reported, then transferred or demoted because of our relationship. Sometimes I wish we could meet at the officers' club just to talk. But the fact remains, Dave, that the complications of our being together aside, I'm a person in transition. Even if I wanted to, I couldn't alter the sequence of my military training. I have to go wherever I'm assigned; I have to complete not just TBS but the next military occupation school, too. After that I don't know where I'll be assigned or even—even what I'll be doing.'' She paused, started to speak, then evidently changed her mind and fell silent.

Again Dave felt shut out.

Maybe that was par for the course. It had only been three weeks since they'd become lovers. Dave stood and put his coffee aside. At her explanations of her feelings, his anger had dissipated. He was flooded with gentleness. ''I'm rushing you, aren't I?''

''It's flattering. I'm glad you care about me so much. But yes, you are.''

Dave was silent. ''All right. I'll try to slow down.'' For her sake, he would have to give her time, give her breathing room. Try not to let everything get so intense.

''I care for you.'' She walked forward to give him a hug.

Dave held her to him tightly. ''And I care for you.''

With time, their love could only grow. "But you're right; maybe it is time we slowed down a bit, got out or, saw others, as well." But that was a feat the no-frat rule made very difficult, at least around Quantico. His next idea offered a solution.

He drew back slightly. "Blythe has been after me to take you down to Williamsburg. She and Percy are going on the Fourth of July. Normally, I'm not much for double-dating, but it would be a historical and educational way to spend the holiday. Want to make it a foursome?"

Mollie's face lit up. "It sounds like fun." With her right palm, she thumped her chest. "As a former schoolteacher, how can I pass up the chance to improve my mind?"

"You can't. Shall I make reservations?"

She smiled and gave her assent. Her relief was tangible as she leaned forward to hug him tightly again. He cherished the change in her mood, from worried and almost guilty to lighthearted and optimistic. He knew it had been tough on her, juggling classes and military training and a new romance. He vowed to lessen the pressures, to somehow make it all up to her. For the duration of the evening, he refused to think about anything else but the fun they would have there together. Colonial Williamsburg, he thought. A step back in time, a step toward a continuing future. Their future.

Just the thought of it felt very right.

Chapter Ten

"So, how does it feel to be getting married in a few months?" Mollie asked Blythe. It was the Fourth of July weekend and Williamsburg was abuzz. While Percy and Dave played a round of golf, Blythe and Mollie were content to sun themselves lazily next to the hotel pool.

"You want the truth? I'm terrified," Blythe said, sipping her mint julep.

"I admit I was surprised to hear you were getting married."

"You weren't the only one," Blythe said with a faintly mystified air.

Mollie watched her curiously. "So why'd you agree?"

Blythe shrugged. "The truth? Mollie, I don't know. Sometimes, looking back on it, I think I must've been a lunatic. But it was such a romantic evening and Percy had been so sweet..."

"You do love him?"

"Yes." Blythe was very firm about that much. "But what that has to do with *marriage,* I don't know."

Mollie laughed. "You really are worked up about this, aren't you?"

"Yes. Part of me thinks I may have made a terrible mistake. Everything is good between Percy and me now.

We're not living together, but in every other way we're very close. I spend weekends with him whenever I can. He stays at my place during the week when he can. I hate to spoil it."

"And you think marriage will ruin what you have?"

"The divorce rate in this country is very high, and among two career couples— Mollie, I don't think I could stand it if we did break up. I'm beginning to count on Percy. Do you know what I mean? I've altered my life for him. I plan everything around him, around us.... Marriage will just deepen that commitment. I feel like I'm investing so much in the idea of us, the relationship. I'm scared what will happen to me if it doesn't work out. If, somehow, I don't live up to his expectations."

"Percy adores you."

"Now. But what about in a few months from now, when the novelty wears off? Mollie, I've run from commitment for so long, I'm not sure I can make a go of this for any length of time."

"Have you told Percy how you feel?"

"I've tried, but I don't think he understands. He's so naturally optimistic, so—so bullheaded! I think he figures if he just wants something to work out, it will; never mind all the variables or hardships."

Mollie chuckled. "Sounds like Dave."

"So how are the two of you getting along?"

"Very well. But I know what you mean about being afraid, Blythe. Dave is beginning to want a commitment from me, too."

"Has he said so?"

"Yes." Mollie thought back to the conversation they'd had on his patio the previous weekend. Part of her had been touched by what he'd said, overjoyed. The other half of her was scared silly. So much so that she identified perfectly with everything Blythe was telling her. ''He also says he's tired of all the sneaking around.''

''You're both officers now.''

''But he still outranks me. I'm a second lieutenant. He's a captain.''

''Yes, but you work in entirely different areas.''

''That doesn't make any difference; not really. I've read the no-frat rule myself. It states specifically that if the fraternization is on the terms of military equality, then it's improper. When I'm with Dave, I'm not saluting him or addressing him as formally as his rank would normally demand. He'd rather be able to live together openly.''

''You know you can't do that. Not and expect to get approval from the military brass. Even if you marry—well, I'm sure the no-frat question will be addressed, if only informally. Thank goodness Percy and I are of equal rank.''

''You're lucky there. Sometimes I think...''

''What?''

''That it would be easier to be alone. Not to have to deal with all the complications. Just to concentrate on my work.''

''I know what you mean there.'' Blythe sighed, glancing down at the diamond solitaire sparkling on her finger.

''But then I think how lonely I'd be without Dave in my life. I really do love him.''

''And I love Percy. So why isn't it easier?''

''I'll be damned if I know!'' Mollie laughed. ''Think maybe we should write to Dear Abby for advice?''

''And Ann Landers, Dr. Joyce Brothers. Maybe even Miss Manners could help.''

They both laughed at that and spent several more minutes thinking up the possible facetious responses the columnists might give to their dilemmas.

"YOU'RE AWFULLY QUIET," Dave remarked later that evening. He and Percy had joined them in the late afternoon. They'd had dinner together at the King's Arms Tavern, the reconstruction of an inn where George Washington had once supped, then split into couples once again. Mollie was enjoying the time alone with Dave as well as the sensation of having slipped back into history, into eighteenth-century America.

The city of Williamsburg had been restored and rebuilt to recapture its heyday from 1699 to 1780. Within the historic area, on previous days, Mollie and Dave had seen a fife-and-drum corps march in the streets. They'd watched blacksmiths, weavers and shoemakers practice their trades. They'd admired handcrafted pieces of silver and ridden in an eighteenth-century horse-drawn coach. In short, their holiday had been both thought provoking and enjoyable.

"Have I been overly quiet? I'm sorry." Instantly contrite, Mollie apologized as they strolled the dark and quiet cobblestone streets. In the distance, a galaxy of fireworks lit up the sky in a dazzling array of colors. But for the moment, the historic district was quiet, blessedly peaceful.

"Anything wrong?"

"No, it's..." Mollie hedged. She wanted to confide in Dave, but how could she? Nonetheless, her dishonesty was weighing on her. She had told Dave she was working on an article for Constance. She had told him she had always wanted to write. But there was much she had left out. The true subject matter of her article, her real reason for joining the marines. Neither of which he could, or would, approve of. Add to that, all the times she had lied to him indirectly by either refusing to tell him what was on her mind or by evasion—by not telling him what she was doing and why.

"Is it TBS, the stress of the second part of the training?"

"No, it's not that, not really. In fact, now it's easier for me. I'm only in class Monday through Friday. The academic atmosphere is more collegiate, less rigidly structured. Instead of being in a barracks with the rest of my platoon, we're in a dormlike facility. I have Greta as my roommate. We even have our own private bath."

"So what's the problem?"

"I'm worried about the future, I guess. I've never been happier in my life. I'm afraid it won't last."

"Us?" His hand tightened possessively on hers.

"Yes."

Exerting pressure on her wrist, he stopped walking and drew her around to face him. In the windows of the colonial bakery beyond, electric candles glowed. The scent of freshly baked bread hung in the still summer air.

"Mollie, I love you. Nothing is going to change that."

And what would happen, her conscience prodded, if Dave were to find out the truth about why she had entered OCS? Would he forgive her duplicity?

Haltingly, without telling him too much, Mollie tried to explain her feelings to him. "I'm not sure if you can understand this, but…for the first twenty-eight years of my life, I spent my life solely trying to live up to other people's expectations. First I tried to please my parents, make them happy, proud of me. They were both teachers, so it followed that I, too, would go into education. On the surface, it seemed a good idea. I wanted to have children eventually, and teaching was a career I could pursue while my children were growing up and still have summers off, holidays, to devote to them."

"Was there ever a point you enjoyed teaching?" he asked.

Mollie hesitated. "I love literature, love writing. But to be perfectly honest, I don't think I'm necessarily cut out to deal with teenagers on an everyday basis. Especially those who don't share my passionate love of words."

"Why didn't you switch to journalism when you were in college?"

"Again, it goes back to my parents. They were so proud of me following in their footsteps. And by the time I realized I wanted to write—well, I had almost finished my junior year. To switch career paths at that point would have meant staying an extra year or so minimum in school. My parents' budget had been strained to the hilt just putting me through the first three years at Ohio State. Still, I thought about it. But about that time I met and began dating my ex-husband. He was in premed. He wanted to study in New York, and he wanted a wife by his side when he did so."

"So you opted for marriage and the more familiar path?"

"Yes, and was unhappy about it from the start. I don't know. Maybe I secretly resented my husband for not being more supportive of me. He alone knew I had doubts about what I was studying, being able to make a lifetime commitment to teaching."

"And yet he encouraged you to teach?"

"He said in New York I would be close to publishing and perhaps could write there, evenings, while he studied or was at the hospital."

"And did you write?"

"Oh, yes, every spare moment." For an instant Mollie forgot whom she was talking to. The depth of her excitement crept into her voice.

"But nothing got published."

"No, nothing. Of course, part of that was my fault.

There's an extremely limited market for short stories, yet I wrote dozens of those. Only to have them returned to me with printed rejection slips. So then I tried my hand at article-writing, poetry. You name it, I explored the field.'' Her endeavor had filled up the lonely hours, kept her in touch with her feelings.

''How did your husband feel about this?''

''He didn't really pay much attention. I was very shy about letting him read what I wrote. And he was wrapped up in his own problems at the hospital.''

''So why the marines instead of going back to college, to journalism school? Mollie, your love of writing comes through when you talk about it.''

''I chose the marines because I'm twenty-eight years old and I needed—need—to be able to support myself. I also knew there was a military occupational specialty that focused on journalism and public affairs.''

''Thinking of signing up for it?''

''I have been, more and more.''

''Have you filled out your 'Dream Sheet' yet?'' he asked, referring to the request-for-duty forms.

''We had the first practice run. I guess we'll have a couple more before the end of TBS, so that if anyone is not able to get into their first choice, they can change to something else. My first choice was Occupational Field 43: Public Affairs. My second was OC Field 02: Intelligence. My third was Personnel.''

''That's quite a variety.''

''Yeah, I know. But I didn't want to get stuck in motor transport or something like that. Anyway, our instructors have said that eighty-five to ninety per cent of the people do get into the field of their choice.''

''What's more of a problem is the location, since we can only specify East Coast, West Coast or overseas. Married couples, on the other hand, are usually better off, as an effort to place them within a fifty-mile radius of each other is made. Of course they can't be in the same batallion or company."

Was that a hint?

"You've got that worried look back again," Dave chided gently.

"I'm sorry."

"Tell me what you're feeling."

She took a deep breath, knowing she owed him at least that much of the truth. "My anxiety gets back to what we were discussing before. For twenty-eight years, I did what others wanted and expected of me. I put my own needs and desires second to everyone else's, to terrible results. I was miserable. When I divorced, I said 'No more.' I was going to work hard, get accepted into the Marine Corps OCS." *Get published.* "I wasn't going to let anyone or anything get in the way or sway me from what I'd set out to do."

"And?"

"And then I met you. And now everything's all confused again." She kicked at a cobblestone with the toe of her shoe. "In some ways—and I don't mean this to hurt you—I feel as if I'm worse off than before for having met you. When I started OCS, everything was so simple. I planned to get through OCS, TBS, job training and then serve my time."

"And then what?"

"It would depend on whether or not I was able to publish. If I couldn't publish—" an unlikely prospect considering Constance's enthusiasm for her article on the military "—then I'd stay in, I guess. Re-enlist for another term of service. Or get out and take a second civilian job." In the distance, the galaxy of fireworks could still be seen and heard as they lit up the sky.

"What you're describing sounds like my life before I met you. Mollie, I was very lonely."

He seemed to be saying he still would be very lonely without her. Mollie knew what he meant. Part of her counted on seeing him every weekend, on talking to him, being with him, making love, holding each other. But his presence, too, was distracting. She hadn't done nearly enough work on her article lately. She was studying and spending more time on her classes at TBS. Except for the letters chock-full of information she regularly wrote Constance, she hadn't done much at all.

"Dave, I care about you—"

"But you care about your career more." For a second, his features hardened.

"That's just it, Dave. I don't want to have to think about where my allegiance is—to a person or a job or my professional future—at this point in my career. I want everything to be simple, as simple as it was when I joined."

His face was a mask of hurt and disbelief. "You're saying you don't want to see me anymore?"

She thought about that option. Although to be romantically unattached would simplify her life, she didn't want to lose him. She didn't want to be without his constant, steady presence. Selfish of her? You bet.

"That's just it," she said softly. "I don't want to be without you. I don't think I could bear it. I know if I couldn't see you, I'd miss you terribly." She would be able to go on. A life shattered by her previous divorce had taught her that. But she wouldn't be nearly as happy. She wouldn't feel as complete as he somehow made her feel.

"I'd miss you if I couldn't see you, too." Dave's hand tightened over hers. He drew her toward him. The flat of his palm rested loosely at her waist. "But I know how you feel. I wouldn't want to give up anything of my career if the situation were reversed." Indeed, in the past he hadn't.

"So where does this leave us?" Mollie whispered.

"Back where we started, taking one day at a time."

"Can you live that way?" she asked.

"For now. Until you finish TBS and get your specific job or MOS training. After that, we'll have to see."

He grinned and slid his palm slowly up her spine. "But for now, this moment, this evening, Lieutenant, you're all mine. Roger?"

"I 'roger' that very well."

Chapter Eleven

"Oh, will you stop being such a stick-in-the-mud?" Greta faced Mollie cantankerously. "You haven't been out with us except for that one time in Quantico. How are you going to learn anything about the other butter bars if you don't give it a try?"

"Look, I know I've been busy—"

"Busy! You've been downright aloof! And where I come from, Lieutenant, that makes you in need of some mandatory socializing."

"Leave it to me to get stuck with a roommate who thinks she's the TBS social director."

"There are a lot of nice men who're also in TBS. You ought to know. You see them in class every day."

"Yeah, and most of them are young enough to be my baby brother."

"Grandma, you're not that much over-the-hill. Besides, there are some older men. Some lawyers who're about your age."

"Spare me any contact with ambitious male lawyers, please."

Greta, seeing she was getting nowhere, tried a more soothing tack. "Mollie, you've got to come over to the officers' club with us for at least one Friday night talkathon. Please? We can walk over. Any time you get tired, you can walk right back. What else have you got to do, anyway?''

"Study, do my laundry.'' Make notes for her magazine article. An article that had been grievously neglected.

"I suppose Saturday you have plans to go into Washington, D.C., to sightsee again?''

"You have to admit I have seen more of the historical sights than anyone else in the platoon.''

Greta groaned. "Don't remind me.'' She muttered a short, explicit oath. "Schoolteachers. Never outgrow being one, huh, Mollie?''

Mollie's weekend activities in D.C. were anything but schoolmarmish, although she and Dave had managed to do a lot of touristy things in between the times they spent alone.

Greta continued her appeal. "Please come with us. I'll be on my best behavior, I promise. I won't push any eligible men at you. I won't try and force you to stay if you're not having a good time, once we're there. All I'm asking you is to give it a try. Talk to some of the men in our classes. Be one of the group for a change; get to know what's on everyone's mind.''

Greta did have a point. Mollie had been neglecting the group lately in favor of spending time with Dave. And it was a part of her article she very much needed to cover, at least in her notes. After all, wasn't the article—the proposition of making it the best it could be—the reason why she was here at Quantico?

"Okay, I'll go with you,'' Mollie said. "Just give me a moment to freshen up.''

Greta smiled her delight at Mollie's capitulation.

Half an hour later, ensconced in Harry Lee Hall, Greta was still smiling—though this time at a tableful of male lieutenants, the oldest of whom, to Mollie's dismay, was about twenty-three. Apparently, none of the lawyers had shown up. Mollie felt old again, old and tired of the subterfuge. But forcing herself to enjoy her time off and to conduct some off-the-cuff interviews, she picked the most outgoing of the group, and concentrated on finding out all she could about his feelings on OCS, TBS, the marines in general, as well as more personal information as to why he had joined and whether he intended to make a lifetime career commitment to the Marine Corps.

Mollie got plenty of background information for her article, indeed ten times more than she needed, as she slowly nursed a cold beer into a warm, flat beverage. But unfortunately, by the time she was through, her interviewee had misinterpreted the intensity of her interest in him. "You know, I noticed you right away, at the beginning of OCS," he said, downing his third beer of the evening. Though not really inebriated, the stocky marine had loosened up quite a bit since the evening began.

"Really? Why?" Mollie was beginning to regret ever striking up a conversation with the ebullient lieutenant. Getting away from him, she saw, was not going to be easy.

"I don't know. Just something different about you. Something more serious...determined. I don't know. Whatever it was, I liked it." He paused. "You...seeing anyone serious, Mollie?"

"Well, as a matter of fact..." Mollie began.

Greta, horning in on the conversation, said, "She's divorced."

"That so?" The lieutenant was watching Mollie again.

"Yes, I'm divorced." She was also getting out of there. Now. Mollie began fishing in her pocket for change.

"You're not leaving, are you?" the lieutenant asked.

"I'm afraid so. I have to...study." And write up all he had told her before she forgot what had been said.

"I could help you study. Hell, we could do it together."

Studying wasn't the only thing the lieutenant had on his mind, Mollie decided. God, this was getting complicated. "Uh...thanks, but no." She was ready to pay her bill and make a hasty—if polite—departure before things got out of hand. Unfortunately, no sooner had she looked up again and around the room in search of the cash register than Dave Talmadge entered the club.

Mollie swore inwardly. And then swore again. Of all the people she hadn't needed, or wanted, to run into that evening, Dave topped the list. It was especially bad, her being there then, with the fun-loving group, because she'd insisted earlier in the week she needed to stay in her room and study rather than spend the time with Dave, as he had wanted.

Briefly, Mollie considered ducking, hiding, running to the ladies' room and staying there until closing. But knowing that would only draw more attention to herself, she could only brazen it out and hope Dave would see...what? That she was out carousing rather than being on a date with him or studying, as she had said?

No way was Mollie going to get out of this one easily, she decided. No way.

Across the room, Dave stood framed in the doorway. It took him less than ten seconds to spot Mollie. He looked simultaneously happy to see her, after a week of absence from each other, and dismayed to see she was partying with a group of her co-workers. Automatically, his mouth thinned in disapproval.

Mollie wanted to explain then and there what was going on, but there was no way she could approach him. It was too public. She flinched inwardly as she saw the continued disappointment on Dave's face. In less than a second, he had her tried, convicted and hung. She had to admit, though, the evidence against her was damning. And getting worse with every instant that passed. Mollie turned her attention back to the lieutenant she was with and what he was saying.

"Look, I know you've got to go; so do I. But so soon? How about letting me buy you another drink? Or—"

"No, really—" Mollie looked quickly past the lieutenant to Dave. He was striding toward Mollie lazily, his steps both loose and deliberately contained, as if he were pacing himself to take the maximum amount of time and the least amount of effort to walk by her. She swallowed as he came even with her, his eyes boring down on her disapprovingly, while his mouth remained implacable, expressionless.

The lieutenant glanced at Dave over his shoulder. Seeing it was a captain passing them, he turned back to Mollie, still bent on cajoling her into spending more time with him.

As music filtered through the club's intercom, the ardent lieutenant stood and pulled out her chair. "How about a dance? Just one dance before you go."

For a second, Mollie stared at the young lieutenant in complete bewilderment. A dance? No one had been dancing that evening. There wasn't really any dance floor to speak of. If they swayed together, anyway, they really would make a spectacle of themselves.

Aware Dave was somewhere to the left of her, watching her every move, Mollie shook her head. She had to get out of there, but she had to do it without hurting the young lieutenant's feelings or making Dave any madder at her than he apparently already was.

"Listen," she began, nervously wetting her abruptly

parched lips. ‘‘Normally I would but…ah…’’ Oh, brother. Mollie couldn’t even string two words together coherently, she was so rattled. ‘‘A…uh…a dance isn’t really…’’ All the while she was talking, or trying to, she was thinking, *Where is Dave? What is he thinking? How am I ever going to explain this without first explaining the book?* Either way, she lost. And lost…and lost.

The marine grinned, thinking her female confusion was all due to him, not to Dave’s presence. Suavely, he placed a hand around her wrist, his other about her waist. With no further warning, Mollie was pulled unceremoniously against him. ‘‘Sure you do. Every woman likes to dance. Isn’t that so, Greta?’’ he asked over Mollie’s shoulder.

‘‘We sure do,’’ Greta agreed, getting to her feet and slipping into the arms of another marine.

To Mollie’s chagrin, her young admirer led her farther from their table; others in the group got up and also began to dance. Several times during the endless song, Mollie was treated to a glimpse of Dave’s face. He was seated alone, watching her surreptitiously. Although his eyes traveled around the club several times, they always returned to her. And when they were fastened on her, they were very unfriendly indeed. Once, beseechingly, Mollie tried to convey her innocence. He glowered back at her implacably. She decided the only action she could take would be to leave. As quickly as possible. Alone.

As soon as the song ended, she extricated herself from the young lieutenant’s arms. ‘‘I’ve got to go.’’ Her tone was firm, spurred and strengthened by Dave’s disapproval.

‘‘You’re sure?’’

‘‘Yes.’’ Mollie strode forward to pay for her drink.

‘‘About tomorrow—’’ He followed after her.

‘‘I’ve got plans. Talking to you was very nice.’’

‘‘Maybe we could do it again sometime?’’

Mollie hesitated just long enough to let him know it wasn't a likely prospect. And then smiling, bid him good evening. She left him gaping after her.

Thankfully, the young lieutenant didn't follow Mollie out of Harry Lee Hall. Neither did Dave. Mollie figured it was just as well. She would have to explain to Dave—as quickly as possible. But it was an explanation that would have to be given in private.

"WHAT THE HELL is going on with you?" Percy demanded, a scant half hour later. He walked into his apartment. Dave, hands shoved into his pockets, followed, watching as Percy switched on some lights.

"What do you mean?" Dave was in the worst mood he'd ever been in his life.

"I'll tell you what I mean! First, I get a message you want to meet me at O-club for a drink. I go there and get a message you're here."

"Change in plans," Dave said tersely as he sat down, then stood up. His balled fists rested briefly on his waist, then dropped to his sides. He paced back and forth like a prizefighter getting ready to enter the ring. All without a word or glance at Percy.

"Oh?"

"It was nothing." Still uncommonly agitated, Dave shook off Percy's question.

"Don't want to talk about it?"

"That's right." Dave's jaw went rigid.

"Mind me asking why not?" Percy circled closer, using the same care one would employ to tackle a wounded bear.

"Yes. Damn her, anyway." Dave finally favored his friend with a sidelong glance. God, but he felt like a fool! How long had that been going on? he wondered. Mollie, claiming to be off studying when in reality she was out drinking with her friends. He felt betrayed. And angry as hell, both at her and at himself, for letting it happen.

"Damn who?" Percy dared two steps nearer, no more. They still stood a good three feet apart.

"Mollie," Dave replied, still feeling like a keg of dynamite about to go off. "She was at the O-club when I got there, with another guy. Someone in her class at TBS, apparently. At least they all looked like they were recent grads of OCS."

"Second lieutenants?"

"All of them."

Percy did some rapid thinking. He debated silently before he finally spoke. "Maybe you misinterpreted the situation."

Dave had thought of that and promptly discarded it. Whatever Mollie had been up to had been planned, not accidental. Beyond that, if she'd wanted merely to go out drinking on a Friday night, why hadn't she called him up? They couldn't have met at the O-club on base, but they could have taken in any number of bars in the D.C. area with little or no chance of being seen together. Why hadn't she called? Dave fumed. Because she hadn't wanted to be with him. She'd wanted to be with her group—or worse yet, that other kid. A kid, by the way, who couldn't have been more than twenty-two or twenty-three! He bit off a long string of curses, finally filling a baffled Percy in tersely on what had happened to make him so enraged. "She was dancing with some guy." He made a sound of disgust. "It was obvious if I hadn't appeared he would have been all over her like a bad smell."

"Oh."

Dave resumed his pacing back and forth. "In addition to which, she looked guilty as hell when I got there, like

I'd caught her with her hand in the cookie jar.'' As he talked, he slammed a fist into the palm of his hand. Again and again.

''Double oh.''

Dave shot Percy an angry look.

Percy got the message and backed off, shelving any other wise remark he might've been tempted to make.

''Well, what did you want to talk to me about?'' Percy asked.

Dave shrugged in bewilderment. His teeth were tightly clenched, and he was restless and edgy. ''I don't know. At the moment I—'' All he could think of was Mollie. He wanted an explanation. Damn it all, he wanted an apology, on bended knee and her solemn word of honor that it would never happen again! But then who was he to demand such a commitment from her? Sure, she'd said she loved him. She'd made love with him. But what did that really mean to her? Anything except a way to pass the time, a way to get through officer training? She'd made it clear enough while they were in Williamsburg that her career came first, that she didn't want to have to cater to any man in any regard, that she really wanted to think only of herself, as she had before they'd met. Then he had accepted it. Yet if this was what she meant— Was it? He couldn't believe it was. He also couldn't believe she'd actually been out drinking and dancing with another guy.

''Maybe you should talk to her,'' Percy suggested finally.

''She's hardly had time to make up a decent story.'' Dave's tone was steely with a wry humor he didn't begin to feel.

''Maybe she doesn't need to make up a story.''

''Maybe.''

"You're really not going to forgive her for this, are you?"

"I don't know," Dave replied sourly. He was certain he wasn't in much of a mood to listen to anything she had to say. Nor did he suspect he would be anytime soon.

"Look, I'd like to help, but—"

"This is a matter between Mollie and me."

"Right."

"Got plans for the rest of the evening?" Dave had the sudden urge to go out and get smashed, to drink himself into oblivion. Hardly proper military behavior. For the first and only time in his life, he didn't care.

"Blythe and I have a date." Percy paused. "You're welcome to tag along."

Appreciating Percy's offer, Dave flashed a reluctant grin and prepared to take his leave. "Somehow, buddy, I doubt my sister would appreciate me making it a threesome. Another time?"

"You got it. And Dave, if you need someone to talk to—"

"I'll know where to come. Thanks for listening, Percy." Dave shut the door quietly behind him. And swore again.

MOLLIE WAS A BUNDLE OF NERVES as she made the drive to Dave's apartment complex. Weeks earlier, he had given her a key to his place. Having a car on the base had made seeing Dave much easier. Once at his apartment, she wasn't at all sure what she should do, considering how they had parted and what he'd seen—or thought he'd witnessed—in Harry Lee Hall. Should she go in to his place and wait for him? Or sit out in the car, wait for him to come home and talk to him then? What if he didn't come home? What if he brought someone with him? The questions were endless, and all served to further unnerve her.

Finally, at around eight-thirty, Dave's car swung into the lot. Mollie watched as he guided it expertly into place. She was out of her car, approaching him on foot, before he'd gone three steps toward his door.

He glanced at her, halted in surprise, then momentarily resumed his steps. Looking straight ahead, he neither waved nor spoke to her or indicated in any way he knew she was there. He was carrying a six-pack of beer and a carton of chicken in his hands. And yet she could tell by the stiffening of his spine and the determined thrust of his chin that he was all too aware of her presence.

She rushed to catch up with him, struggling to keep pace. "We've got to talk." She wasted no time with preliminary greetings.

One corner of his mouth quirked up in a mocking smile. "I don't think there's anything to say."

"I do." She was desperate, and it carried through in her tone.

He gave no notice, merely shifted both beer and chicken to his left hand and unlocked the door with his right. Mollie shot in ahead of him, very much aware he could have kept her out if he had wanted to. She was determined to give him no chance. They had to straighten out this mess now, before it got any worse, before he jumped to any more erroneous conclusions.

"Get your studying done?" he ground out with exaggerated solicitousness.

His question surprised her. Mollie swallowed. "No."

A muscle twitched involuntarily in his cheek. "I don't wonder you still have work to do."

"Dave, listen to me...." She trailed after him, watching as he put away the chicken and beer.

"Why should I? Why should I believe anything you have to say at this point?" He whirled toward her with a violence that was intimidating.

Mollie's breath stalled in her chest. A thin film of tears moistened her eyes. It was frustration making her cry, she told herself, sheer frustration. "You should listen to me because I love you." She spoke in a low, controlled tone.

"You have a damned funny way of showing it."

"I got roped into going there by Greta!"

"You don't make it a habit every Friday night?"

"No, I don't. And I don't dance with other men, either."

He shifted his head but bit off whatever he was first tempted to say. "How consoling."

"Will you stop the sarcasm and listen to me? I know you're angry with me. You have every right to be. But believe me, there is no reason for you to be jealous!"

"No reason!" He approached her swiftly, and grabbing her roughly, shook her exasperatedly. "I walk into the O-club on Quantico by a fluke, at loose ends on a Friday night because I can't see you because you're supposed to be studying. And there you are, drinking and dancing...."

"I told you. I can explain." The tears Mollie had been holding in suddenly flooded her eyes and spilled down her cheeks.

"So explain." He let her go as roughly and unexpectedly as he had grabbed her.

Mollie took a deep breath. "The whole time I've been at OCS and TBS, I've stood apart from the others. Part of it is my age, the fact I'm older than ninety percent of the others in my class. And part of it is my attitude. I'm one of the team on the drill field, but apart from that, when it comes to anything social, I'm a party spoiler. I never go out drinking with the others. I come to Washington to be with you. But they don't know that. They think I'm simply sightseeing. Tonight, when Greta accused me of being antisocial, I thought there might be some merit to it. So I went."

"And that guy you were with?"

"While we were there, a few male lieutenants joined our group. I spent some time talking to the guy you saw me dancing with."

"What about?" Dave's tone was terse but calmer.

His increasing reasonableness gave Mollie courage. "Largely, the differences in training between the men and the women. I was curious about what they did in physical training and we didn't. Obviously he got the wrong idea about my—interest—and that's when you came in and he asked me to dance."

Dave might have quieted his temper, but he was looking about as forgiving as a stone.

"And this urge to know more about the men's program, to go out with the girls, just came over you tonight, out of the blue," he ascertained grimly.

He was acting like a prosecuting attorney. Mollie's own temper began to soar. With difficulty, she kept her voice level as she replied, "I told you. Greta pushed me into going."

"And you wouldn't have gone otherwise." He slanted her a scornful glance.

Mollie held her own. "No, I wouldn't have."

A moment passed. Neither won the staring match that ensued, but he seemed to respect the fact she didn't look down or look away from him. Finally, it seemed, the truth of her innocence was getting through to him. Yet he had his doubts. "You're telling me your interest in this other guy wasn't genuine?" Jealousy was evident in his expression.

"Of course it was genuine. As far as it went. He just thought it went a little further than it did."

"And you gave him no…encouragement?"

Mollie clenched her jaw and focused on a drawer next to Dave's hip. The wood blurred, came into focus, blurred again. "I listened. Perhaps that's a commodity he's had in limited supply recently—at least from a woman." Mollie glanced back up at Dave, relieved to be able to relate with perfect honesty. "I don't know what his thoughts were. I do know that as soon as I realized he had misinterpreted my attention to what he was saying and had developed some man/woman interest in me, I determined to just exit gracefully. I was in the process of trying to break away from him when you entered the club. He realized it and rather forcefully asked me to dance. I agreed because I couldn't see any graceful way out of it. I didn't want to hurt his feelings."

Dave frowned again. His shoulders became rigid. "And you didn't care about mine."

"I care very much about your feelings. That's why I'm here."

He didn't move, didn't speak. Mollie could tell he wanted to believe her.

"Look, if the situation were reversed and I caught you dancing with some great-looking woman when I expected you to be here in your apartment studying, I'd be similarly upset. But damn it, Dave, I didn't want to be dancing with that guy. You should have trusted me. You should have looked at the expression on my face."

He crossed his arms. "I saw it. I was also married to a woman who cheated on me. I know the first rule of infidelity. And that's lie, lie, lie and keep on lying." He gritted his teeth, and his eyes were suspiciously liquid.

"For all I knew, you could have been— Hell, maybe you're an actress...for my benefit."

What could Mollie say to that? She couldn't deny his suspicion, because in a sense she *was* an actress—at least for the sake of advancing her career. She'd successfully feigned a gung-ho attitude in order to get into the marines, only to ironically later discover she really did have what it takes to be an officer. The butter bar in the O-club had been right. She was a natural officer. And damn it, she was proud of it, proud of being a marine. But she also wanted to be a writer. And she was so close to achieving her dream....

Dave was next to her without warning. His voice was gentle now. "What are you thinking?"

"Nothing."

"Stop shutting me out. You do that constantly. Did it ever occur to you I might be able to trust you more if you didn't lapse into long silences or periods of moodiness or refuse to talk about the future?"

Tears flooded Mollie's eyes for the second time that night, and she dashed at them in aggravation. "I do trust you, Dave, but there are times when I can't articulate what I'm feeling."

"Bull. You say you trust me. You say you love me. Well, not enough, apparently. Hell, I don't even know what that article you went all the way to South Carolina to write is about. Or if it got published."

"I don't know, either." Mollie rapidly shifted gears, adapting the neutral, careful tone she used to talk guardedly about her real career, her writing. "I'm going to New York next week to meet with Constance. We're going to discuss it in detail then."

His brows drew together in a frown. "I thought you

were going to know in a week or two if it passed. That was in June." Two months ago.

"It did and it didn't. Apparently there are complications. They want me to do some additional work on it." Mollie told him as much as she was able.

"How long have you known this?" Dave was unexpectedly sympathetic. He seemed to know intuitively how much this chance meant to her.

"Since yesterday morning. I got a letter from Constance." It had been a curiously buoyant note, and just as mysterious.

"How are you going to get there?"

"I'll drive to the airport in D.C. and take the shuttle. It'll be faster.

"I'll go with you."

"No—"

"Plans again? What is it this time? You have to study?"

How was it he knew instinctively when she was evading or covering up or just plain and simply feeling guilty about her duplicity? Mollie thought. "No, I don't have any plans except to see Constance."

"I see." He didn't believe her.

"You can go with me if you want," she offered. "You would be bored, sitting alone in a hotel room—"

"Fine. I'll go with you and be bored."

"You need to keep tabs on me that much?"

"You want that much for me not to?"

Mollie understood the depths of his jealousy; she just didn't think she could deal with that and everything else she had going, too. "This is ridiculous. I'm leaving."

She got as far as the door before he caught up with her. She expected him to be rough—as physical as he had been before. His hands were gentle, expressing tenderness, regret, even love.

"Mollie, don't go. I'm sorry. I am." He held her until his warmth transmitted into her. There was something stark and lonely in his voice, something she couldn't deny or turn her back on. And again the tears started. She, who never ever cried, was sobbing buckets. And he was holding her, holding her until the unexpected flow of tears stopped and they could talk rationally, unemotionally, again.

There was so much she wanted him to understand, so much she wanted to give to him. "Dave—"

He quieted her explanation with a touch of his finger against her lips. "It's not necessary for you to explain any more. I believe you. I do. It's not what happened tonight so much that's getting to me—although that's part of it." He paused long enough to draw a ragged breath. "It's this constant sneaking around that's driving me crazy. I want to be with you, but I want it to be open and aboveboard. I want everyone to know you belong to me and I to you so there'll be no confusion, so you can tell another guy to get lost, or if it comes down to it, let me tell him. I want us to be able to live together, to get up every morning and go to bed every night."

"The only way we could do that would be to get married."

"Exactly—"

"Dave—"

"Don't answer me yet. Just think about it. Think about how crazy this is making the both of us."

Mollie promised, and then she had no more time to think. His mouth was already covering hers. They made up with a series of kisses, tender, drugging, persuasive, repentant, until the world had steadied and they both felt they had come home again, to love.

Chapter Twelve

"Mollie, the article is everything I had hoped it would be, and much much more," Constance Vanderbilt said in early September as she finished reading the pages Mollie had turned in. "Your writing is smooth, polished, professional. And yet it's emotional, too. Reading your prose, I can readily understand and identify with the pride candidates feel upon graduating from OCS. It must have been a very emotional moment for you when you received your commission."

"Yes, it was," Mollie reflected. She had dressed as a civilian that weekend, yet oddly enough she still felt very much a marine. Being in a creative nonmilitary environment only intensified the sensation.

"How many more weeks before you graduate?"

"I've got approximately three months of TBS left," Mollie said.

"As you know, I initially planned to publish your article in two sections, with one part concentrating on your experiences at OCS, the other at TBS. But looking at what you've given me, plus all your personal letters with stories about what's happened to you and others in your platoon... Mollie, I think you ought to consider writing a book—as well as the article for *Super Women*, of course."

The thought of attempting such a lengthy project both alarmed and intrigued Mollie. She did some quick calculations. "I've got at least that much in notes and anecdotes alone. Add what I've learned about the training of officers in the marines—sure, I could do that!" She paused, considering the possibilities. Just as suddenly her mood took a downward turn. "But—" Dampening Mollie's excitement were the problems undertaking a project like that would generate. Ethically, legally, she could be putting herself in trouble.

"Great." Constance reached for the notepad on her desk. It was a Saturday, and the editorial offices of *Super Women* magazine were abnormally quiet. "I have a list of some book editors I think would be interested in your project. You'd have to submit a formal proposal, of course. Probably at least one hundred pages of the manuscript to get an actual sale."

Mollie leaned forward in her chair. Everything was happening so fast. She'd hardly had time to absorb Constance's suggestion, but it didn't take Mollie long to see the problems inherent in such a tremendously involved undertaking. "I'm not sure I'd be safe from libel if I were to print even half of what I have." And if she didn't print the juicier items about the other officer candidates in her company, would she still have enough information to sustain a book?

"As far as the personal stories about others you've worked with, to avoid being sued for libel, you could go one of two ways. Either change enough about each person's story—alter their age, background, name, description—to successfully muddle up who is who, perhaps even combine several candidates' characteristics into only one or two actual candidates. Or you could go the way of signed release forms. Formally ask permission. I'd advise the first option though. Frankly, they might refuse to give permission. And if they did—well, you might just open up problems where you don't necessarily need to have any."

"It's not just getting sued for libel I'm worried about."

"What, then?" Constance looked perplexed.

"The military." Her superiors. Dave.

"What would it take to get permission from the military?"

"I don't know. I think I'd have to go through the public affairs office."

"Would they censor anything you wrote?"

"They'd certainly make sure I didn't print any classified information. Beyond that...I don't know." Mollie felt restless, unsettled.

"Well, we'll tackle all that after you've quit the marines," Constance said.

After I quit. Mollie tumbled the words about in her mind. Never had the option she'd been counting on all the long months since entering OCS and TBS seemed so unpalatable. "You mean before I finish TBS?"

"You want to finish for the sake of your writing project?"

"Yes." *And for myself,* Mollie thought. For reasons she didn't quite understand. She only knew Quantico had begun to seem like home to her. That when she was there, she felt as if she belonged.

"All right, you can resign directly after TBS," Constance said.

Mollie decided to level with her editor. "Frankly, Constance, I'm not sure I want to quit the marines, then, either," Mollie replied carefully.

Constance did a double take. "Run that by me again?"

"They've spent so much money training me. I feel I

have an obligation to pay back some of that money and effort on their part by going on active duty. At least for a while.'' Embarrassed, Mollie got up to pace the length of the office. She felt her cheeks grow hot. She knew she was acting like a Girl Scout, but she couldn't help it.

Constance was watching Mollie curiously. After a moment the editor shrugged. ''So serve some time in the military if that will ease your conscience,'' Constance admonished. ''Your experience as an officer on active duty will only add yet another dimension to the magazine article. We'll be able to tell our readers what it's like after training, as well. How long do you think it would take you to complete the second part of the article for *Super Women*?''

''I think I could have the section about my TBS training finished in January. After that, well, it would depend on how much further you wanted me to go with it.''

Constance frowned. ''January is a little longer than I wanted to wait for the second half. Can you get at least part of it to me by November first?''

Mollie nodded affirmatively.

Constance continued. ''I know this article is going to be a smashing success when it runs. You'll probably get a lot more work.''

''You're that confident?''

Constance nodded. ''Your letters have been very entertaining and informative. The subject matter is timely; it's something that hasn't already been done to death.... Yes, I think it will be well received. If there is a problem, it will probably come when we have to decide what to keep for the final draft and what to cut. That probably will be hard for you, Mollie, because you've gathered so much wonderful information. But not to worry.'' Constance smiled reassuringly. "Whatever we don't use for the magazine can probably be published later, in the book."

"Provided I get a book contract."

"You will," Constance said confidently.

Both women fell silent as they mulled over the possibilities. For Mollie, what was happening was like a dream come true. It was a nightmare. All she could think about was Dave and what his reaction would be if he knew what she was doing.

"HOW DID THE INTERVIEW with Constance go?" Dave asked a short time later as Mollie entered the hotel room they were sharing. It was late afternoon and he was dressed to go out for dinner. He'd been watching a football game when she entered, but he switched it off in favor of talking to her.

Mollie sat down opposite him, on the other double bed.

"Constance likes what I've done so much she thinks I ought to try and expand the material into a book-length work. She's even given me a list of book publishers, tips on how to submit a partial manuscript."

"That's great."

"Yes." And it was also a way Mollie could use all of the material she'd gathered about the officer training program.

"What about your article for *Super Women*?"

"I've promised to have a rough draft of the second half of the magazine article ready for Constance's perusal by November first."

He gave her a searching, sympathetic glance. "Feeling deadline pressure?"

More than you know, Mollie thought. "Yes."

"You once told me becoming a published writer was

a dream you'd had since childhood. Do you still feel that way?''

''Yes, I do, more than ever. But at the same time, over the months of training, I've slowly become a marine. I think like an officer in the military, act like one. I don't want to quit the marines, Dave. And Constance... Constance thinks I should consider resigning my commission, now that my publishing career is taking off.''

Dave stared at her in stunned silence. ''Sweetheart, I hate to break it to you and Constance, but I don't think you could quit now if you wanted to. Oh, sure, you can hand in your resignation anytime up until the time you graduate from OCS and receive your butter bars, but after that, you're expected to honor whatever contract you made with your recruiter. If you don't...well, you'd probably be facing a dishonorable discharge.''

Mollie's jaw clenched stubbornly. ''I don't want a dishonorable discharge.'' Neither did she want to give up the chance to be published. Yet what was she to do? ''And I enlisted for three years,'' Mollie murmured.

''And now your editor wants you to renege on that promise; is that it?''

He was looking at her with decreasing respect. Yet Mollie couldn't help but answer honestly. ''Part of me does want out—now. The part that's a writer. For the rest of me, it's unthinkable. Mostly I feel torn.''

Dave was silent for several moments. ''Is there any reason you couldn't do both?'' Dave asked. ''Write a book and the *Super Women* article and serve out your time in the marines?''

''I'm afraid if I try to do both, I'll end up losing everything, that neither my writing nor my performance in the marines will be considered my best or that by even attempting to write a book while serving would be seen as a conflict of interest by the military.''

''Is there a conflict of interest?''

Mollie avoided his eyes, saying carefully, ''The subject matter of the writing project is in part about me, my experiences, since I've been divorced.'' She faltered a bit, trying to speak only the truth, yet keep from him knowledge that would upset him. ''I'm on active duty in the marines now...I'd be surprised in a way if they didn't consider it a conflict of interest. If only because in order to do both, I'd probably be burning the candle at both ends.''

''Is there any reason you couldn't put off publishing the book until your time in the marines is completed? Write slowly, give it the same amount of time and attention you would any other off-duty interest or hobby while you serve out your tour? Maybe just do the article for *Super Women*?''

''I've thought of that.'' Mollie sighed. ''Publishing is such a timely business. It's so hard to be writing something saleable at exactly the time it's hot. Usually, by the time you finish an article on the subject that's holding the public's interest, there have already been twenty other articles printed. So you're left holding the bag, so to speak. This is the first time I've ever had a project on the mark enough to get published. The idea that my editor thinks I have enough to manage a book sale, too—it's a very exciting feeling! I want to have everything, to be a published author in more than one medium. I don't want to just do the article if I could do the article and a book both.''

''Maybe you should go to the public affairs office and talk to them.''

And what would her superiors say? Mollie wondered. It wouldn't take much intelligence to figure out she'd been up to this all along, that there'd been a very good reason she'd kept such a detailed diary. "I think I'll wait until after I'm actually offered the contract for the article and maybe the book." Thus far, for Mollie, everything was still in the talking stage.

"I wouldn't sign anything before you talk to them," Dave warned.

Mollie knew he was acting in her best interest, handing out that advice. And that his judgment in this instance was sound. "I won't," she murmured. "But I'm far from that stage right now. I haven't even written a proposal yet." Nor would *Super Women* put her under actual contract until the entire work was handed in, in publishable form.

Mollie reasoned she didn't have to go to public affairs until she'd had time to think her position through, to see if she was even capable of putting a book together. Although she felt she was able to do so, she felt more comfortable doing the work first, then going to public affairs. That way she'd have time to think through her own position first, to do some research on other marines who'd had articles published. Were there any? Mollie thought so, but she would have to look it up to be certain. Besides that, if she delayed going to public affairs as long as possible, she'd also have more time to spend with Dave. On the chance this whole business did blow up in her face—well, suffice it to say, she knew if it did, she would more than likely lose Dave. She wasn't willing to give up her time with him, not yet. Maybe—just maybe—not ever.

"Does that thoughtful look mean you're feeling better now?" Dave asked, snapping her from her reverie.

Mollie's shoulders relaxed; she nodded. Her mood brightened as she realized she did have quite a bit to be happy about.

"Great. I think this calls for a celebration, then."

Mollie grinned. "I'm all for that."

"ANY THOUGHTS about where you'd like to have dinner?" Dave asked half an hour later, after Mollie'd been given a chance to freshen up.

Mollie picked up her purse. "Well, not right offhand—"

"Good, then I know exactly where we want to go."

He was excited! "Hungry?" She arched her brows teasingly.

"Starved. And I know this place over on Sixty-Fourth Street that serves homemade manicotti! I ate there once when I was in New York a couple of years ago."

"You like fresh pasta?"

"Love it."

Mollie marveled that she was so in love with this man, and he with her, and there was still so much they didn't know about each other. "You can make it yourself, you know," Mollie said, as together they walked out the door of the hotel room and approached the elevator.

Dave shrugged off her suggestion. "Too much trouble. I'm not much in the kitchen. Oh, I can manage sandwiches, steaks, heat up anything in a can," he continued as he hailed a cab for them.

"I know. I've seen your kitchen, remember? It's ill equipped to do anything but the most basic cooking. Not that I'm much of a gourmet myself. I've never even owned a Cuisinart or an omelet pan."

"Well, tonight get your taste buds ready, because this is going to be a gastronomic experience you'll never forget."

He was right. The food was wonderful. As was the wine—and the company. Dave was charming and expansive. They talked not about either's work or problems but about funny experiences in their youths. Mollie was still laughing at his stories about the various pets he and Blythe had owned when they left the restaurant. It was only eleven o'clock; the night was still young. "Having a good time?" Dave asked.

"The best. The excitement of the city always energizes me." She was drunk on her success, the increasing fulfillment she felt in her relationship with Dave, the wonderful time they were having.

"Glad you brought me with you?" Dave asked, lacing an arm about her waist and drawing her against him. Above them, multicolored neon lights sparkled against the black evening sky. She stood on tiptoe and brushed her lips across his cheek, then lower, across his jaw. "You're the best traveling companion I've ever had," Mollie confessed softly. And she was very, very glad they'd met.

Chapter Thirteen

"I hope you don't mind doing something different this weekend. I thought you might be tired of sightseeing in Washington."

Mollie stretched languorously in the seat beside him, basking in the early-morning September sunshine streaming into the car. Two weeks had passed since Mollie had talked to Constance. She was making good progress on her outline. Unable to work on it the weekends she'd spent with Dave, though, she'd taken to writing early in the morning, in her dorm room, while Greta slept. She found she got more done that way in less time. And she still had her weekends and evenings to study her regular TBS work. Not that the two subjects were very different. The topics were endlessly interrelated. "You want the truth?" Mollie asked, turning her attention back to what he was saying.

"Nothing but."

"I've really liked playing tourist. Oh, before this I'd been to Washington once with a couple of schoolteacher friends to see the sights. But we only got as far as the Washington Monument, the Capitol, the Smithsonian. I never had time to go to Arlington Cemetery and see the changing of the guards or the Tomb of the Unknown Soldier or stop and read the names engraved on the Vietnam Memorial. If it hadn't been for you, I still probably wouldn't have ventured into D.C. much."

"But you're glad you did?"

"Very."

"I still haven't taken you to see the FBI building."

"Yeah, well..." Mollie shifted uncomfortably in her seat and tried to concentrate on the rural Virginia landscape they were speedily leaving behind. "Since it's only open nine to five, Monday through Fridays, doesn't look like I will, either." She smothered a yawn and kept her glance turned to the scenery. She could sense him looking at her, but he said nothing more in response.

Did he know how grateful she had been that they couldn't arrange the tour? she wondered. Or how she had avoided even talking about the establishment where they showed the latest criminal-investigation techniques? It was foolish of her to fear going there. She had no criminal record, but there was the nagging feeling of dishonesty plaguing her these days. She felt like a criminal for lying to Dave. She felt badly about enlisting in the Marine Corps for purposes that would benefit her first, her country and those depending on her a very distant second. What she had done was fraud. She could remedy that by serving out her three-year enlistment and hence live up to the contractual obligation she'd made with her recruiter. But she could never negate what she had knowingly done in her heart, and that was lie her way into the marines to realize her writer's ambitions.

Dave's low voice cut into her thoughts. "You surprise me, Lt. Devlin. You're not generally so easily led. By now I thought you'd be bursting with curiosity about where we're going!"

Mollie laughed, glad for the reprieve from her conscience. She swiveled around to Dave, a reckless smile playing on her face. "You mean just because you insisted on meeting at dawn...and the back of your car is overflowing with camping gear? Sleeping bags, tent, a cooler, two bags of groceries and two packs? Now why would I question that?"

"I don't know. Why would you?" He picked up her playful mood.

"It's fairly obvious we're going camping."

"Ah, but where are we going camping?"

"Uh...the Blue Ridge mountains."

"Close. We'll be in the foothills, anyway. We're going to a little place in Culpeper County."

"A town?"

"My place."

"Your place!" She faced him in shock. He'd never said anything about owning any property. Matter of fact, she'd got the impression he was as rootless as she currently was.

"Yep. Several years ago, I put a down payment on twenty acres of land." He spoke casually, but nonetheless a ray of pride shone in his voice. "It's not much. It's rocky and overgrown with weeds and scrub. There's no electricity there currently, no city water or sewer. But it does have a well on it—water comes from a hand pump outside the burned-out shell of a house. I should say, what's left of the house."

"Which is?"

"Part of a cement floor and the fireplace. I've torn down the rest of it. What didn't collapse on its own, anyway."

"The house had already burned down when you bought the place?"

"Yes. The owners chose not to rebuild. It seems they were never out here much, anyway, and just used the place for a weekend retreat. Rather than go to the trouble of rebuilding, they decided to put the property up for sale. I knew the moment I saw the place I wanted it. Despite the problems with the house itself, the land was everything I've ever imagined a potential homesite to be—beautiful, easily accessible, yet at the same time off the beaten track enough to be very private."

"How often do you get out there?"

"Before I met you? At least once a month."

"Have you told Blythe about this?"

"Yeah. She went out with me once and termed it 'Dave Talmadge's Folly.' She thinks I'll give it up."

"And will you?"

"Well, I'm no farmer—not that this land could really be tamed, anyway. But I do love the country. And I want a place where I can retire someday. It's not much; I want you to know that. But someday it's going to be my home."

"What prompted you to buy it?" Mollie asked as seconds drew out and he said nothing more; indeed, he acted as if he were suddenly almost embarrassed for having revealed so much of himself to her.

"I guess I'm at the point in my life where I need something more permanent than an apartment." He slanted her a curious glance and changed the subject around to her. "I know you went to Ohio State. Did you spend all your formative years there, too?"

"Yes, I lived there in a small town all my life before coming to New York as an adult."

"What was your house like?"

"Very roomy. It had a wood frame and was painted white, with black shutters and a glossy red door. There was a huge wraparound front porch that covered three sides of the house and a tiny back stoop. My bedroom was on the second floor."

"What do you miss most about it?"

"The scents, I guess. Wood burning on a cold winter's day. Opening the door, smelling cinnamon cookies or roast beef. My mother was a great cook. She really enjoyed homemaking. What about you? What was your house like?"

"Blythe and I grew up in a suburb of Cleveland, in a small brick ranch house."

"What was it like inside?"

"Crowded. Mother always had a committee meeting there—she was always actively involved in preventing, sustaining or eliminating something. Pollution. Crime. Juvenile delinquency. Muscular dystrophy. You name an issue or charity, she tackled it."

"And you resented that?"

"Not her good works specifically. But bear in mind all four of us lived in less than a thousand square feet of house. The backyard was very tiny, as was the front. I never felt I had enough breathing space. Sometimes I used to go to the library or the park after school just to hear the silence, to be able to study in peace."

"And Blythe?"

"She often found refuge at a girlfriend's house or the library."

"What about your dad?"

"He was a fireman. He'd been in the army but quit. My mother wanted him home. I always felt he regretted resigning from the service. It was like the best times he ever had were when he was in the service, although I know he enjoyed working at the fire station. Maybe it was the same type of environment. All male; at least at that point in time it was. The guys ate and slept there for twenty-four-hour shifts. Of course, maybe his absences were why my mother felt such a pressing need to fill up the house with others, to occupy herself. She didn't have a career. She needed something, and as Blythe and I grew older, she turned to community service. I'll say this; she was happy in what she did."

And her son and daughter were essentially both loners who had difficulty establishing or trusting intimacy. A fluke? Mollie wondered. A biologically inherited facet of their characters? Or something deeper? At times she felt such need emanating from Dave, a need that echoed her own yearning to be loved, held, treasured simply for being oneself.

"Well, here we are," Dave said minutes later, turning the car up a narrow gravel lane.

The land was exactly as he had described it, Mollie noted. Overgrown with weeds and littered with huge boulders. The terrain was hilly and peppered with trees. At the highest point, toward the rear of the property, was the area where the house had once stood. The remains were few and yet Mollie saw such promise reflected there. Such hope. For the future, for herself.

"Dave, it's beautiful! You didn't mention there were wildflowers. Mountain laurel, Indian paintbrush, rhododendron and violets..."

"That was my surprise." He walked over to pick her a fragrant bouquet from the flowers still blooming in partial shade. Strolling back toward her, he presented her with a bouquet. Mollie buried her nose in the fragrance of the silky multicolored blossoms.

"This is wonderful." Mollie sighed. It was the best reprieve she could think of from the rigors of her TBS studies and her self-imposed writing schedule.

"You really think so?"

"Yes." His land was a writer's paradise. Quiet, peaceful, no distractions. For a second, Mollie closed her eyes and envisioned herself finishing her book there, with Dave at her side. Now that would be heaven, wouldn't it?

Beaming at her pleasure, he began unloading her belongings from the car. "We'll set up camp here while it's still light. I packed sandwiches for lunch. This evening, we can light a fire and cook in the fireplace."

The afternoon passed lazily. For a change, Mollie let herself forget the demands of school and her writing. She concentrated only on Dave and the happiness simply being with him gave her. They walked among the flowers, scouring every inch of his property, examining where fences had been trampled or torn down by storms, where squirrels and birds nested. In the early evening, they walked back to the campsite, hand in hand. Dave built a fire while Mollie pumped water from the well. Later, she worked on assembling a salad and putting potatoes on to bake while he went to see about gathering more kindling. Darkness fell. Dave didn't come back.

At first Mollie convinced herself she was silly to worry, but when he didn't answer her shouts for him, indeed no sound at all save the crickets and cicadas and rustling of the wind was forthcoming, she began to panic. Putting the salad into the cooler for safekeeping, she picked up the Coleman lantern. Only when she lifted it did she see the envelope and compass tucked safely beneath it. Her name was inscribed on the envelope in Dave's bold scrawl. Mollie was swearing even as she put down the lantern and sat cross-legged on the cement to open it. *Damn it, Dave,* she cursed out loud, *what game are you up to now?*

The note read:

Mollie sweetheart,
We know you can survive a night compass course and a day compass course. You proved that in OCS. The question is: Can you survive a scavenger hunt for love?

I knew you'd want to take the test, like a true marine. So follow the instructions clearly and you shall be rewarded. I'll be waiting for you.

Love,
Dave.

Her first thought was *I am not going to do this. No way.*

Then, why not? It should be fun. Moreover, she knew if she didn't follow the instructions, he was liable never to come out of hiding.

Step one said, "Take fifteen steps backwards, due north of the campsite. Three hops due northwest from there. Six giant steps east from there."

Grumbling but counting and using the instructions, she ended up six feet short of the base of a huge oak tree. Mollie searched the tree limbs above her, half expecting to see Dave ensconced cozily above her. Nothing. She backtracked and covered the surrounding territory. If he was there, observing, he was well hidden and not moving or making a sound. She stomped forward again, beginning to lose her temper. What if she never found the appointed items? Finally, in the grass due east of the tree, she saw a ribbon-wrapped knapsack. Not an ordinary knapsack, it was bright pink—the kind little girls carried to school on their backs—and sported a huge daisy decal. It was empty—except for a new set of instructions, this one more complicated than the last.

She swore again, this time very loudly, but her tirade was peppered with chuckles. Damn the man, anyway.

Eight leapfrog lengths later and three equally confusing changes of direction, she found a second gift—a foil-wrapped bottle of perfume. The flowery fragrance was one of her favorites. With it came a third set of directions, harder to follow than the last, yet by now Mollie was eager to get to the end of the trail, and grinning wildly, she followed the directions explicitly, glad she had a Coleman lantern to light the way.

Located in a strand of wildflowers was a plastic-wrapped item. Mollie knelt to open it and found a long, old-fashioned flannel nightgown. It was high necked and long sleeved, bordered with rows of delicate white lace and covered with tiny violets. It was feminine and warm, a hopelessly intimate and intuitive gift. Precisely the sort of garment she would buy for herself, for long winter evenings alone.

With it, came the note that read: "Only one more journey. Up to it? Dave."

The final instructions were easy. "Take three steps forward, close your eyes and count to ten."

Mollie did as ordered. It was no surprise when she found herself wrapped in Dave's arms and hugged against his frame. His lips touched her hair. "Surprised?" he asked gently.

"Very." Mollie returned his hug and cuddled closer. "How did you ever work this out?"

"I thought of it last week. Had everything arranged; just needed to wait until you were occupied elsewhere, helping get dinner, before I set it into play."

"Thank you for the gifts. They're wonderful."

"You're wonderful."

They walked back to the campsite arm in arm.

Dinner was late, and they were both famished. Later, they unrolled their sleeping bags to fashion a double bed. ''Model the nightgown for me?'' he asked.

Mollie grinned. ''With pleasure.''

Chapter Fourteen

On October 15, Mollie submitted a partial manuscript and outline for completion to one of the book publishers Constance had recommended. She also turned in the additional pages Constance had requested for the second half of the *Super Women* article. Then, feeling she could delay no longer, on October 26 she made an evening appointment with a lieutenant colonel in the public affairs office. The senior officer was sympathetic and not nearly as surprised as Mollie had thought he might be by her revelation that she had always wanted to write.

"So what I want to know is this," Mollie finished carefully. "If I were to have the chance to publish in a national magazine or a newspaper or even write a book, could I do so?"

"You find you want to get back to writing?"

"Actually, sir, I've never quite given it up."

He smiled. "As long as it is about nonmilitary matters, we would have no objection to your doing so."

"What if I wanted to write about my time in the marines? Or...or do a short story about going through OCS?" Mollie was improvising.

"There we'd have a problem. You see, even in fiction, there's a tendency for the public to accept whatever is presented to them as fact—even though it may only be one person's view. And frankly your perceptions, or any other marine's, may not coincide with the official outlook of the Marine Corps. So we have to be very careful there.''

''In other words, in an instance like that, permission would be denied,'' Mollie ascertained with growing trepidation. What was she going to do now? She'd finished the first section of her work, and though she was still waiting for a reaction from Constance—one she hoped to get from her editor in person when she went to New York the first weekend in November—Mollie was sure she was going to be offered a contract.

''Probably permission would be denied,'' the lieutenant colonel affirmed, jerking Mollie back to reality.

''But...well, it seems to me I've heard talk...since being in OCS and TBS, of people in other classes, before ours, writing to hometown newspapers and such about their days here at Quantico.''

''Occasionally that happens—usually without permission from this office, because the offenders don't know it's against regulations. Were they to come forward, it's possible their article would be reviewed and permission granted for it to be published.''

And equally possible that permission would be denied, Mollie thought, cursing roundly. ''What happens to those people...who publish without permission...and don't know it.''

''That depends on what they print. If it is inconsequential, nothing. The offending officer or enlisted person would be counseled on the correct procedure to follow.''

''And if it were classified?''

''That's another matter. They'd be tried in a military court.''

"What if it were middle-of-the-road information?"

"Like what?"

Mollie was silent, trying to come up with a suitably unincriminating example. "I don't know. Uh, a fictionalized account of OCS training or life in the marines. Or a nonfiction overview of life in the military. Could something like that conceivably be granted permission to publish?"

"I don't know. My guess is we'd be back to a perception problem on the part of the public."

"So permission would be denied."

The lieutenant colonel hesitated. "Probably."

Mollie was silent.

"Why are you so interested in this, Lieutenant Devlin?"

Again Mollie grappled for the right words, trying to tell the truth, yet miserably aware of all she was omitting.

"As I said earlier, I'm still interested in writing, as a hobby—I've kept a diary for a long time—and as a profession. I wanted to be sure about what I could and could not write about while I was in the marines."

"Stick to nonmilitary topics and you'll be fine. However, if you do receive an opportunity to have your work published while you are in the marines, it wouldn't hurt to let your public affairs office know, even if it has nothing to do with military matters at all. If nothing else, you could get your accomplishment written up in a base newspaper."

"Thanks." Mollie stood. She returned the lieutenant colonel's smile. She'd never felt worse.

There was little doubt in her mind that if she tried to get her articles published as written, she would be denied official permission, for they were written with an overview that covered the good, the bad, the occasional pettiness, and sometimes semiridiculous military protocol. If she were to omit all the objectional parts, she wouldn't have an incisive article. She'd have a public relations pamphlet for the marines. Timely and topical a subject as hers was, it wouldn't get published in that syrupy form. Not by Constance Vanderbilt, and not by anyone else. So what was she going to do? Give up a lifelong dream of becoming a published writer? Or try to resign from her stint in the marines and hope they would let her go—honorable discharge or no. Mollie didn't know. She did realize she'd never been more unhappy in her life, less sure of herself or of what was right and what was wrong. It was a damning fix she'd gotten herself into. What was worse, she couldn't discuss it with Dave or turn to anyone else for advice.

Over the next few days, Mollie's conscience continued to haunt her. Yet despite the tension she was under due to her effort to continue her deception, strangely enough her daily writing and journal keeping had never gone better. With Constance's faith in her came a renewed sense of her own inner strength as a writer. She realized belatedly she was talented and that writing gave her a pleasure she got from nothing else. But the rose she had sought for so long was at the end of a stem covered with prickly thorns. Mollie didn't know if she had the agility to keep on nimbly jumping around to keep from getting stuck. She did realize every time she saw Dave that she felt a little more guilty for keeping the truth from him. Her deception was made worse by his being so trusting—accepting her reluctance to discuss much of her current work in progress with nary a qualm or question.

It was almost as if she had expected their mutual state of limbo to go on forever. It was with a shock that it ended.

"You're leaving for Europe?" Mollie faced Dave in shock the last day of October. A feeling of unreality came over her as she watched him start to pack, yet on the surface it couldn't have been a more normal setting. It was a Sunday afternoon; they'd just spent the weekend together and were still in his apartment. Outside, the autumn day was crisp, clear and cool. It was perfect weather, a beautiful day, and he was leaving her. Just that swiftly and easily.

"My flight leaves tonight around ten." Dave was busy stuffing belongings into a single duffel bag.

"Why didn't you tell me?"

He straightened, then turned slowly toward her and held her glance. "I didn't want what time we had together before I left spent lamenting my absence the next couple of weeks."

"And if you'd told me, that would've been all we'd done," she said softly, understanding.

He nodded affirmatively, his mouth tightening. For a second she saw the frustration he, too, was feeling. This assignment of his couldn't have come at a worse time.

"If it's any consolation, I really don't want to go."

Molly didn't want him to go, either. "But you really don't have any choice, do you?"

He favored her with a lopsided smile. "I'm in the marines. When duty calls..."

Mollie smiled. She knew his orders were beyond their control. She also knew he could take care of himself in any situation. There was no reason for her to worry about him while he was away. But she couldn't help it. Apprehension for his safety and continued well-being suffused her.

With effort, she controlled her inner anxiety and concentrated on the specifics of his assignment. "How long will you be gone?"

"I don't know. Maybe three weeks. I should be back before you graduate from TBS." He relayed the news in a matter-of-fact tone of voice, but there was misery and regret in his eyes.

"And Percy and Blythe's wedding?"

He hesitated, looking even more unhappy about this impending departure. "I'll try and make it. If I can't..." He shrugged and exhaled wearily. "Blythe and Percy both understand part of my job means going whenever, wherever, I'm needed."

On an intellectual level, Mollie could understand and cope with what was happening. On an emotional level, she found the going to be much rougher. She didn't want to go on without him, even for a short while. She'd come to rely on his reassuring presence, his love, his tenderness.

But she didn't have a choice, she reminded herself sternly. "Is what you're going to be doing dangerous?"

There was a brief pause, a fraction of a second too long. "No."

"Dave—"

"Mollie, don't ask me any more. I can't tell you anything. It's all classified. Every bit of it."

How did others do it? she wondered. How did they live with officers whose work was so confidential it couldn't even be discussed? Part of her felt very left out and alone. Her more pragmatic side was stoically accepting. So there would be a few weeks of loneliness. He would be back. And she would be waiting for him when he did come home. Together they'd make up for lost time. What was important now was that he know that she loved him and would wait for him, however long it took. She swallowed hard. "I'm going to miss you."

"And I'll miss you." He walked forward to swallow her in a hug. His lips brushed the top of her head. "When I get back, we'll talk." His words held a world of promise.

Mollie had never been a dependent sort of woman. She'd always liked to be very much on her own. But now she found that was changing. She wanted to be as much a part of his life as he was of hers; she wanted them to go on together as a team. She saw it was possible. That possibility filled her with hope.

"I'm going to hold you to that promise, Dave Talmadge," she teased.

He grinned and ruffled her hair. "You couldn't get me to break it if you tried."

"SO THE UPSHOT of all this is the public affairs office won't let you publish unless they review whatever you write and approve of everything you say," Constance said over a business lunch at Tavern on the Green in New York.

"Right. Which would leave me with a rosy view even a fairy-tale character wouldn't accept."

"Well, you know what you have to do, don't you? You have to resign from the military as soon as you've finished the article for *Super Women.* Or at the very latest, directly before the article hits the newsstands."

"Which would mean the longest I could serve on active duty would be about a year of my three-year commitment."

"Yes."

"What if they won't let me resign?"

"Accept a dishonorable discharge; get out that way. Believe me, in the long run, once you're famous, it won't hurt you in the publishing field. Having a dishonorable discharge slapped on you for what you've done may even help the article."

But it would be hard for Mollie to cope with personally. It would cheapen her somehow, lessen her self-esteem. She was a commissioned officer now, a person of responsibility and authority. She had worked hard to get where she was; ironically enough, she found she did not want to give up her commission, nor did she want to renege on her commitment to serve her country.

Inwardly still struggling with pangs of conscience, Mollie forced herself to concentrate on her future as a writer. She mentally envisioned the success that would come with publishing the *Super Women* article. But strangely enough, the motivation she needed to pursue her literary success was no longer within her, at least not in the no-holds-barred way it had been before she had joined the marines.

Constance became very still as she watched the play of emotions on her protégée's face. "Mollie, you're not still having qualms—"

"I've been thinking of ways to get around alienating or offending the Marine Corps. What if I were to delay publication of the magazine article several years...to give me time to serve out my contract first, to meet my obligation?"

"I can't guarantee someone else wouldn't publish a similar article first. It's a question of timing, Mollie, of being in the right place at the right time with the right material. You're there now. If you wait, you might lose your chance to break into print, and I would hate to see what happens to you, especially after all you've risked to get where you are."

It was precisely because of what she had risked and done, and become, that Mollie found herself unable to continue on the path she had originally and ambitiously slated for herself.

"I don't want to lose my chance to get published, either," Mollie confessed. Neither did she want to face disgrace and failure in the Marine Corps. "I don't want a dishonorable discharge."

"From what you're telling me, the public affairs office is not going to give you much choice. Have you submitted anything?"

"No, but I know what they'd say."

"No."

"At the very least. I'd probably be out on my ear, anyway." Mollie guessed, her mood becoming blacker and blacker.

Constance put down her fork. "I know what it is. It's all this honor and country and duty business, isn't it? Mollie, that's just propaganda, to get you to do what they want you to do, to get you to follow orders blindly without thinking it out for yourself first!"

"No, it's not, Constance. It's true, they have established formal standards of conduct, but that's only because the prestige of the Marine Corps depends greatly on the appearance of its officers." Briefly, Mollie told her editor the story of Nosy Nellie and the Limburger cheese, how the impetuous actions of a few had affected the reputation of the entire platoon. "I learned then that there is never any justified relinquishing of responsibility. We're all morally accountable for what we say and do, especially in regards to others. Since then I've also had TBS classes on standards and conduct. I've learned that integrity has no degrees. Something is either right or it's wrong. I have to go with what I feel inside."

Constance slanted Mollie a concerned look. "And this feels wrong to you?"

"I discovered during OCS that I'm not cut out for deception. And I don't like being ashamed of myself for my actions or those of the people around me. I'm just not good at lying or deceiving. I don't feel good about it. It haunts me. Keeps me from concentrating as fully as I should."

"All right. Maybe what you've learned there is not all propaganda." Constance tried another approach. "But listen to me, Mollie. I've dealt with writers a long time now. It's natural for them to get worked up about whatever they're writing about. If it's a save-the-whales campaign, you can bet that writer will be out combing the coastlines and marching in picket lines while he's doing the story. But when the story fades, so does much of the writer's enthusiasm for the subject matter. Maybe not all of it. But much of that go-get-'em attitude does fade, only to be redirected to the next story."

"You think that's what I'm doing?" For the first time, Mollie was uncertain. Maybe this was writer's enthusiasm. Heaven knew she'd always felt her articles were terrific before, even after they didn't sell or get published.

"Who wouldn't have turned into a marine in your place? Mollie, you took an incredible dare, joining the marines and going through officer's training just to get a story. Your expectations have been fulfilled beyond your wildest dreams. You've not only proved you can succeed in the marine environment, a monumental challenge in itself, but you're going to have a two-part article in a nationwide periodical."

"Then the magazine is definitely going to buy my article?"

"As soon as it's put into the proper form. I've shown what you've sent me to our editor in chief, including the partial section on TBS. She likes it very much and wants to go with it, with the stipulation that a few changes are made. Changes I agree with. She wants a slightly different slant...a more controversial— Mollie, there's no need for you to look worried. The work is nothing you can't handle; I'm positive of it. I'll be sending you the revisions in a couple of weeks. When you've completed the work satisfactorily, a contract will be issued, along with payment for the first article."

"And the second article?"

"Will need to be revised before we go to contract, too."

"When would I be published?"

"Assuming you could get the work done within the next several months? The article would probably run anywhere from three to six months from when the final revisions are completed."

Mollie sighed tremulously. She forced herself to concentrate on her original goal. "To think, I'll be a published writer, actually see my words on the pages of *Super Women* magazine. It does sound too good to be true." If only she didn't feel so guilty!

"It's a chance in a lifetime, so don't blow it. Now drink your champagne," Constance ordered. "Then we'll talk about the article. I'll give you an idea of what we at *Super Women* would like to see done to make it more interesting and incisive."

Chapter Fifteen

Dave folded his long legs into the narrow compartment between seats of the transatlantic jetliner. He was glad to be going home. The past three weeks had seemed like an eternity to him.

Always in the past he'd enjoyed taking assignments in other parts of the world. Not this time. His most recent assignment, to serve on a special task force to help tighten airport security for American tourists and service personnel traveling in Europe, had been both challenging and satisfying. And yet he'd been lonelier than hell. Mollie had been on his mind constantly. The few times he'd managed to talk to her on the phone hadn't been nearly enough. And though she'd been glad to hear from him, he'd heard the undertone of loneliness in her voice, too.

Odd that he'd known her just seven short months, seen her only weekends when her schedule allowed, but in that time she'd become the most important element in his life. She was there in his fantasies, his dreams, included in his every aspiration or hope for the future. Did she realize it? he wondered. Did she have any clue as to how much he loved her? He'd whispered the words countless times when they'd made love, but other than that—Mollie had a habit of shying away from intensely personal conversations and all talk of the future. Not that he could blame her, he guessed. Knowing she was bound to be moving on soon, without him, what could be said about the future that wasn't bound to depress both of them?

With any other woman, Dave would have accepted that twist of fate with casual regret. With Mollie, just the thought of her leaving was enough to throw him into the blackest of moods. Especially when he knew now it was easier than ever for marines to have a two-career marriage. Mollie knew full well a future was there for them for the taking if they wanted it. But she hadn't mentioned it, or given him much of an opportunity to discuss the range of possibilities, because she wasn't sure they had a future. Not one that would allow her to be everything she was capable of.

He had no intention of holding her back. He would just have to make her understand that. They would have to get past their mutual anxieties about marriage in general, past the traumas of their individual divorces, and go on with their lives. Together.

His course of action decided, Dave relaxed. He'd be home in a matter of hours. Exhausted, no doubt, but home again. Once he was through customs, he could drive to his place. With any luck he'd be there before dinner Saturday evening, Washington, D.C., time.

Unfortunately, Mollie knew nothing of his plans. He'd been on standby for the past four hours, not sure he could even get a flight out. When he had, there'd been no time to call her, only time enough to board the airplane. It wouldn't stop to refuel until they reached D.C. And by then, well he might as well surprise her—at the very least get home and take a shower and shave. Then they'd have dinner together, make love, hold each other. After that, the time would come to talk seriously.

If luck was on his side, Mollie would already be at his apartment, house-sitting as on previous weekends. Hopefully, by the time he arrived, she'd have her studying done.

It was high time they faced what was happening in their lives, to both of them. It was time they made a more permanent commitment.

MOLLIE SAT at Dave's kitchen table, her sweat-sock-covered feet hooked around the chair legs, her elbows braced on the table. In front of her was a revision letter from Constance regarding the magazine article.

She'd been reading the words for two days now, and she still didn't feel any better about the revisions that had been suggested. Were her feelings a writer's resistance to outside interference in one's work? she wondered bleakly. Or was it simply that she'd lost her journalist's perspective somewhere along the way? Mollie didn't know what the answer was. But the suggestions Constance had made had devastated her.

In her effort to comply with the suggestions, Mollie had highlighted the major points of the letter in yellow marker. They read: "We're *not* writing a romance here. I *know* you've fallen in love with the military, but some perspective, please... We need to see much, much more of the downside of your life as a marine.... The classroom instructor, for instance, is not nearly flawed enough! She comes across as almost superhuman, consistently fair-minded. Can this be true?"

On down the four-page letter, Mollie read, "On the positive side, your descriptions of the first day at camp were excellent! I loved the harassment by the drill instructor...the feeling you were most definitely not a ragtag group of ninnies and cowards. That she was the jerk. Your reaction to the clothing given you…the fact you'd be wearing it for days on end, week after week. This is what we need more of…raw emotion…and again, especially anything negative. What about your colleagues? Anything juicy about the candidates that might be included? It's imperative for the magazine, as well as your future, Mollie, that we sell a lot of copies, and controversial material will do that."

Mollie leaned back in her chair. If she were unscrupulous, uncaring, definitely not a friend of the other butter bars in her platoon, there was much she could say. She could tell about Greta's broken-up marriage, her deep hurt that her marine husband couldn't cope with the idea of Greta also wanting to become a marine and not just remain a helpmate to him. She could talk about Greta's wildness since the divorce, her penchant for betting on everything and anything, her occasional drinking in excess, her bold talk where men were concerned—but the cold fact was that Greta never went home with any of them. She could start digging into everyone's past—secretly, of course—and probably unearth a skeleton in every closet. Who among them hadn't done something she was embarrassed about? Something saleable, in a tabloid sense.

But that wasn't what Mollie wanted to write about. Mollie was no innocent. She knew it took a certain sensationalism or controversy to keep a reader turning the pages. Constance was right in her evaluation of what Mollie had turned in thus far in the article.

And also right in her final summation: "I'm sorry not to be able to offer you a contract at this point, Mollie. But first we must see more indication of truly saleable elements, of controversy that will make the article truly hard-hitting and incisive. I know this goes against the grain with you, dwelling on the negative every bit as much as the positive, if not more, but you've got to get down and dirty...."

Down and dirty, Mollie thought. What an apt phrase for what they now wanted her to do. And how ironic, after months of officer training and note-taking, to find she couldn't do it.

Oh, she still had a magazine article, maybe even a book left in her. But not the kind *Super Women* magazine wanted her to write.

So what was she going to do?

As far as Mollie could figure, she had three options. She could talk to Constance about the slant of the article and try to get them to change it, to see military personnel as all heroes of the storybook sort. She could accept a rejection from *Super Women* magazine and try to sell the work, written her way, to another publisher, or she could give up the idea of doing the project altogether.

If she gave up the writing project, she could serve out her time in the marines, not jeopardize and instead hopefully somehow maintain her relationship with Dave, and later pursue her journalism career with the experience she'd gained in the military.

But if she gave up the sale to *Super Women*, she would also be giving up her one shot at literary success, the only one she had truly had. So what it came down to was this: what was more important to her, her relationship with Dave or her ambition?

Miserably, Mollie put her head on the table. The truth of the matter was, she didn't know; she still didn't know. Dave had said he loved her. He hadn't mentioned marriage lately. For all she knew, he could be perfectly willing to let her move on in mid-December as scheduled and have someone else take her place. In his heart and in his bed. By even flirting with the idea of giving up her ambition for him, for a code of honor that at least before had been nebulous at best, was she throwing her life, her whole future away? Was she succumbing to some romance of the military that was nothing more than a writer's fascination with her subject? Mollie didn't think so. But the truth was, she couldn't be sure. And until she was, she supposed she would just have to start revising.

It's better to be safe than sorry, she schooled herself determinedly, typing madly. Better to be safe than sorry.

"GOD, I HATE IT. I can't do it! I just can't!" Mollie stared at the slanderous prose she had written, the scattered pages of outline in her hand. The revised manuscript she had proposed was highly saleable, and it sickened her. "I've torn apart everyone I care about here. The people in my platoon, my superiors, my company commander, even the lieutenant colonel in the public affairs office at Quantico. I've even talked about how easy it is to get around the no-frat rule and used my assignation with Dave as an example. I've sold my soul up the river. I've never felt lower in my life."

Mollie wiped a stray tear from the corner of her eye. "This really isn't going to work," she whispered. "I'm going to lose everything I've wanted for so long. And all because of my stupid allegiance to a code of values that months ago I didn't even understand."

And yet there was no denying she did understand those same values now. And there was no turning back. One didn't magically "unbecome" a marine. You either were for God and your country and all those patriotic expressions, or you weren't. You were part of a team, a whole, or you weren't. Mollie was part of that team. It had taken her efforts to stray from the fold to prove it to her. But now she knew. She was a marine. She was a writer. She was both. She could no longer separate the two.

Holding the papers in her hand, Mollie prepared to tear the slanderous outline up. But before she could act she heard a key in the lock. Within a split second, the door handle turned and the door swung open. Mollie was left standing and holding the condemning papers in her hand.

Damn, she thought. *I'm in trouble now.* "Well, are you just going to stand there?" Dave said, tossing his duffel bag across the room carelessly and holding his arms wide open. "Or are you going to come over here and give me a welcome-home hug?"

"I'm going to give you a welcome-home hug!" Mollie tossed the papers aside, facedown on the table, and ran across the room to his arms. He was harder and stronger than she remembered. She closed her eyes, reveling in the feel and touch and scent of him.

"God, I missed you." He squeezed her so tight against him she could hardly breathe. His lips touched her hair, then burrowed into the soft, silky thickness as he inhaled the flowery scent of her shampoo.

Tears of happiness misted Mollie's eyes. She hugged him back, as fiercely as she could. He released her, just enough so that they might kiss. Long, breathless moments later, they found themselves in the bedroom. Between bits and pieces of conversation and adoring looks, they undressed themselves slowly and then made love, again and yet again.

DAVE SIGHED beside her. "If I didn't know better, I'd think I was in heaven."

"Ditto here," Mollie confessed. "I don't think I even knew how much I missed you until I saw you walk through that front door."

"Does that mean you were glad to see me?"

"Couldn't you tell?"

"What? That little interlude just now?"

The "little interlude" had lasted hours. They were still stuck together like glue, as if to let one another very far out of sight would mean to be alone and lonely again. Mollie smiled and playfully bit into his shoulder.

"No," she said with a grin, "not that 'little interlude'...but...just..." Without warning, her throat closed up. She couldn't get out another word. She was all emotion, all love for him.

"I missed you, too." Without warning, his arms tightened around her. He held her close. "Enough to know I don't want to be without you again. Not for very long, anyway. Mollie, I know it's fairly sudden...that we haven't known each other for very long, just over half a year, but...I want you in my life. Permanently. If we weren't in the military, we wouldn't have to get married. But we are and I—oh, to hell with it. Damn it, Mollie, I want you as my wife. I want to be your husband. I never thought I'd say those words again. Not if I was standing on the end of the plank and the only thing between me and twenty-eight hungry sharks was a tunnel full of air, but I am saying those words. And I mean them, more than I've ever meant anything in my life. I love you and want you to marry me. So—" He stopped long enough to take a breath "—what's it going to be? Yes or no?"

In that instant, Mollie saw his mild panic, at the thought of losing her, and she knew his love mirrored her own. They would be together not because it was convenient or in line with military regulations but because they wanted to be. More than anything else in their lives.

"The answer is yes. As soon as it's permissible for me to get married."

"After TBS?"

"Should we wait that long?"

"Or after your next MOS school?"

"I'd rather be married before."

"So would I."

"But if not, I could hack it."

"So could I. I like flying, driving, any form of transportation that gets me closer to you."

"Roger that."

"So..." He folded his hands lazily behind his head, now that it was settled, and looked up at the ceiling. "Hungry?"

"I think we missed dinner, didn't we?" Mollie grinned.

"Mmm...and then some. Not that I minded." He glanced at his watch. It was nine-thirty. "We could go out. I want to get cleaned up first...a shower."

"So do I. But since this is your first night back, why don't we just stay here. I could rustle us up something quick to eat." *And clean up the incriminating papers in the kitchen,* she thought, beginning to panic again.

"You sure you don't mind?" He furrowed his brow.

"Not at all." Mollie slipped from the bed, and pulled on her bathrobe. "Go ahead and shower. When you come out, I'll have supper ready."

She gave him no chance to argue and left the room quickly, shutting the door behind her. Once in the living room, she rushed into the kitchen. She had just picked up the revised outline when the bedroom door opened and Dave dashed across the living room toward her. He had a sheet wrapped loosely around his waist. He had a grin the size of the Atlantic on his face. "You didn't think you were going to get away from me that easily, did you?" he teased.

"Dave!" Mollie gulped. She held the papers, facedown to her chest.

"What is this? After hours of lovemaking you're suddenly a shy maiden?" Dave's expression radiated his confusion. Wresting the papers from her hand without really looking at her, he put them aside. Unfortunately, part of the group missed the table and slithered to the floor. Mollie couldn't help it. She turned white, then red, as Dave's eyes focused on the typewritten pages. "What the...?" Too late—he'd seen enough. His name, she guessed, that of Mollie's company commander, the heading that proclaimed it a proposal for *Super Women.*

"I can explain," Mollie said swiftly.

"I'll bet."

She tightened the robe around her with fingers that trembled.

He had speed-reading capabilities. Or maybe it was just the adrenaline flowing through him at that moment. But in less than two minutes he'd scanned every scattered page. Mollie stood back, away from him, knowing he needed time to register his shock before he would even begin to listen to her. The main thing was for her to remain calm.

"So, while you've been house-sitting you've also been...what...composing this muck?"

"I'm not going to use it."

"How comforting! What are you going to use?"

"If you'll sit down, I'll explain."

He moved past her, toward the table, She moved swiftly, putting herself between Dave and the rest of the papers. Hands on her waist, he lifted her aside, and using a long arm as a barrier, kept her from stopping him from perusing them openly. In a few seconds' time he had again zeroed in on everything important, most especially the revision letter from Constance.

"So now we really know what you've been working on—an exposé about marine life?" He turned toward her. The paper in his hand fluttered down to the tabletop. It was an unexpectedly passive action, and because it was so overly controlled, especially unnerving. Mollie almost would have preferred a scalding outburst to this icy calm.

"Dave—"

"Just answer the question, Mollie. The article you've been writing all along—about your experiences as a single woman after divorce—was really about the marines. You're a muckraker."

"They want me to be."

"You are."

"I'm not doing what that outline says. I tried it. I realized I couldn't go through with it, not the way they wanted me to. I'm going to talk to Constance, Dave. I'm going to turn down the offer."

"Is that supposed to make me feel better?"

"Yes."

Just that swiftly, he moved. All fire and fury, he grabbed her robe by the lapels and shook her—once. His hands closed urgently over her shoulders. "Damn it, you lied to me! Not once!" He shook her again. "But over and over and over!"

Tears filled her eyes. She was losing him; she could see it. "I didn't mean to...."

"Didn't mean to! What the hell is that? Some sort of namby-pamby excuse! There is no middle ground for something like this!"

"There is!"

"No, Mollie, there isn't. And if you don't know that, I don't want anything to do with you, not ever again."

"Dave—"

He turned his back on her and folded his arms across his chest. "Get out."

She swallowed hard, distressed by the bleak acceptance she saw on his face. "Please…"

He whirled toward her, his expression savage. "Get out, I said! Before I lose what little control of my temper I have and throw you out!" He meant what he said.

Knowing he'd been pushed to his limits, Mollie went into the bedroom. She locked the door and began to dress. Her fingers trembled so badly she couldn't manage the buttons. Finally, after several trials and errors, she was dressed. She had shoes on, not tied on, but on. Her clothes were stuffed into her own duffel bag. When she came out, she saw that her papers were nowhere in sight.

"Where—"

"I'm not giving them back. You know what you did was against regulation." In her absence he had dressed also, using clothes from his duffel bag. The sheet he'd worn was crumpled up into a ball in the corner of the living room.

"I talked to the public affairs office—"

"You didn't tell them this…."

"Not in so many words, no, but…"

"I'll give you a day—twenty-four hours to talk to them."

"Tomorrow's Sunday."

"So find someone. Because Monday morning, first thing, I'm turning all this in."

"Dave—"

"You may have forgotten, or maybe you just knew and never understood, what honor is all about. But I haven't. I've screwed up in my love affair with you. I'll be the first to admit it, but no more. I'll be damned if I stand idly by and watch you mutilate everything the Marine Corps stands for in some cheap travesty of an exposé!"

"Dave—"

"Twenty-four hours, Mollie. No more, no less. Now get out."

She had no choice. Tears blurring her eyes, she left.

Chapter Sixteen

"I can't believe Dave's still furious with you," Blythe lamented. The day of her wedding had finally arrived, and she was busily adjusting her veil. "After all, it worked out okay. You were able to straighten out the whole mess with the public affairs office."

"Yes. I won't be able to publish with *Super Women*—"

"But you are getting published in a military newspaper. And you still have the option of publishing with any other magazine."

"Provided the public affairs office approves the material first."

"They've done that, haven't they?"

"Yes, and I've already sent my proposed article out to several magazines. I should hear back in a couple months. Hopefully, anyway."

"You'd think Dave would come around." Blythe scowled.

"I lied to him."

"So? He ought to understand the depth and difficulty of your situation."

Mollie shrugged. She was no longer sure of anything. "I made a mistake."

"We all make mistakes," Blythe said, readjusting her

veil with a frown. "Dave doesn't have to treat you like a leper. Especially when you graduate from TBS next week. Where are you going for your training?"

"Fort Harrison, Indiana. I've been assigned a military occupational specialty of public affairs. The school is ten weeks. After that, I'm not sure where I'll be stationed."

Blythe was silent. "Look, I know you've been depressed. But Dave will come around. Give him time."

"I'm trying...." Mollie felt her throat tighten up, but no tears appeared in her eyes. She had sworn to herself she wouldn't cry over him, and she hadn't. But the loss was telling on her. Never in her life had she felt more depressed, more hopeless about the future.

The bride gave Mollie a searching glance. "That stupid brother of mine. I ought to kick him—"

"Blythe!"

"Some things never change, and sibling irascibility is high on the list!"

"I THINK YOU'RE MAKING a giant mistake if you don't use this opportunity to at least talk to Mollie," Percy began in the small waiting room off the sanctuary of the chapel.

"Blythe put you up to this?" Dave asked, retying his tie for the hundredth time that day.

"I would've spoken to you even if she hadn't made me promise."

"Aha!" Dave lifted his index finger and pointed it straight up in the air before aiming it directly at Percy, pistol style. "Well, tell Blythe to forget it. What Mollie and I had is over."

"Because of the article?"

"Because I can't trust her." Dave's tone was as grim as his mood.

Percy was silent. "She lied to you about the article—"

"Yes, she did."

"That doesn't have to mean the end of the world. I know she's sorry."

"What good does her being sorry do if I can't trust her? You don't know the woman like I do, Percy. She's an excellent con artist when she wants to be. She can carry out a practical joke or a gag better than any woman I've ever met!"

"Precisely why the two of you should be together instead of apart. You're a lot alike. You've pulled your fair share of pranks, Dave. The majority of them lately on Mollie. You're in love with her, buddy. That hasn't changed. It isn't ever going to."

Dave should have been arguing but he couldn't. Everything Percy said was right. He did love Mollie. Their time apart had only strengthened the feelings he had for her.

"I don't know if we can go on," Dave said quietly at last. He walked to the window and stood looking out at the bleak November landscape. Inside the church, all was cozy and warm. The fragrant smell of flowers was in the air.

He turned, jamming his hands in his pockets. "The last time we were together, I said some ugly things to her." The truth was that he wasn't sure she could, or would, forgive him, either.

"So did she, I bet."

"Not really."

"She still loves you."

Dave said nothing.

"Talk to her," Percy encouraged.

"I'll think about it," Dave promised. But that was all he was going to do. Until he saw for himself and gauged her mood.

MOLLIE STOOD next to Blythe. Dave was on the other side of Percy. Though she should have been listening to the wedding vows, she was adrift with thoughts of Dave. Was it too late? He didn't look happy. She didn't feel happy. Would he ever be able to trust her again? Did she even have the courage to approach him after what she had done, the way she had lied?

There were no easy answers, and the eight days that had lapsed made the prickly situation all the more difficult.

The wedding was intimate and lovely. A small, private reception was held in a festively decorated banquet room of a local hotel. Percy's family was overjoyed to finally welcome Blythe to the family. Blythe and Percy were both radiantly happy. Mollie was glad for them both, as was Dave.

But how Dave felt about Mollie was another matter. It seemed he glanced at her constantly. He even approached her several times. They talked about inconsequential matters. They were interrupted often. By Percy, Blythe, his family, guests. Finally, it was all she could do to get through it, to pretend her heart wasn't broken and that she didn't love or care for him anymore. Finally, near the end of the evening, Mollie succumbed to temptation, and slipping out of the room, took the bottle of champagne she been drinking and a glass. Not long after, Dave followed.

"Planning to get smashed on this happy occasion?"

"You're doing your best to drive me to it."

"Don't you wish." His voice was faintly sarcastic. Not nearly as angry as she had expected.

Mollie turned toward him. If only he'd give her a sign, a hint that he was willing to forgive her! "You wouldn't know what I wished," she said quietly, then continued, her temper rising. "You've never listened long enough to—"

"To what?" Without warning, his tone gentled. He approached her slowly, step by step.

"Nothing." Mollie turned away. She blinked hard to dispel the moisture gathering in her eyes.

"I talked to Blythe," Dave continued softly. "She told me you gave up the *Super Women* opportunity and had arranged for your article to be published in a military newsletter instead."

Mollie glanced at him over her shoulder. He did look handsome this evening. "So?"

"So I'm glad you made the right decision, that's all." He stuck his hands in his pockets.

An awkward moment passed.

Mollie didn't know whether it was too much champagne or just his presence, but she was getting more surly by the moment. "So who asked you?"

"You didn't." Without warning, he grinned again and started to laugh.

Mollie observed him keenly, with the same care she would approach any lunatic. His eyes looked suspiciously moist, she decided, or maybe her eyes were.

"You're getting smashed," he said softly.

"Am...not." For the first time, Mollie knew how Greta must've felt, losing her husband because he couldn't accept what or who she was.

"You are, too, getting smashed." He started to take the glass from her hand.

She moved the glass and bottle out of reach. Cantankerous now, she whirled on him, the alcohol bolstering her confidence. "Don't even try it, soldier. I'm a marine. I know how to protect myself." *I am slightly smashed,* she thought. She hadn't imbibed that much, either. The bottle was still half full. It must be that her stomach was empty, that she hadn't eaten all day and was upset at seeing Dave again.

"I can see you're armed and dangerous."

His tone was so droll she winced. Mollie was reminded suddenly of the night he had played the practical joke on her in the clinic. She'd fallen for him then. Maybe even sooner. But her adoration hadn't gotten her anywhere. She shored up her defenses. She wasn't going to let him hurt her again. "Don't patronize me."

He blinked, as if taken aback. "At least let me escort you back to the base," he urged quietly.

"Are you kidding? That's a two-hour drive!"

"You don't want Percy's parents to see you inebriated, do you?"

"Well, no—" Mollie knew he knew she wasn't that smashed, that in a half hour—if she stopped drinking, and she had—she would be stone cold sober.

Taking advantage of her momentary acquiescence, he said, "I'll just tell them we're leaving."

Blythe came out to give Mollie a hug goodbye. "Way to go, kid. He's really coming around."

"Dave—?" Mollie croaked.

"Who else?" Blythe glanced at the empty champagne glass Mollie was still holding in front of her like a shield. Blythe frowned. "You really should lay off the sauce, Mollie. It's not good for you to drink in excess."

Mollie glanced around for the champagne bottle, but it had disappeared. It figured, she thought, now that she was tempted to get a refill. "Your brother's not good for me, either." That fact hadn't kept her away from him. Though it probably should have.

Blythe grinned indulgently and patted Mollie's shoulder. "Good night, Mollie. And thanks for being my maid of honor."

"Anytime," Mollie said in a resigned voice, aware Dave was once again at her elbow, hovering over her like a combination nurse and bodyguard. Dave fought a laugh, clueing Mollie in on the inanity of what she'd just said.

"No, I don't mean that," Mollie corrected. She stiffened her spine and squared her shoulders, aware of the shivers of fatigue that had started coursing through her. Without warning, she was feeling tipsy again; her vision was pleasantly out of focus, as if someone had placed a special lens over a camera. The kind they used to make older actresses look younger on the screen than they were in real life. She struggled to finish her thought. "I don't want you to get married again."

Blythe laughed and exchanged worried looks with her brother. "Neither do I." Then she elbowed Dave in the ribs, as if to say Mollie's condition was all his fault.

Dave was silent as they walked to the car. Try as she might, Mollie was unable to come up with anything to say, either.

Her false aura of safety was fading with the alcohol. Still, determined to look nonchalant and unaffected by his presence, she had kept up her most diffident front. Hence, she sat casually; her lacy dress was flowing around her. She had kicked off her high-heeled sandals and tucked her feet up under her.

Dave waited until they were on the freeway before he spoke. "Are you sorry you lost the chance to be published in *Super Women* magazine?"

"No, I don't care about that."

"Your friend Constance mad at you?"

"No. She was sorry I didn't get to write the article for them, since it was my idea and all. But they've hired another writer to do the same job—more or less, anyway. I guess the person they hired won't actually join the military but will interview about twenty women who've gone through basic, both enlisted recruits at the Marine Corps's Parris island facility and officer candidates at OCS. The public affairs office is going to mediate the whole process. Ironically enough, I'll be spotlighted in the article. Some of my journal entries will be used, but I won't get credit for the article. Nor will I be interviewing and writing up the rest of the personal stories."

"Are you upset about that?"

"No. I went about writing the article unethically. I should have been straight with the marines."

"If you had, they never would have let you enter OCS."

"I know." Mollie stared out at the blackness of night. The silence, the fact he was listening to her, gave her the license to admit, "I think that's why I went about it the way I did. I think maybe all along I really wanted to join the marines, but I was afraid I'd fail...afraid people would find out and laugh at me. Doing the article secretly was my safety net to keep me from falling too far. Not until I began to realize I didn't need a safety net did I begin to see how wrong I was to do what I did. It bordered on fraud, Dave, enlisting just to write an article. I don't know. I'm ashamed to admit it, but my ambition was so strong... For a while there, I almost lost sight of myself."

"Maybe we both did."

"What do you mean?"

"I've been wrong, too, Mollie. I should have listened to you."

She slanted him a mock-reproachful glance. "Yep, you should have."

"Maybe we can call a truce?" He reached over to briefly squeeze her hand.

A truce or the renewal of their love affair? she wondered as he released his grip on her fingers. Mollie wasn't sure what he meant, and he didn't explain. Suddenly aware of all the hurt still between them, they fell silent.

It was Dave who finally began to talk again. "This article of Constance's. It's going to be quite different from what they first envisioned doing, isn't it?"

"Yes," Mollie acknowledged wanly. "But it's all the marines will let them do. I guess it was pointed out to Constance and her publisher that if they presented anything inaccurate, it might later find its way to court in the way of a libel suit."

"I didn't think Constance was that sort of person, not from how you described her."

"She's not. She's actually very nice and is still my friend. But she's under the same kind of pressure to produce controversy from her boss that I was under from her. She's trying to keep her own job. Magazines have been having a tough time of it lately. Mailing costs are up; subscriptions are down. Readers are very demanding. They want something they can sink their teeth into."

"I hear you're going to specialize in public affairs?"

"Yes."

"It's what you want?"

She nodded.

"I'm happy for you."

"Thanks."

The conversation dwindled off after that, for obvious reasons. Mollie was exhausted, as was Dave. And it was hard to talk further without getting more personal. Besides, the ever-escalating, late-night freeway traffic demanded all his attention.

Mollie fell asleep. She awoke, her head against his shoulder. Dave slowed the car to a halt. They were in front of his apartment building.

"I thought you were taking me back to the base." Mollie struggled to sit up.

"I want to talk. I need to talk. I'm afraid if we wait, we'll just put it off or forget about it entirely. You've meant too much to me for me to let that happen."

Mollie faced him skeptically, wanting to believe him, not trusting her own hopes for a reconciliation not to color matters unrealistically or misleadingly. "You were quite willing to let me go off without conversing before the wedding."

"Before the wedding I was a fool," he said roughly, giving her no chance to reply.

He got out of the car and came around to get her. He wrapped his arm around her waist as they traversed the short distance to his door. "Coffee?"

Mollie put a hand to her now aching head. "And two aspirin, please."

He laughed, soft and low, and it was a welcome sound to her ravaged nerves. Suddenly, it was as if they were drifting back into normality. It was easy for her to forgive him. She knew how deeply she'd hurt him, that if the situation had been reversed, she would've been just as angry. And most of all, she was glad they were going to have a chance. She wanted to part friends. If nothing more, maybe they could at least hold on to that.

He returned with the aspirin and coffee and a glass of water for her to take the pills. "Too much champagne will do that to you every time, sport."

"Thanks for the advice," she intoned wryly.

He sat across from her. She was curled up on the end of his sofa, her legs tucked under her, an afghan across her lap. He cradled his coffee cup between both hands. Feeling shy, she looked down and focused on the steam rising from his mug.

"I don't think it's enough for me to just say I'm sorry," he said quietly. "I've behaved like a total jerk."

"Yeah, you did." She grinned, lifting the coffee to her lips. She was beginning to feel more lighthearted than she had since they'd broken up, just being there with him. "But it was a trait we both shared."

"Think if we worked on it we could get rid of that personality trait?"

"I don't know. We may have to call Blythe in to do major surgery."

"I'm serious."

"I know."

"I want to pick up where we left off. I don't know if it's possible."

Mollie lifted her glance to his. In him, she saw everything she had ever wanted. She felt so in love with him it scared her. She determined to go slow. "I think it is. But I think maybe we both have to do some growing. Even if we do get back together, our life together isn't going to be perfect. I don't even want to think about the possibility, but at the same time, I know I'm bound to disappoint you. And you're probably going to disappoint me, as well. I need to know that together we have the strength to get through it. That you won't ever walk out on me again."

"I promise."

"Not even for half an hour?"

He took a breath. "Mollie, I have quite a temper...."

"I noticed the night in the infirmary. But I can't live with a man who walks—" Mollie's voice caught emotionally. She'd been deserted once, by her previous husband. Not again. "That's the kind of threat I can't live with," she finished finally.

"Okay, I'll stay even if we fight, but we'll have to work out some sort of a system so you'll know when I'm too hot to handle and need to be left alone."

"You can wear a sign that says Don't Feed the Bear."

"Okay, then you've got a deal. But by the same token, I need a promise from you, too. I need you to level with me at all times about what you're doing and feeling. I can't promise I'll always understand. But I need to know that you trust me, that you care enough to at least be a hundred percent honest with me, to give us the chance to try and work things out no matter how great a problem may seem or how angry or disappointed you think I'll be. Whether it's in you or a career choice you want to make or something as simple as an overdrawn bank account."

"I'll level with you."

Mollie paled, thinking about the specifics of combining a marriage with their military careers. "What about the no-frat rule?"

"Because we work in different areas, and haven't compromised the chain of authority in any way, I don't think there's going to be a problem. We'll both have to go to our COs and explain, but it's my understanding that in similar cases there's no official objection. We won't be stationed together, but we'll be within commuting distance."

"Then our fraternization won't hurt our careers?"

Dave paused. "It could be listed on our fitness reports, with a reference to poor judgment in our personal lives—something like that. But I think, considering the situation, that would be as much of a reprimand as either of us would get at this point. Had you worked for me directly and had I given you a promotion that wasn't earned...well, then, Mollie, we both would've been in hot water.''

She laughed at his teasing tone. ''Would you have given me a promotion I didn't earn?''

''No.''

''I didn't think so.''

''What about having children?''

''Women marines are granted maternity leaves now.''

''No kidding?''

''No kidding.''

''So maybe someday...''

''When the time is right...'' she affirmed.

Slowly, he stood and walked across the room. He held out a hand. She took it. ''I asked you this before,'' Dave said softly when they were standing face-to-face. ''I'm asking you again. Will you marry me?''

''Yes.''

He hugged her to him, letting actions, his love, speak for him.

Happier than she could ever remember feeling, Mollie murmured into his shirtfront, ''Dreams do come true.''

He laughed softly, answering, ''And dares pay off.''

''This dare did.'' Mollie smiled and hugged him harder. ''It sure did.''